CEMETERY WORLD

JE GURLEY

SEVERED PRESS
HOBART TASMANIA

CEMETERY WORLD

Copyright © 2017 JE Gurley
Copyright © 2017 by Severed Press

WWW.SEVEREDPRESS.COM

ISBN: 978-1-925711-01-1

FOREWORD

A dwarf sun, red and baleful, almost invisible against the black backdrop of the empty void between galaxies, beckons the intrepid explorers onward. Separated from its brethren in the Milky Way galaxy by hundreds of light years, the star pursues a path that will eventually deliver it into the inescapable clutches of the massive, swirling black hole lying in wait like a spider in its web of gravity threads in the galaxy's heart. There, its grisly fate is inevitable, ripped apart by unimaginable tidal forces, digested, and ultimately spewed back out into the galaxy as radiation.

The red dwarf is alone, but not without purpose. At a distance of 100 million kilometers, about the distance from Sol to the planet Venus, an ebony band encircles the star like a promise. The ring is so dark it seems to drink up the sun's light. What race would create such an edifice where no one could see it? What alien mind thought in terms of billions of years? How could humans, a species newly thrust upon the stage of interstellar travel, a species that flitted through their brief lives in the blink of a cosmic eye, comprehend the magnificent object's builders? Did mankind dare stare into the eyes of God?

1

Kari Stone lifted her head and stared heavenward, but she saw no sky, no clouds, and no birds; just a swollen, blood-filled orb frozen perpetually directly above her, glaring down at her like some angry, one-eyed colossus. To her east, spinward on the Band, the shadowy structure rose up in an arc, glistening like a storm cloud in the sun before vanishing into the deep blackness of space. The knowledge that the Band continued until its far end, 205 million kilometers away on the far side of the sun, climbing directly over her head, disconcerted her. Rationally, she knew gravity prevented it falling down on her, but her mind had difficulty accepting that fact. Standing there, she felt minuscule, out of place and out of time, just as she had felt standing before every other Architect artifact she had viewed.

The long-vanished race of builders, known as Architects, had left little to memorialize their passing. The few monuments so far discovered had proven gargantuan, like the Band, built on a scale so grandiose that even the attempt would have been an impossible undertaking by lesser beings. The Band stretched 620 million kilometers in length and over 1,000 kilometers in width, a continuous ring of a material harder than any known substance encircling the red giant star humans had named Cyclops. At a mere two kilometers in thickness, the Band was an ebony ribbon wrapped around a crimson marble. No one could fathom how the Band had managed to remain in position the estimated 500 million years since its construction, much less calculate the unimaginable power required to set its incredible mass into motion.

In 150 years of exploration of their small corner of the galaxy, humans had discovered evidence of only two other sentient species. Both humanoid species had reached the equivalent of Earth's Early Bronze Age before disappearing. Speculation on their demise ranged from pandemic disease to natural disaster. They had left samples of their writing and images of themselves in the form of statues, stone carvings, and metal funerary objects, but little else. So far, neither language had been deciphered. Both species had been long-dead memories before

Earth's first land creatures crawled from the primordial sea. The discoveries elicited little interest in most humans other than ardent archaeologists eager for a new field of study and theologians put on the defensive as the fundamental tenets of their religious dogma came under tighter scrutiny.

However, the discovery of a third species, one capable of feats far beyond anything mankind might ever hope to achieve, struck the world with a sense of awe and wonder, and just a little fear, invigorating a new age of exploration, one in which Kari Stone had eagerly enlisted.

"A penny for your thoughts."

The voice over her suit com startled Kari from her reverie. It had been hours since she had heard anything but her own labored breathing. "Wha ...? Oh, it's you, Ken," she said, turning around awkwardly in the bulky excursion suit to recognize the white-suited figure of Ken Hitochi, the ship's engineer. She envied him in his U.N. Navy excursion suit; so much sleeker and trimmer than hers. Designed to double as battle armor, his helmet was narrower, and the larger faceplate offered a wider view. The module containing his oxygen supply and CO_2 scrubber snuggled into the back of his suit, while hers rested uncomfortably in the crook of her lower back like an overstuffed purse. His fit him like a tailored suit. Hers was an off-the-rack bargain basement model provided from the meager funds allowed the archaeological team. The air recycler constantly whistled in her ear, and did little to eliminate body odors.

The low gravity, only half of Earth normal 1-G, gave him a loping gait over the black plain, as he closed the hundred yards or so that separated them. Because of the lack of perspective created by the pervasive black background, Hitochi seemed to grow in stature rather than draw nearer. His white suit bore black scorch marks from his attempts to penetrate the walls of a building with a laser drill. She abhorred such crude attempts. It reminded her of early archaeologists using sledgehammers to smash through the walls of ancient tombs in Egypt's Valley of the Kings. It was ... sacrilegious. Unfortunately, the Band had left them little choice.

The filter of her helmet visor, which allowed her to stare at Cyclops without searing her retinas, gave Hitochi a wispy, slightly out of focus appearance, like an apparition. *How appropriate in such a dead place,* she thought. Several people had reported seeing ghosts or apparitions in various places around the City, shadowy objects floating above the surface or popping in and out of walls. She attributed the unusual sightings to the perpetual gloom, the absolute dead silence, and the lack of any discernible movement on the Band. The isolation didn't help. The mind played tricks on the eyes in an attempt to make sense of the lack of normal sensations. It was beginning to affect her as well.

She could not see his face through his reflective visor. She keyed the communications view screen inside her helmet with her sleeve suit controls and dialed his internal helmet camera. His face appeared in the lower right-hand corner of her visor. His dark brown, almond-shaped eyes twinkled at her in the low-resolution light, but she noted the disappointment on his haggard face.

"I don't have a penny's worth of ideas about it," she answered. "Whatever a penny is," she added.

Hitochi grinned at her. She thought he should smile more. He was a handsome man – fair-featured and muscular – but he seemed unsure of his value to the expedition and did not often display his feelings.

"Uh, an ancient U.S. and Great Britain coin," he explained, "made of copper and practically worthless." When she showed no further interest in his impromptu history lesson, he nodded at the collection of buildings around them. The nearest structure, a towering dome measuring nearly a kilometer in height and five kilometers in diameter, perfectly smooth and featureless, held his gaze. "It's beyond anything I could have imagined. It's almost magical."

"Maybe it is," Kari said only half-jokingly. "Any technology this advanced is beyond our comprehension and as close to magic as we can come."

"Well, we know one thing. The Band is older by far than anything else we've discovered by them."

"Oh, I thought Kirkurk said some of the constructs looked rather recent."

Hitochi flared his nostrils and narrowed his eyes. "Kirkurk!" he spat through clenched jaw. Everyone on the team, including Neville Kirkurk, knew of his dislike for the team's outspoken leader. Kari had no great love for the team's leader, but was more circumspect in her remarks. She hoped Hitochi had limited broadcast to her suit alone. She checked and saw only the proximal suit-to-suit channel was in use, activated automatically when two excursion suits were within range of infrared laser communications.

"Some are," he continued, "if you consider five million years younger than the rest of the Band recent. Evidently, the Architects continued adding to the Band right up until the time they disappeared. The Dome is one such recent addition, he claims."

His snort of derision demonstrated his disbelief in most of Kirkurk's claims. Kari's estimate of Kirkurk's assertions was slightly higher. He was pompous, condescending, and wrapped up in his own carefully projected public persona as the leading authority on Architects, but she did not dismiss his observations out of hand. He had earned his reputation.

She looked over at the black hemisphere rising into the dark sky like a bubble blown from the vast obsidian plain surrounding them. The Dome was neither the Band's tallest structure nor its largest, but it was the most prominent, the only dome on the Band's surface and according to Kirkurk, the most recent. Unlike any other group of structures on the Band, the Dome stood apart, surrounded by a flat, featureless black plain. They had all reasoned that its size and position made it the likeliest target for their exploration efforts. So far, it had foiled all attempts to penetrate its secrets.

"To think a species created this artifact as their first undertaking in space," she said, rocking on her heels in her excitement. Her voice was wistful and filled with awe. She noticed Hitochi's quick grin, but ignored him. He had heard it all before. "They must have waited millennia before leaving their world, perfecting their sciences and art. They didn't venture into space out of idle curiosity but with a definite purpose." She turned back to face Hitochi, an unnecessary gesture since she could see him on her com screen no matter which direction she faced. It just seemed more personal. "Has anyone gained entrance yet?" She wasn't sure why she asked. If anyone had broken through the seemingly impervious material, excited chatter would fill the com channels.

"Not yet," he replied, shaking his head. "We may never find a way inside. It seems impossible. The material is composed of intricately woven lattices of crystalline metal embedded within a force-field matrix. It's not really a metal at all. I'm not certain it's truly a solid. I'm baffled. The laser doesn't even warm the surface. The material dissipates the heat too quickly. It's much denser than anything we've ever encountered. Diamond drill bits don't scratch it. It's impervious to acids, x-rays, sound waves ... Hell; I even kicked it with no results except a bruised toe. They intended this thing to last for eternity."

She smiled at his attempt at humor. "Like a memorial in a cemetery," she mused.

"Sometimes this place gives me the same willies I get in graveyard. I catch myself looking over my shoulder."

"Oh, really? Why?" she asked, curious about his reasoning. Did the environment create the mood, or did the person's mood color the environment, reshaping it in their mind's image? Some people shunned cemeteries. Others thought them peaceful and serene. Cemeteries didn't bother her. Cemeteries, tombs, and ancient burial grounds were mere workplaces for archaeologists. Maybe the ghost stories were getting to him. "Try whistling," she suggested.

Hitochi's face twisted into a quizzical expression. "Whistling?"

"Yeah, whistling. Like this." Kari pursed her lips and whistled. The loud, high-pitched sound echoed inside her helmet. Her demonstration startled Hitochi, who took a step backwards.

"Why would I whistle?" he asked.

"You've never heard the expression 'whistling past a graveyard'?"

"Never."

She chuckled. "Whistling warns away the ghosts."

He smiled. "Oh, now I see. I'll try that next time." He turned to view the City. "It doesn't look like a city as I would imagine one. There are no statues, no parks, no plants, and no writing of any kind. There's not even any art unless you count the buildings themselves. It's as if they wanted this place to remain anonymous. That's why they stuck it way the hell out here outside the galaxy proper. They wanted to be left alone." He lifted his arms and dropped them. "And yet, here we are."

"Maybe it's a museum. Wouldn't that be wonderful? The things they could teach us."

She could not keep the wistful tone from her voice. In the 50 years since the discovery of the first Architect artifact, no one had uncovered a single inscription or depiction that shed light on the Architect culture. It was as if they had explored the galaxy, left a few bizarre but enticing monuments, and disappeared into history, folding the millennia over them like a funeral shroud. The discovery of a library or a mother lode of artifacts had been the object of every expedition to an Architect construct. It had been the driving force behind their expedition beyond the edge of the galaxy.

Hitochi laughed. "You sound like an Interventionist. I would be satisfied knowing how in Hades they made this black crystal material."

She was sure he meant it in a joking manner, but his remark about the Interventionists annoyed her. The Church of Celestial Intervention claimed the Architects were progenitors of all life in the galaxy, seeding it with the essential elements necessary for intelligent life and stepping in at times to assist or bring down a race they helped create. As a Christian – at least she had been raised a Christian – Kari abhorred such an idea. The Architects were an advanced race, certainly, but they were no more gods than the Egyptian pharaohs were gods. She suspected there might be a few Interventionists among the crew, but they kept their ideas to themselves and caused no trouble.

Hitochi glanced up at the sun, convulsing like a living thing in the center of the sky above the Band. "Surely they didn't evolve under a red dwarf sun. They seem so … so … human-like."

"We have no idea what they looked like," she reminded him. "Maybe they were six-meter-long slugs."

"Intelligent escargot – yeah, I like that." He snickered. He pretended to search the surface of the Band. "Maybe we should look for slime trails." He sighed, a soft exhalation of breath amplified by the com link. It sounded as if his suit was deflating. "Oh, well. We had better get back to the ship. The lights go out in 20 minutes."

Since their arrival, they had discovered the same unknown dampening field that shielded the Band from the sun's deadly radiation also blocked the sunlight over the entire Band every 14 hours. Speculation abounded that the cycle reflected the day/night cycle of the Architects, but there was no proof. Hitochi pointed out that it could have easily been a necessary cycling of the machinery based on heat exchange ratios or necessary for regular maintenance. Kari suspected something more … alien involved.

She hated that the ancient builder species had no name other than Architect. Many had been proposed and shot down just as quickly. Archaeologists, even journalists, resisted naming them, hoping the next great discovery would reveal a clue to their identity. The Architects had left no writing or images, but that had not stopped the press and the media from idle speculation. Kari had seen them depicted as three-eyed scarecrow giants, four-armed slavering simians, and glowing, floating orbs of pure energy. Other than the Band, they had left no structures resembling habitable buildings. Even here, they left no doorways or windows, and no way to judge the Architects' shape or size. It was as if they wished to strut their hour upon the stage, and then vanish into the wings leaving only the memory of their character to endure.

In their survey of the Band, they had discovered 9,281 individual Cities, the unofficial designation for the numerous groupings of buildings scattered asymmetrically across the sunward surface of the Band. Each City consisted of 11 or 29 buildings. A few people made great significance of the fact that 11, 29, and 9,281 were prime numbers and saw hidden messages in the irregular placement of the Cities. Kari saw a lack of balance that might drive mad someone suffering from OCD, but suspected deciphering neither the numbers nor the placement would reveal great secrets. They were just numbers. The Architects were mysterious enough without adding mysticism or numerology to the mix.

Slowly, like a dark mist spreading across the sky, the ruddy light of the sun faded – an eclipse without a planet. Directly overhead was only darkness, but toward the edge of the far horizon, a sprinkling of stars, the fringe of the distant Milky Way Galaxy, shone as if through a silk veil. She felt a sudden shiver, as her suit heaters fought to keep up with the sudden drop in ambient temperature.

She unlinked her connection to Hitochi's helmet camera to clear her screen and dialed up an infrared filter. The filter offered a contrast in the failing light between the ultra-black material of the Band and the vacuum surrounding it. With their suit lamps, they could see each other, but the low-power beams did not illuminate the light-absorbing material of the Band. She did not fear running into anything in the dark since there were no obstacles to trip over, but the light made placing her feet easier.

Her lamp reflected from the recoilless, high-velocity flechette pistol attached to Hitochi's suit. Guns made her nervous. The act of going armed on a lifeless artifact struck her as absurd.

"Why must you wear that ridiculous thing?" she asked.

"All officers are to remain armed at all times while outside the ship," he quoted in a rote voice bearing a striking similarity to the resonant, lilting voice of Captain Sidthuri. "Orders from the captain," he added in his own voice.

"It's silly."

"Oh, I don't know," he said, drawing his pistol and brandishing it. "It could come in mighty handy against Architect ghosts. Better than whistling."

She suppressed a shudder at the thought of Architect ghosts. "Don't even joke about it."

He sighed in defeat and re-holstered his weapon.

Something about the inky darkness, perhaps the vague shape of the buildings rising like macabre ebony ghosts, dispelled any serenity a normal night might hold. She could not see anyone sitting around a campfire roasting marshmallows and telling ghost stories in such a place. Such an idea bordered on the profane.

The ship, a shiny, bright needle with odd bulges containing the FTL Jump engines at the needle's eye, gave the impression of a blemish on the dark, unmarred surface of the Band. Dwarfed by the smallest building of the City, it represented home in an alien land, their only link with Earth. By mutual consent and for reasons of safety, all work ceased at dusk. As night fell, everyone had sought the familiar comfort of the ship and the two portable inflated domes sitting beside it.

On the long journey from Earth, the small ship had seemed uncomfortably overcrowded with 15 team members and a crew of 20 Navy and Marine personnel. Now, it felt cozy and safe, a bit of home in an unfamiliar place. The artificial gravity generators on the ship and in the temporary twin domes erected beside it offered respite from the Band's disconcerting .5 Gs. The former ship's lounge, converted into an operations center, became the impromptu first stop of the evening, a spot to have a cocktail and a bit of gossip, while team leaders filed their reports and organized the next day's activities.

Deidre Gibbons, as usual, was the center of attention, at least among the younger male members of the crew. Kari was jealous of the newswoman's ready wit and statuesque beauty. Few people knew she had a last name. Her millions of viewers knew her only as Deidre. Not that she was all show; she had earned her place on the team as official chronographer with her series of incisive, in-depth reports on the Architects. Kari liked that her admiration of and curiosity about the Architects matched hers.

As one of only five females on the ship, Kari knew she should attempt to become closer to Deidre, but she felt ugly next to the beautiful, vivacious videographer. At a full-figured 5'9", a curly skullcap of jet-black curly locks, bronzed skin, and eyes as dark and sultry as raven's wing, Deidre presented the perfect appealing newscaster for male viewers. *Dreamy Deidre.*

Kari was not ugly. In the mirror, she saw a 5'5" brunette, somewhat mousey but with fair features, hair cropped short for convenience rather than as a fashion statement, and eyes as green as a spring meadow. She had drawn her fair share of attention from the men on the outbound trip, but her dedication to her work had invited more than a few comments about her standoffish attitude. A few of the men had labeled her a cold fish, an epithet she resented. She considered herself dedicated, not aloof. Ken Hitochi was one of the few men with whom she felt comfortable. Perhaps it was because he, too, saw something magical in the Architects.

She winced each time Deidre called Kirkurk by his first name, Neville, instead of Doctor Kirkurk or even Mister Kirkurk, as befitted his status as the expedition's civilian leader. She fawned over him, leaning closer, and clasping his forearm as she spoke, making sure her large breasts pressed against him. Kirkurk ate it up like a spoon-fed puppy, his eyes never leaving her body even when speaking with someone else. Kari wondered if he had become one of her numerous sexual conquests.

Kari despised touchers, people with the need to clasp your arm or lean in close when conversing. To her, it was an invasion of privacy, an uninvited, intimidating intimacy. Some thought it prudish. She considered it good manners. In the close quarters of the ship, a certain amount of loss of personal space became unavoidable, but now, it felt contrived, as if she were marking her territory, like a dog pissing on a tree. Kari laughed at the image the thought conjured in her mind of Deidre hiking her leg.

Josh Luntz strolled over to her with wearing a pair of gym shorts that hugged his sculpted buttocks like a second skin and a cut-off T-shirt accentuating his washboard abs. He had been working out in the ship's gymnasium and hadn't bothered changing clothes for the gathering, but his hair was still damp from showering. She glanced around for an escape, but she had trapped herself in a corner of the small lounge. His golden locks and muscular build had made the tall photographer a favorite of the celebrity vids back on Earth almost as much as his talent as a photographer. Kari begrudgingly envied his knack for capturing the essence of any subject for posterity, but detested his overzealous attentions.

She thought he tried too hard aboard ship to project his carefully honed image as everyone's friend, as if the expedition's small size intimidated him more than a large, impersonal crowd of fans. As usual, he held a cocktail glass in his hand, but she seldom saw him actually take a sip. She had reached the conclusion that the drink was a prop, and like the people around him, only served to accentuate his performance – a perpetual photo op.

He smiled at her, flashing his perfect, white, even teeth. His sparking sapphire-blue eyes flecked with specks of gold reminded her of opals. They gleamed as he gazed at her, making her skin tingle. "I saw you and Ken together earlier. Anything going on there?"

Her cheeks flushed and her heart quickened. In spite of herself, Luntz's looks and charm affected her on a basic level over which she had little control. She was certain he was aware of his effect on women and was enjoying the effect he had on her. She caught a faint whiff of cologne. Even his hair smelled of a floral shampoo. "Ken is a friend. That's all."

"Then why won't you accept my invitation to dinner?" he asked with a slight pout on his lips and downcast eyes. After a few seconds, he raised his gaze and smiled.

"I don't want to be another notch on your bedpost." Kari eyes flicked to Deidre. "Like some others I know."

He threw back his head and laughed a musical tone that had become his trademark in his public appearances. "Oh, Kari dear. You need to lighten up. The Architects are long dead. You'll never meet one. Don't save your virginity for them. Live a little before you become a musty, old artifact yourself."

Her face reddened at a few titters from those who had overheard their conversation. Burning from his remark, a rebuke that hit too close to home, she stalked off. She was not a virgin, but felt defending herself by proclaiming the fact to the gathering was too personal and would be almost an admission of guilt. She pushed past some of the Navy crew still on duty, ignoring them as she steamed from Luntz's remark.

Alone in the ship's small library, she opened her flatscreen and read over her notes, paying little attention to them. After a while, she noticed she had highlighted the word 'cemetery' twice. Something Hitochi said had struck a chord within her. If the buildings were monuments to the dead, why were there no carvings or memorials? Her frustration mounted. How does one think like an alien?

The Architects had first conquered space half a billion years earlier during Earth's Paleozoic Era of the Late Cambrian Period when alga, arthropods, and trilobites ruled the early seas. For nearly five million years, they explored the galaxy before inexplicably abandoning it and returning to their unknown home world. Had they lost their sense of mystery? Had they learned all there was to know? Or, more ominously, had something they found among the stars frightened them into a retreat? What would make humans return to Earth, never to venture forth again? The thought frightened her.

She reviewed the Architect artifacts so far discovered. The first one was the Ice World circling a gas giant around Syracuse I, discovered 55 years earlier. The size of Earth's moon, the globe of cometary ice from the system's Oort Cloud was a delicately carved series of interlocking spirals. The design itself was awe inspiring, but the light of the yellow sun turned it into a work of art, a glittering jewel visible for millions of kilometers.

The second discovery, the Water World orbiting Beta Secundus, rivaled any Earthly paradise. Moss-covered islands dotted its crystal blue waters, perfectly symmetrical steppingstones creating an emerald pathway encircling the planet. The sterile water at a uniform depth across the planet was free of any impurities and tasted slightly of honey and lime. It was a Zen garden world in space.

Numbers three and four had been discovered together, two ultra-dense moonlets on a continuous circuit of twin suns, so positioned that upon each circuit around their respective stars they came into perfect alignment, singing out in subsonic frequencies well below the normal range of human hearing. To Kari, who had heard the song on recordings, it was both hauntingly beautiful and melancholy, like a dirge performed by suicidal whales. Because of the long, elliptical orbits of the moonlets, the song had played only a dozen times since mankind had first walked erect.

Most impressive of all was artifact number five, the Kaleidoscope Nebula, every star in the center of the dwarf nursery nebula so positioned that their combined gravity fields induced the dense, colorful gases of the nebula to swirl and writhe like a dancing wraith. The outermost stars ran the color spectrum from white, to red, to blue, creating a slow kaleidoscopic effect over the eons as the stars matured and changed color.

Now, with the discovery of the Band, artifact number six had become the most puzzling of them all. It had existed for hundreds of millennia before the other five were constructed. What was the connection between the Band and the other artifacts? Why would the Architects undertake such a massive project just before retreating? Understanding them was the key to unlocking the secrets of the Band.

Deidre slunk into the library and leaned the bulkhead with her arms crossed beneath her breasts. She sighed aloud. "You need to lighten up, Kari."

"What do you mean?" Kari asked, conveying her annoyance at Deidre's disturbing her by her sharp tone.

"Josh is interested in you, and so is Ken, but you act as though you were in mourning for your damned vanished Architects."

Deidre's slurring of her words spoke of one too many cocktails, but her condescending tone when mentioning the Architects shocked Kari, and to a degree, angered her. "*My* Architects. You made a dozen vids about them. I thought they fascinated you."

Deidre shrugged. "Once, maybe, when they were new and different. Viewers are always interested in them, so it made for a good story. That's my interest, the story. Personally, I couldn't care less about them. *Veni, vidi, vici.*"

"What?" she asked.

"I came, I saw, I conquered. It's Latin, a dead language. I thought if anybody would recognize it, you would."

The barb stung deeply, but Kari shook it off. "I know the Architects are long gone. It's just ... well, they interest me."

Deidre lit a cigarette. Kari noticed she had chosen a cinnamon scented, non-carcinogenic, synthetic tobacco blend that was popular in trendy social circles on Earth. *Of course, she would.* She held the cigarette between two long fingers with her elbow resting on her ample right breast. Her LED nail polish flashed through a beach scene with gulls skimming crashing waves, making Kari homesick for just a moment. Deidre took a puff, let the pungent smoke slowly roll out of her open mouth, and said, "Live with ghosts, and you'll lie with ghosts. Why not try joining the living for a while?"

"Like you?" she shot at Deidre.

Deidre's sharp laughter almost drew blood. "Sweetie, you can never be like me, but you could try to act more like a woman than a funeral director."

Deidre sauntered off, leaving Kari smoldering with rage. She wanted to strike out, relieve some tension, but her upbringing prevented her. *No, not my upbringing. I'm just too damned timid. Maybe she's right.* That realization hurt more than Deidre's barb about the Architects.

"Damn her to hell," she swore, the worse curse she could force herself to utter, and slammed her flatscreen closed.

2

Each evening, the two science teams met before dinner to discuss the day's progress in the larger of the two inflatable domes erected beside the ship. Building A, as they named it to differentiate it from the Band Dome, was the only space large enough to accommodate all of them. It housed the kitchen and cafeteria, a library, the entertainment center, and a dormitory for most of the male members of the science teams. Building B, connected by an airlock, accommodated the labs and small, shared cabins for the four female members of the expedition and some of the senior staff.

Since no one had gained entrance into the alien buildings, the sessions quickly degenerated into beer-and-bullshit sessions, a reason to extend the cocktail hour. Sometimes, as tonight, the captain joined them. He sat in a chair across the room from the others wearing his always-immaculate ship's captain uniform, as aloof as a judge. On the table beside him sat three empty beer cans, curious, she thought, for the usually casual drinker. He held a fourth in his beefy hand.

As usual, Kirkurk philosophized about the Architects. He spoke as if he were standing behind a lecture podium at a university rather than sitting in a folding chair at a folding table. "They were magnificent, like gods. They manipulated forces we can't imagine just for the creation of beauty. I think they eventually evolved into incorporeal beings, pure energy life forms. They might be watching us right now."

Kari suppressed a shudder. Alone on the surface, she sometimes felt as if she were being observed. She often caught herself turning around expecting to see someone in the shadows, but the unidentified Band material cast no shadows.

Champiri Sung, the team's chief biologist, voiced his opinion for the tenth time since arriving on the Band. Sung was a small man, quiet and observant. Unlike Kirkurk, he held no high opinion of the Architects.

"True, the Pembina"– Kari winced at Sung's constant use of the Malay word for builders instead of Architects, an affectation he refused to give up, perhaps thinking it annoyed Kirkurk —"were great builders, at least on a cosmic scale, but we have found no evidence they even lived in our galaxy. They may have simply passed through our galaxy on an eons-long journey across the universe. The artifacts they left might be their version of a roadside sign riddled with bullet holes, a kind of 'Kilroy was here' thumbing their noses at emergent civilizations."

"Nonsense," Kirkurk huffed. "They must have derived the same pleasure from their creations as we do. That makes them like us in at least that way. You don't scrawl graffiti for five million years."

Sung shrugged. "It's all conjecture. Unless we manage to get inside one of the structures, we might as well take photographs and go home, like frustrated tourists."

Captain Sidthuri cleared his throat. Like Sung, he was a small man, thin and gaunt cheeked, but in spite of his small stature, he wore his authority about like a cloak. Everyone in the room turned to look at him. "On that subject, I would like to address you. We have been here almost two months, five weeks exploring the Band and three weeks trying to enter the Dome, with no results. The longer we remain, the longer the return journey becomes. It might be prudent to gather data, return to Earth, and organize a larger effort – three or four ships to establish a permanent base."

"No, we can't!" The words erupted from Kari's throat before she even had time to consider them. She damned herself for speaking out, but his proposal appalled her.

Sidthuri and Kirkurk both eyed her as if noticing her presence for the first time. The sudden attention caught her off guard. She tried to will herself invisible, but it was too late.

Sidthuri spoke. "And what is your reasoning, Miss Stone?"

She stared at him, trying not to let him intimidate her. "Reasoning? We're here already. We envisioned a lengthy stay, four or five months. Why the hurry to quit?"

"We anticipated visible results for the time invested. Do you have any to report?" He paused for a few seconds. "I thought not." His eyes swept the room in a challenge. "Do any of you have anything to add to the knowledge we gleaned during the first weeks?" He nodded at the silence. "I'm a military man. My superiors ordered me on this expedition against my recommendation. The *Worthington* is a *Europa*-Class frigate, not especially large or fast, but against the pirates in the Sigma system, she could make a difference. Sitting here accomplishing nothing is a burden on the taxpayers and a drain on military resources."

He finished his beer and set the can on the table with his collection of empties; then, used his forearm to shove them out of the way. "As I said, my orders are to explore the Band, but from what I have observed, it might be more prudent to leave behind probes to catalogue the Cities, collect data, and investigate any anomalies. A better-equipped second expedition on a civilian ship could utilize the collected data and not waste time." He looked around the gathering. "If any of you have a proposal to make it worth the time and effort to remain longer, I will be glad to review it. Otherwise, I have to consider all the options."

Kari settled back in her seat with her legs tucked up under her, shoulders drooping, suddenly tearing eyes downcast. She could feel the others' attention on her but resisted the impulse to look up. Her disappointment that no one else spoke up in her defense silenced any protests she wanted to offer. She knew Hitochi agreed with her, but why hadn't he voiced his opinions? Was he so eager to return to Earth after only five months, less than two on site?

The *Worthington* might have been a small ship to her captain, but to Kari, whose earlier expeditions had been aboard tiny, privately charted vessels, the frigate was enormous. Over 150 meters long and 50 meters wide, the *Worthington*'s three decks boasted a gymnasium, a squash court, a library, a theater, a galley, labs, and comfortable if not spacious quarters for the crew and passengers. Her powerful nuclear engines rapidly propelled her to secure translation points where her infinite gravity drive modules created a pinpoint wormhole with which she bypassed light years of space in one translation. The outbound voyage had taken 15 jumps and 80 days, 12 of those days in a slow, careful approach to the Band.

Because the Band and its companion sun travelled in a long arc outside the Milky Way Galaxy on a journey that would eventually take it into the galaxy's core to be disintegrated by the gravity distortions of the black hole lurking there, it now moved away from the galaxy. Each week spent on the Band translated into several added days in return time. The reason for the Band's eccentric orbit lent credence to her idea the Band was a gigantic mausoleum; a cemetery world designed to transport its occupants to a final resting place in the heart of the galaxy, to be digested and spewed out as stardust in the endless cycle of creation, a kind of cosmic cremation.

The Band's origins were still a mystery, but it had been crawling along its path for almost as long as the Architects had first explored space. The tremendous power needed to construct such a marvel paled in comparison to the force necessary to alter the path of a red dwarf star. Stabilizing a red dwarf for the length of the journey involved an immeasurable output of energy. With all the marvels around them, she found it incomprehensible that the captain wanted to leave.

The discussion broke up as the dinner chime sounded. The meals were highly anticipated after sucking at suit rations through a straw all day. The food was always tasty if unimaginative and unvaried, but she found she had no appetite. The aroma of freshly baked garlic bread and lasagna, usually one of her favorites, turned her stomach. She went directly to her quarters, eager for a few minutes of solitude. She was glad Deidre was still dining. She didn't have to worry about Deidre cajoling her into leaving so she could bring someone to the room they shared.

Kari would have changed assignments to room with Amanda Collins, but the astrophysicist had recently become involved with Dale McLaren, one of the sailors, during the long voyage and now shared a cabin with him. She lamented the fact that, as a lowly archaeologist, she did not rate a single-occupancy cabin. Leanu Mbala, the only other civilian female, shared her cabin with one of the Matsui 20-terabyte computers compiling data from the remote surveillance drones scattered along the Band's length.

Her solitude was not to be, as a short while later a soft tap at the door broke her chain of thought.

"Come in," she answered before thinking, a polite habit difficult to break, though she really did not want to entertain company, especially if it was Luntz.

Hitochi entered, now clad in a crisp white coverall, his lieutenant's bars gleaming on his shoulders, and the U.N. Navy patch above his left breast pocket. She tried not to think of him as Navy, but inside the ship, his bearing was decidedly military.

"May I sit?" he asked.

She gestured to Deidre's empty bed, unmade as usual. "Sit."

Hitochi pushed aside the bed sheets, eyed a pair of lacy underwear for a moment, and covered them with the sheet. Kari suppressed a smile. He brushed his hand through his short black hair and said, "I know the captain's announcement upset you, but you have to see it from his viewpoint."

She resented Hitochi's making excuses for Captain Sidthuri. "Must I? He didn't want this assignment, and he'll do anything to prove he was right."

Hitochi shook his head. "No, he's not that petty. That's why he was drinking more than usual. He had to screw up his resolve. He's used to results, and we've discovered nothing an unmanned probe couldn't have at less cost."

"It's only been seven weeks," she protested.

"Almost eight," he corrected her, and then held out his hands in surrender at her stern look of disapproval. "I agree with you. I'm an engineer. This Architect Band material fascinates me. If I could discover its properties and how to manufacture it, our ships could explore the heart of a sun."

"Why didn't you speak up tonight?"

He sucked in his lower lip for a moment and shook his head. "He's my superior officer. You don't piss off your captain. He's allowed me an extraordinary amount of leeway to explore the Band. I don't want to jeopardize that."

His admission amplified her guilt at being derisive to him. She did the same thing with Kirkurk for the same reason.

"For you, it's just an engineering problem."

"I am an engineer," he answered quickly.

"But you care nothing for its builders," she said, carefully choosing her words.

His eyes jerked away from her to stare at his feet. "Well, I ... I'm curious, of course, but ..."

She sighed at his deflection. "That's the difference between us. I want to know about them, not their constructs. How did they live their lives? Did they have families, pets, listen to music? Did they believe in a higher power? What drove them to create such magnificent structures? Why did they retreat from space? Were they happy?"

Hitochi looked at her curiously. "Happy? That's an odd question."

She shook her head. "No, it's not. We think they created the artifacts for their beauty, to enjoy them, but what if there is a deeper significance behind them? What if they created the artifacts for a specific purpose? Wouldn't that change our view of the Architects?"

He tilted his head slightly. "A specific purpose? What purpose?"

She grimaced and squirmed in her chair, uncomfortable with the question. "I don't know. It's just a feeling." She pulled up a scene of the Band on her flatscreen. "The Band is different from the other artifacts. They created the artifacts for others to enjoy, not for themselves. They created the Band for themselves, a memorial, a Cemetery World."

Hitochi rolled his eyes and wiggled his fingers in the air. "Cemetery. Woo. Creepy." He became more serious. "Look, I'm in no hurry to leave. I can learn a lot here, but I'm a naval officer. Our primary purpose is to protect the commercial corridors against pirates and smugglers. Captain Sidthuri is a decorated veteran. He hates inaction, especially when other vessels are fighting in our stead while we're out here ..." He fumbled for a word.

"Wasting time," she said, supplying the word she thought he meant.

From the beginning, Kari had resented hitching a ride to the Band on a military vessel. Science and military seldom mixed. However, the enormous distance involved required a large vessel, which only the Navy possessed. She stared at the image of the Band on her screen, trying to decipher the deeper meaning the Architects had intended for their creation. It always came just within her grasp before slipping away like a wisp of smoke.

"This is important, too important to ignore," she insisted.

"No one is ignoring it. Maybe he's right. Maybe we need a larger expedition better equipped for a long stay. God knows we need physicists and engineers more qualified than me. We didn't know what to expect out here. This stuff is way over my head."

Hitochi was right, and that irked her. When an unmanned FTL probe had picked up spatial discrepancies near a small red dwarf star beyond the edge of the galaxy four years earlier, the united governments of Earth had deemed it too distant and too costly to investigate. Not until the probe transmitted faint images from five-light-years distance of an artificial construct likely of Architect origin did they relent. An expedition was mounted, but they had not expected the Band. They all faced challenges for which they were unprepared.

"You're doing an excellent job. Besides ..." She paused. "I might not be chosen for the next expedition," she confessed. It was the truth and admitting it hurt. She had gotten her position because many Architect archaeologists did not want to spend a year in the void. Now, the venture had become less archaeological and more technical oriented. "The answer is here, and I intend to find it, now, while I can."

She felt he wanted to laugh at her but refrained from doing so. She silently thanked him for allowing her that small scrap of dignity. She pointed at the Band beneath the dome. "The Architects built the Band first, and then the other artifacts much later, almost as an afterthought. The artifacts started us searching for their creators, and the search led here. The Architects began here and ended here. There must be a reason."

Hitochi studied her for a moment. Rather than Lutz's lecherous looks, Hitochi's penetrating gaze excited her and made her acutely aware that he found her desirable. "Do you think the Architects originated here?"

She marveled that he could read her thoughts. "From the Band? No." She paused. She had never voiced her thoughts about the Architects' origins. She decided to use Hitochi as a sounding board. "What if they created the Band from planets of the Cyclops solar system, including their home world? As their sun cooled to red, the Band was a more efficient means of collecting energy."

Hitochi nodded. "As an engineer, I understand that, but what about the artifacts? Where do they fit in? If they could explore space, why devote so much energy to transforming a dying world? Why not simply choose a new one?"

"It was their home, Ken, like Earth is our home. It will always be home no matter how far mankind expands into space. The Architects changed toward the end, became more introspective. The artifacts are sign posts to something … wonderful."

Her inability to express her feelings about the Architects frustrated her. She knew how she felt and knew she was right, but could not find the words to convince anyone else.

Hitochi stared at her a long moment before finally smiling. "I have to turn to," he said. "See you tomorrow."

She sighed as he stood to leave. If she had failed to convince him, how could she sway the others to her cause? At the door, he said, "Fitzhugh is going to search for an entrance on the underside of the Band tomorrow, a backdoor. Maybe he'll have better luck."

"Maybe," she answered with little enthusiasm.

The reverse side of the Band facing away from the sun was seamless and unadorned except for an identical dome directly below the dome they were exploring. From its dimensions and location, Bonner Fitzhugh, the team's only qualified structural engineer, had proposed both domes were actually part of a much larger sphere. If so, the sphere melded seamlessly into the material of the Band as if carved from it. He and a handful of others had wanted to begin the explorations there, deeming it the most obvious place to start, but Kirkurk and Captain Sidthuri had vetoed the idea in favor of the sunward-side Dome. Kirk ridiculed Fitzhugh's idea as 'sneaking in through the backdoor.' She wished Fitzhugh luck, but she agreed with Kirkurk in this instance. The answer lay on the sunward side of the Band.

After Hitochi had gone, she mentally kicked herself for being so standoffish. He had attempted several times to get close to her during the voyage, and unlike Luntz's glib attentions, she felt his interest was genuine and his intentions honorable. Yet, she had turned him aside each time. They were alone in her cabin. She should have made a move on him. She was certain he would have responded. Why hadn't she? *Because I'm a cold fish, that's why.* Why was she being so obstinate and cold? Was it because she was so driven, or was she so driven because she was incapable of returning simple human emotions, more comfortable delving into dead things, as Deidre had accused?

Disappointed in the day's results on all fronts, she mumbled, "Lights off," to extinguish the light above her bed, lay down fully clothed, and let sleep take her.

3

Kahoku Mani badly wanted a cigar. His suit helmet could dispense a safer substitute nicotine vapor through his oxygen line, but he missed the taste of tobacco and the feel of a fat stogie in his hands. It was a filthy habit, but his grandfather had smoked two packs of cigarettes a day, and his father had smoked a pipe. It was a Mani family tradition, as was sailing. His great grandfather had been a navigator on a solar-sail schooner plying the trade route between Oahu, Tahiti, and San Francisco. His grandfather had been a bosun's mate on the U.S. destroyer *Anderson* during the Five-Day War between the U.S. and the Philippines in 2115. His father had been a mechanic on a near-system ore freighter on the Earth-Titan run.

Kahoku, whose name meant 'star' in Hawaiian, had followed family tradition and enlisted in the United Nations Navy. He had seen a dozen worlds, but so far, he had made no mark for which his ancestors would be proud. He had thought himself destined for great things. Now, he was standing in the dark on an alien artifact wishing he had a cigar.

Why they needed guards in such an obviously dead place was beyond him, but he had pulled the duty. He continued his slow circuit around the ship, wishing with every bouncing step he was in his bunk listening to classic blues on his pod. As a teenager, he had enjoyed long walks around his island home of Hawai'i, often while listening to the blues. Most of all, he enjoyed the feel of the sun on his skin and a tropical breeze on his face. Here, there was no wind, no tropical sun. He was as far from his home as any human had ever been, and all he could think was how good a cigar would taste.

One leg of his circuit brought him very near the Dome. Even in the deep darkness, visible only by the majesty of the Milky Way behind it, the Dome appeared mysterious and intimidating, like a silent Kilauea, ready to erupt at any moment. He waved his suit light across the structure. The ebony substance devoured it as if hungry for light. So far, the scientists had sat around scratching their heads at their discovery, thwarted by the Band's mysteries. Kahoku took things like that in stride.

The gods did not intend man to know everything. Without mystery, what in life was worth the effort of living?

As he stood staring at the Dome, a dark mirage hovering just this side of disappearing altogether in the darkness, he moved his right leg around to ease the chaffing around his crotch where perspiration collected. "Damn suit. They could stick a camera out here to stand watch, and I could be back in the ship and out of this sweatbox." No amount of effort relieved his annoying itch.

A rush of dizziness swept over him. He staggered a few steps before planting both feet firmly on the ground. At first, he thought his ministrations to his itchy crotch had overtaxed him. He shook his head to clear it and checked his suit biometric readings, mystified to see his oxygen level was dropping. In fact, all his suit readings were nose-diving, including power. His suit lights dimmed to total darkness.

"What a time for a suit malfunction," he moaned.

He tried his com link but heard only the distressing hiss of static. He was not quite in a panic, but he began to wish he were somewhere else, like with a deeply tanned *wahini* at Maninowali Beach at Kua Bay with its white sugar-sand beach and crystal-clear water. He began the long trek back to the ship, moving at a slow pace to conserve oxygen.

He sensed rather than saw something approaching him. It was a deeper blackness imposed on the darkness surrounding him. It was probably a trick of the eye, like black spots after staring at a bright light, but his orders were to report anything strange. The darkness had no distinct shape. It was more like a pulsating mist, folding in on itself and rushing forward. Each pulse brought it nearer. He had heard the rumors of ghosts on the Band but had ignored them as ridiculous. Now, he wondered if they could be true.

He maneuvered to place the mist between himself and the ship, hoping to see it more clearly defined against the lights of the ship. The mist coalesced, became smaller and denser, hovering a few centimeters above the dark material of the Band. Eyes formed first, red and pulsating like bubbling molten pools of lava in Kilauea's cauldron. Dark filaments danced around the head, like a woman's long, silky hair in the breeze. He smiled as he recognized her.

"*Aloha oe, Tutu Pele*," he said in greeting. "*Ka wahini 'ai honua*," he added, calling her the earth-eating woman, his people's name for Pele.

The shadow swooped down on him, enfolding him in her dark embrace. He could not move. He did not fight. *Pele* was a goddess. She meant him no harm. He was in the air, moving toward the Dome at breakneck speed. He closed his eyes, waiting for the crush of impact, but none came. He was inside the Dome, passing through walls and floors, moving quickly deeper into the bowels of the structure toward an unknown destination.

Minutes later, the shadow Pele dropped him on the floor of a dark space. His suit light flickered on, illuminating oddly shaped objects around him. With a start, he realized they were bones. He knew then his captor was not *Pele,* but as he stared at the shadow creature, he felt no fear, only curiosity. The fear didn't come until the shadow solidified, reached inside his chest with a black hand, and ripped out his still beating heart.

4

The sound of claxons awakened Kari from a fitful sleep filled with dark images and strange sensations in which she fled down long, shadowed corridors pursued by creatures she could not see, but who whispered to her in an unknown language. At first, she thought the shrill blaring was a part of her dream still haunting her mind, but the claxon's intensity soon roused her to full wakefulness. She fought off the intense chill that had gripped her during her nightmare.

She spoke the light into life and saw that Deidre, as usual, was not in her bed. Kari wondered briefly whose bed she was sharing. The klaxon continued blaring. She checked her watch. It was just past 4:00 a.m., well before the usual wake up call. She grabbed a bottle of water, splashed some on her face to dispel the vestiges of sleep, and slipped on her ship's softboots. Outside, she stopped the first person she saw, Les Mailors, a team biochemist. His pale blue eyes, too large for his thin-as-a-rail body, were ablaze with excitement.

"What's going on, Les?"

He barely slowed down as he replied, "Air. The Band is producing an atmosphere like Earth's." Before she could inquire further, he disappeared down the corridor into his lab. *Passageways aboard ship, not corridors*, she reminded herself.

"Air," she whispered, and smiled. "They know we're here."

* * * *

Six hours after it had begun the mysterious process, the Band had produced sufficient atmosphere to negate the necessity for environmental suits. Atmospheric pressure and the mixture of gases was almost an exact duplicate of Earth's at sea level. The temperature was that of a spring day in New York City, cool but mild. Even the gravity had increased to .98G. Kari was delighted.

There was a dark side to the news, however. Kahoku Mani, the big Hawaiian ensign with whom she had spoken several times, had disappeared while on guard duty. Video from the outside security cameras had been inexplicably blank. Kari could not help but connect the disappearance of the crewmember with the appearance of an atmosphere.

Captain Sidthuri ordered an immediate lockdown of the ship, suspension of all work, and a search for Kahoku. The search teams returned an hour later after having found no trace of the missing Hawaiian. It took all of Kirkurk's formidable powers of persuasion to convince the captain to allow his team outside the ship. Kari cycled through the airlock before he could change his mind.

She brushed her naked hand against the ebony material of the Dome for the first time, expecting it to be cold, but found it surprisingly warm to the touch.

"It feels like velvet," she said to Hitochi, who had accompanied her. "Not at all hard. It tingles."

"It's some kind of single-molecule surface tension field," Hitochi explained. "Make any attempt to penetrate it, and it becomes solid." He smiled and touched the wall of the Dome. "It's much nicer working without a suit. I wonder how they did it. Probes indicate only this section of the Band contains air. Beyond a certain distance, the vacuum of space reasserts itself."

"They want us here," she replied. She pointed to the Band beneath her feet. "Right here."

"I hope they do, for Kahoku's sake, but perhaps they simply breathe the same type of atmosphere we do, and we inadvertently triggered an automated sequence of some kind."

"Maybe," she conceded, annoyed by Hitochi's cold logic, "but I prefer to think they want us here." Like Hitochi, she worried for Kahoku's safety, but the thrill of being able to walk around unencumbered by a bulky environment suit overrode any slight fear she might have.

She knew she was right. She could see no other option. The Architects had sent them an invitation. The fact that the Architects had created an atmosphere duplicating Earth's was less important to her than the timing of the sequence of events. First, Captain Sidthuri had suggested leaving; then, Kahoku had vanished. The next day an atmosphere appeared. They were under observation, perhaps since they entered the system.

"There's no smell," she commented, taking a deep breath of the virgin air. After months of breathing recycled ship's air, it was a welcomed change. The air scrubbers could never fully remove the slight smell of ozone, the cooking odors, or perspiration.

"There's nothing here to create an odor. It's a manufactured atmosphere. It's a sterile world."

She disagreed. "No, not sterile, just uncontaminated."

Hitochi looked puzzled. "What's the difference?"

"Sterile means lifeless." She swept her arms around her. "This place has known life. Uncontaminated means it no longer bears the marks of life. It has been scrubbed clean."

"Well, I suppose the sun has done that, but we'll contaminate it soon enough with all our germs."

She frowned at the thought. How would the Architects react to invading germs? Had they considered Kahoku a germ? She shook her head. "No, surely they have a way to prevent cross-contamination."

Hitochi cocked his head and arched one eyebrow as he stared at her. "You give them a lot of credit."

"Considering what they've accomplished, I would think decontaminating alien germs would be a trivial matter."

"You may be right. Just don't be too disappointed if this entire structure is solid."

His words struck her deeply. She had not even contemplated that possibility. Could the Band be just another massive object, like the twin Singing Moons or the Ice Planet? No, the Band was different. She could sense it. The answers they sought were within the impervious black shell, like a chocolate treat in a plastic Easter egg.

"This is what we've searched for, and they want us to discover its secrets."

Hitochi did not appear persuaded by her reasoning. "You're reading too much into the production of a breathable atmosphere."

She considered Hitochi's statement for a moment before shaking her head. "No, they know we're here. Taking Kahoku proves that."

Hitochi shrugged. "Whatever. Maybe Fitzhugh will find something. His group is leaving soon in one of the small shuttles."

She noticed Hitochi's attempt to defuse the situation by changing the subject and let it slide. She could never convince him if she pushed him too hard. "Now?" she asked. "That's odd."

"Why? Fitzhugh is determined to prove Kirkurk wrong and beat him inside."

"I would think finding Kahoku would take precedence."

Hitochi paused before answering, "Not to Fitzhugh."

Kari knew that was true enough. Fitzhugh was as cold as they came, worse even than Kirkurk. Kirkurk was a pain and an intellectual snob, but Fitzhugh's disdain for people was legendary. Almost as bad was his dismissal of Architect wonders as anything other than marvels of engineering. For that alone, Kari despised him.

"What are you doing?" she asked, as Hitochi dug through the equipment case he carried.

He pulled out a gravimetric probe, a thin rod attached to a small, hand-held box. "I'm going to check out that dimple in front of the Dome."

The dimple, a three-meter-in-diameter bowl-shaped depression in the flat surface of the Band near the Dome, was the only visible deformity they had discovered marring the ebony material. So far, it had withstood all efforts to fathom its secrets. One theory held it was an entrance into the Band. Another, one to which neither Kari nor Hitochi subscribed, suggested the dimple was the result of a meteor strike. Kari was no expert on meteor strikes, but she doubted the impact would have left such a regular mark. Nor for that matter, did she believe such an impact would scar the Band's impervious material.

"I'll come with you."

As they walked the half-kilometer to the dimple, carefully skirting the edge of the Dome, she imagined the Architects were inside the Dome, watching her through dark windows. She resisted the impulse to stop and wave lest Hitochi thought her crazy. The short journey was a joy free of the heavy suits. Unfettered, she wanted to dance. There was no wind, but the feel of air against her face as she walked brought a smile to her lips. Closing her eyes, she could well imagine a stroll through Central Park in her native New York. She made a quick *déboulé* in a tight circle, stepping with one leg and turning to land on the toes of her other foot.

Hitochi stopped and stared at her with a mixture of shock and wonder. "What are you doing?"

She fought down the exhilaration of freedom pounding in her chest. She felt light enough to float away from the surface. She imagined herself pirouetting against the backdrop of stars as the Band slowly spun below her, an ebony stage. She wondered if Hitochi danced but was too embarrassed to ask.

"Dancing. I took ballet as a child. I was never very good or very graceful. I felt like the ugly duckling that never turned into a swan."

"You're no ugly duckling," he said, smiling.

A hot flush of embarrassment colored her cheeks. She turned away before he could see. "Thank you," she whispered.

They walked the rest of the way in silence. At the dimple, Hitochi's professional manner reasserted itself. Kari tried to match his curiosity. Observing the 30-centimeter-deep depression, she remarked on the uniformity of its features. "It's not a meteor scar."

Hitochi waved the probe over the dimple's smooth surface. "No. It looks like a natural feature, not an event inspired one. There is no fusing or deformation of the material. What's this?" he said suddenly. He backed up slowly, running the probe over the spot he had just surveyed. "I don't believe it," he laughed.

His excitement was contagious. Her eyes danced over the dimple. "What is it?"

"I examined this area two days ago. The readings were neutral. Now, I'm picking up a spike in the gravimetric index." He lifted his foot experimentally. "You can even feel the difference, almost a ten percent increase."

"What does it mean?"

He looked at her and smiled impishly. "I have no idea, but it's wonderful."

For ten minutes, Hitochi examined the dimple with different instruments, sometimes on his hands and knees. He carefully scanned the entire perimeter; then, did it again. During that time, the gravity anomaly increased another ten percent.

"Whatever's occurring," he said, "it's happening quickly."

Before they could continue their conversation, the com units on their belts burst into life with an All Call signal, the signal to call in to the ship. Hitochi keyed his mic and spoke into it.

"This is Hitochi."

Kari couldn't hear the voice on the other end on her com link, meaning Hitochi had chosen the military channel, but watching his expression, she knew it must be something big. He drew his eyebrows together, narrowed his gaze downward, and drew his lips into a tight line. He raked one hand through his hair.

Finally, she could stand the suspense no longer. "What is it? What's going on?" she demanded.

"One of the probes detected a large energy fluctuation centered nearby." He glanced down at his feet. "Right here, I imagine."

Contact! Kari's excitement fought with her apprehension. Perhaps the Architects were going to swat them away like an annoying gnat. No, if that were true why alter the environment for them.

"What do we do?" she asked.

"The captain suggests returning to the ship."

That was the last thing Kari wanted to do. She felt no fear, only a vague sense of being on the verge of something wonderful.

"We can't go back," she said, surprised at the determination in her voice.

Hitochi watched the dial on one of his meters with a puzzled expression on his face. "I don't think it would matter. The energy readings are localized and are dissipating."

"What could it be?" Kari asked; then covered her mouth with her hand in surprise. "Look!"

She pointed to the dimple. The outer edges shimmered slightly, and then the entire dimple glistened as if wet. As she watched, the dimple bulged upward or filled in with some black liquid substance – she could not decide which – until it was level with the Band's surface. The shimmer abated and once again became solid, but left a distinctive ring where the perimeter of the dimple had been.

Hitochi knelt by the edge and used another device from his equipment bag; then, tapped it with his knuckles. "Solid. There's no residual radiation, no heat. The edges didn't melt. The dimple … transformed. Amazing."

They waited, but nothing happened. Once again, Hitochi scanned it with his gravimetric probe.

"Almost Earth normal," he announced, ".98-G."

Trying to suppress her fear, Kari slowly walked to the disc and stood on it. From its center, a small circular rod the diameter of her leg emerged, stopping when it rose to waist level. The top of the ebony rod glowed from within with a brilliant topaz light. She stared at it, mesmerized by its beauty. It was the first light, ornamentation, or color other than black she had seen on the Band. *Now, we're getting somewhere.* Hitochi joined her on the disc, looking at her as if expecting her to do something more.

"Do we dare?" she asked, feeling giddy and fighting the urge to giggle like a silly schoolgirl. "Or do we wait for the others?"

Hitochi reached out his hand toward the glowing topaz light; then, stopped and sighed. "We have to wait. If this is an entrance, as I suspect, we'll need a well-equipped team to enter." He grinned at her impatience. "It's been here half a billion years. A few hours shouldn't matter."

She burned inside with eagerness to see what the strange glowing rod did, but knew something as significant as their discovery should be examined closely. As much as she wanted to continue, she agreed with Hitochi's assessment. "Okay. We wait."

They stepped off the disc and returned to the ship.

5

After much arguing among both teams and the military, Captain Sidthuri pulled rank and decided the initial insertion team would consist of only eight people – Kirkurk, Sung, Mailors, and Fitzhugh as technical experts, Luntz as photographer, and Deidre as video chronicler. Because of Kahoku's disappearance, the captain insisted on two armed marines accompanying them. Fitzhugh, as smug and annoying as ever, refused to go, insisting the captain allow him to undertake his exploration of the underside of the Band. Sidthuri relented and chose Hitochi to replace him.

Kari vehemently protested her exclusion from the team, but Kirkurk ignored her until Hitochi reminded him that she had initially discovered the entrance and suggested she join them as his engineering assistant, if not as an archaeologist. To her surprise and immense relief, Kirkurk agreed.

The captain, over Kirkurk's protests, insisted they all wear full excursion suits as a safety measure. As much as she enjoyed the freedom without a suit, Kari thought the precaution warranted. They could not assume the atmosphere extended below the surface. Neither, Hitochi reminded them, could they assume the atmosphere was a permanent feature created solely for their benefit. Its purpose, while beneficial to the humans, could be part of the Band's automated maintenance, as was the day/night cycle or the solar radiation shield.

Two hours after the dimple transformed, the small caravan, properly equipped and heavily laden with extra oxygen tanks, lights, and equipment, trekked to the disc. The consensus was that the disc was some sort of elevator, although several members of the team suggested a race as advanced as the Architects might use teleportation or some other exotic form of transport. Kari wasn't certain she wanted her body zapped from one place to another, but she doubted the Architects would have gone to all the trouble with the dimple to teleport them inside.

The two marines went first. One laid his palm on top of the rod. Nothing happened. He tried several times with the same lack of results.

The others muttered their bitter disappointment, but Kari had an idea. The pillar had reacted to her bare hand.

"Try removing your glove," she suggested.

The marine looked to Hitochi, who nodded his approval. Removing the glove, he once more placed his hand atop the rod. Still, nothing happened. Kari was dismayed. Kirkurk glared at her for wasting their time. On a hunch, she stepped forward, removed her glove, and after a moment's hesitation, grasped the top of the rod with her hand. The deep topaz light pulsed a few times before changing to a lighter azure hue. Everyone stepped back, as the disc sank into the surface of the Band. After it had descended a few meters, she removed her hand and the disc stopped. She placed her hand on it again, and it rose.

Hitochi looked at her with an unspoken question on his face.

"I was the first to touch it. Maybe it imprinted on me some way."

Kirkurk looked at those gathered around him. Deidre's video camera was running, panning the crowd. Never one to miss an opportunity to extol his own importance, Kirkurk stared into the camera through his helmet and said, "We take these first steps of discovery so that mankind might further his long journey into knowledge." Kari recognized his liberal interpretation of Neil Armstrong's words upon his first steps on the moon. She doubted anyone else was aware of the near plagiarism. She also doubted Kirkurk was aware the glare of his helmet visor had obscured his face. She decided not to mention it to him for fear he would want to do it all over again. She was too eager to get on with it.

After loading all the equipment onto the disc, it became very crowded with the addition of the nine-member team of explorers. The crush of bodies forced Kari up against Josh Luntz, who grinned at her and leaned close until their helmets touched.

"I'm so glad you came," he said so no one else could hear. "This should be an interesting experience."

She felt as if he was mentally undressing her through her suit. She pulled away as far as she could, a matter of only a few centimeters, but he got the message and backed away still grinning. She placed her hand on the rod, and the disc dropped as if someone had yanked the floor from beneath her feet, but she felt no disconcerting acceleration. Only by focusing on the lip of the circular opening quickly receding above her could she determine the rapid rate of descent. The perfectly round shaft glowed with a diffuse azure light that matched the top of the control rod. After 500 meters, she had observed no markings on the smooth wall.

By the time they reached a depth of a full kilometer, she wondered if the disc was conveying them to the very bottom of the Band. Was Fitzhugh correct? Was the real entrance on the shadowed side? Finally, the elevator stopped, so softly she did not realize at first it was no longer descending. They faced a blank black wall all around them.

"What do we do now?" Deidre asked.

Kari touched the wall with her hand and felt a strange sensation in her head, like someone tickling her brain. On an impulse, she removed her glove and touched it again. As if cued by her bare flesh, a section of the wall vanished, as if it had merely been an illusion. The suddenness startled her.

"I'll be damned," Hitochi commented and smiled at her. "You have the touch."

She wondered about that. Why was the Band accepting her hand imprint and not the others? The thought unnerved her somewhat. Beyond the elevator shaft laid a wide, curving corridor whose sides, floor, and ceiling were so black it masked the corridor's true length. She was disappointed Kahoku wasn't there to greet them as an emissary chosen by the Architects. She worried about him.

Hitochi checked the atmosphere readings. "There's no air here," he said. "I don't understand why no atmosphere is bleeding from the elevator shaft into the corridor."

"Don't worry," Kirkurk assured him, "our suits hold eight hours of air, and the extra tanks are good for six additional hours. We will explore for six hours maximum, replenish our tanks, and head back to the ship." He held up his hand to quell the protests at his time limit. "I insist. I agree with Captain Sidthuri on this matter. Safety first."

The wall reappeared behind them, cutting them off from the shaft. Seconds later, Kari felt the fabric of her suit moving. "Air," she whispered.

Hitochi checked his instrument and nodded. "It's almost Earth normal." Cautiously, he removed his helmet and sniffed. "It's not musty."

She smiled at his reference to the musty air of a tomb. She joined him and removed her helmet. He was right. The air had no odor or taste, but it was assuredly fresh.

"Keep your suits on and your gloves and helmets nearby," Kirkurk warned. "We don't want any nasty surprises."

Kari didn't think the Band's builders would bother with air if they meant them any harm, but she kept her suit on. She stuffed her gloves in her helmet and clipped it to her belt. Their booted footsteps echoed eerily as they marched single file down the corridor behind one of the marines, as if the hard material of the floor and walls partially absorbed the sound. Their suit lights barely illuminated the corridor. The ebony walls sucked the life from the lights like a vampire. The beams illuminated their suits but left only a faint reflection on the walls' surface. It was like prowling the depths of the deepest, darkest coalmine with a candle. The darkened corridor reminded her of her dream. She shivered.

"Chilly?" Hitochi asked.

She shook her head. "Excited," she lied.

As they explored the corridor, her enthusiasm slowly waned. She had hoped they would find a trove of Architect artifacts perfectly preserved in the previously vacuum environment, but to her dismay, they encountered no markings or objects of any kind, no dust to indicate any had decayed over the millennia, or doors leading into other corridors or rooms. The single, featureless corridor wound around dizzyingly for several kilometers, sloping slightly downward. If not for the GPS readings from her suit comp and the fact they had not deviated from the corridor, she would have been hopelessly lost.

"Is this a corridor or just a method of conveying air to the surface of the Band from some reservoir deep within?" Mailors asked.

Mailors' question mirrored Kari's reservations. Had they inadvertently entered one of the Band's ventilation shafts? Was their invitation in reality just a routine maintenance function? Had Kahoku accidentally fallen into another ventilator shaft and lay dead or injured at the bottom? Were they wasting their time, as the captain believed?

Kari's doubt drained her enthusiasm. Where at first her steps had been light and buoyant, driven by her thirst for adventure and the possibility of discovery, now, they were leaden. She trudged along, each step moving her farther from her comfort zone. She glanced at Hitochi. The opportunity of observing the inner workings of the Band had put a fresh sparkle in his eyes. As an engineer, he was in his element. He pushed up close behind the marine leading the procession, eager to see what lay beyond the next turn of the corridor.

"The corridor forms a Fibonacci Spiral," Sung replied.

"Fibonacci Spiral?" Kari asked. "What's that?"

"Certain objects in nature show a mathematical relationship with Fibonacci numbers – a spiral nautilus shell, a flowering artichoke, or the fruitlets of a pineapple. Fibonacci, an Italian mathematician, discovered the number sequence named for him. Each number of a Fibonacci sequence is the sum of the two preceding numbers – 0,1,1,2,3,5,8,13,21,34,55, 89,144, etc."

"Nautilus?" Hitochi repeated, noting one of Sung's examples. He turned to Kari smiling. "Maybe the Architects *were* slugs."

Sung ignored Hitochi's remark. "It is expressed by the equation $F_n = F_{n-} + F_{n-2}$. By my calculation, we should be almost directly beneath where we entered the corridor." He glanced around. "I had hoped there might be something significant here, a marker of some sort. I am extremely disappointed."

"Too easy," Hitochi said. "They want to play games; invite us in, and make us jump through hoops."

"Could it be some kind of intelligence test?" Kari asked, thinking along the same lines.

Kirkurk jumped on her remark with his usual disdain for others' ideas. If he didn't think of it, it was insignificant. "I should think arriving in a Faster-than-Light ship would be proof enough of our intelligence."

"Maybe they have a different definition of intelligence," Kari replied. He did not respond.

They stood around for a few minutes trying to decide their next move. To Kari, it was obvious. They could either continue along the corridor or retrace their steps in defeat. Hitochi was the first to notice the difference in the wall of the corridor and brought it to their attention.

"The energy field is in flux here," he said, reading his instrument. He reached out and touched the wall experimentally. When he removed his hand, an impression of his handprint remained glowing on the dark wall material for several seconds. He swiped the wall with his fingertips, leaving a series of five streaks. They too faded after a few seconds. "It's like a digital chalkboard."

"What do we do," she asked, "write hello?"

Hitochi continued to play with the wall, drawing designs with his fingertip. As she watched, his fingers made a swirl on the screen, giving her an idea.

"Dr. Sung, can you draw a Fibonacci Spiral on the wall?"

He looked at her mystified, but nodded. Using the edge of his flatscreen as a ruler, he drew a large square, and divided it in half, further dividing each consecutive square in half. "I will use dots instead of numbers," he said. "I doubt our alien friends understand Arabic numerals." He placed one dot in each of the two center squares, adding dots until he had 34 in the larger square. "That should be sufficient." He drew a spiral connecting the opposite corners of each square. Kari smiled as she recognized the resemblance to a nautilus shell and to the interlocked spirals of the Ice Moon. "There, a Golden Spiral." Beside the square, he added the formula for the Fibonacci number sequence and for the Golden Spiral, $r = \alpha \varepsilon^{b\theta}$.

He stepped back to examine his results. The spiral continued to glow, growing steadily brighter. Suddenly, the entire wall before them dissolved, as if a mist clearing in the morning sunlight, revealing a large room beyond. Kari gasped in surprise and took an involuntary step backwards. Fighting her fear, she leaned forward and peered into the room. A diffuse blue light illuminated the room from an unknown source with a dim eerie glow, but it did not alter the intense blackness of the walls. The room was barren, devoid of contents or anything to mar the perfect symmetry of the walls. It was just an empty space. Disappointment dampened her initial excitement of discovery.

"Do we enter?" Sung asked.

"Of course," Kirkurk replied. "It would be impolite to ring the doorbell and run away." Making certain Deidre focused the camera on him, he walked inside, head held high, chest pushed out. "There's nothing here," Kirkurk complained to the camera after a few moments. "It's empty." Crestfallen that his triumphant entrance was wasted, he glared at the empty room as if it was a personal affront to his status.

"So was the corridor," Kari reminded him, trying not to let her disappointment consume her.

As soon as all nine of them entered the space, the light level rose slightly. Hitochi was the first to discover the light cast no shadows. He used every instrument in his equipment pack and shook his head in defeat. "I don't know how they manage to produce a light with no apparent source."

Kari noticed several previously undetected empty niches in the wall, visible only from certain angles. *Yes! That's more like it*, she thought. Compelled by her overwhelming curiosity, she walked directly to one of the niches to examine it. She took measurements with her laser, carefully noting them in her comp-log. Each niche measured 97 centimeters high by 29 centimeters wide, but only 5 centimeters deep.

"Those are all prime numbers," Kirkurk announced loudly. "There must be some significance to the numbers, just as there must be with the number of buildings in the Cities."

Sung shook his head. "That is just conjecture on your part. It has no bearing on this matter."

"The niches could not have held anything substantial," Kari mused aloud to silence both Kirkurk and Sung. "It's more like a frame."

"A frame for what?" Sung asked.

"A photo," Hitochi suggested. He touched the back of the depression hoping it would glow just as the wall of the corridor had. Nothing happened. Disappointed, he stepped back.

"Maybe the questions become more difficult," Kari said.

"What would they want to know about us?" Hitochi asked.

"Who we are," Deidre replied.

They all turned to stare at her.

She looked surprised by the attention. "What? Well, I would want to know who was outside my door before I let them inside."

Hitochi pointed to her 3-D video recorder. "Can you project images from your recorder onto the depression?"

Her eyes narrowed slightly, and she cocked her head to one side in annoyance. "Of course I can." She pushed a button and aimed the recorder at the recessed space. An image of Kirkurk entering the room appeared. The niche grabbed the image and began manipulating it, forming a 3-D hologram and turning it, as if inspecting it from all angles.

"Try other images on the other spaces," Hitochi suggested.

"Project an image of an Architect artifact," Kari told her.

Deidre found an image of the Ice World and projected it onto one niche. The image began rotating. Suddenly, script appeared above the image, changing rapidly. The words or numbers were indecipherable geometrical shapes, some overlapping or with curved or straight lines and dots surrounding them. Kari likened them to a combination of Hittite cuneiform and Vedic Sanskrit. She marveled at the sudden response.

"I think it's data about the Ice World. Look, one section of script doesn't change, like a catalog number."

"Are you recording this?" Kirkurk asked.

"Of course," Deidre replied somewhat testily, as if offended that she could not do her job.

"If the number of characters indicates the value of the number, there are many more artifacts than we've discovered thus far," Sung said.

An image began to form in a third indentation. As she recognized it, Kari gasped in revulsion. "It's Kahoku."

It was Kahoku, but not as she remembered him. The big Hawaiian lay unmoving and spread-eagled on the floor of a room somewhere in the Band. Crimson blood stained his suit and helmet. The view changed focus, and Kari saw where the blood originated. Deidre groaned aloud in horror. The chest area of his suit looked as if some wild animal had mauled him. Three parallel gashes ran diagonally from his left shoulder to his right hip. The shattered ends of his ribs marked a hole in his chest where his heart had been. His eyes were open, but Kari knew he was seeing nothing. Kahoku was dead.

"Murderers!" Sung shouted, his lips stretched light and nostrils flared in anger. His eyes remained fixed on the image, as if he could not turn away from the scene of slaughter. "They butchered him."

Kari agreed but could not speak for fear the bile rising in her throat would spew out of her mouth rather than her outrage. Kirkurk reacted differently.

"Perhaps they were examining him," he said, his face betraying no emotion other than curiosity. "Maybe he was already dead, injured in some accident."

"Or maybe they sliced him open while he was still alive and just didn't give a shit," Hitochi growled, eyeing the image with disgust and anger. His hand brushed the weapon at his side. The two marines, sensing a threat, took up positions on opposite sides of the room, holding their larger flechette dart rifles in their arms at ready.

"How do we find him?" Kari asked the others. No one had an answer.

"He could be anywhere," Hitochi finally replied.

Deidre glanced around the room, her eyes widened in fright, the blood drained from her face. Her voice had a worried edge to it, as she said, "We should leave this place."

The words had barely left Deidre's mouth when the opening through which they had entered vanished, replaced by the ebony wall, cutting off their retreat. Deidre rushed to the wall and pounded on it with her fists. "Let me out!" she cried. "Let me out!" She slid down the wall on her back and began sobbing into her hands. "It's a trap."

Kari wondered if they, too, were about to meet Kahoku's fate? Part of her refused to believe the Architects would lay a trap for them.

"Our supplies!" Kirkurk wailed.

Kari realized with a sinking feeling that they had foolishly left their extra oxygen tanks, their tools, and most of their food and water in the corridor while they had examined the room. Now, it was out of reach beyond the black wall. She checked her suit air supply – slightly less than five hours remaining. She fought down the rising panic trying to grip her. She had learned long ago not to sweat the problems over which she had no control and instead concentrate on the ones she did. They could not go back the way they had entered. That appeared to be against the ambiguous rules. Their only logical choice was to move forward.

6

The disappearance of one of his crew only reinforced Captain Sidthuri's deep-seated distrust of the Architects. Any species able to control the incredible power needed to build and transform entire worlds or to construct an object as massive as the Band frightened him. It was anthropomorphizing them based on his personal experiences with his own kind, but no matter how advanced, or how much power at their disposal, the Architects were still susceptible to the same flaws as any other thinking species. He saw the Architects as a possible threat, one he had thought long dead. Now, on the Band, they had awakened something long dormant, and he did not think it was at all benevolent.

When the Band had created an exact duplicate of Earth's atmosphere and gravity, the scientists had considered it an invitation – Welcome to the Band. He smelled a trap baited with a taste of home. After much deliberation and arguing, he had acceded to Kirkurk's demand to enter the Band mainly to get the obstinate and irritating archaeologist out of his hair on the pretense of searching for the missing Ensign Kahoku. He did not share their hope the big Hawaiian was still alive. Kahoku's suit monitor had shown certain biometric ... peculiarities, followed by a surge in adrenalin levels and oxygen consumption. To Sidthuri, that sounded like a frightened man, and it took a lot to frighten the imperturbable Kahoku. Moments later, it ceased transmitting altogether. To Sidthuri, that meant Kahoku was dead.

Kirkurk's foray into the Band served a secondary purpose Sidthuri had not confided to the archaeologist. His team would act as a probing force into the heart of the Band, a lightning rod to draw any attention to them and away from his ship and the small Marine contingent for which he had another mission. Now, he did not know if his plan had worked or failed. He had lost contact with Kirkurk within minutes of his team's entering the Band.

The military-grade environmental suits worn by Lieutenant Hitochi and the two marines enhanced their signal strength to broadcast a real-time feed of each individual's physical condition and of their environment. Covert intelligence had been the real reason he had ordered the team to wear environmental suits, not simple caution. The civilians balked at such an intrusion into their privacy, and he could not order them to do so, but he needed Intel. He disliked working in the dark, but darkness was all the Band had to offer.

Kirkurk's team had entered the Band and descended the elevator shaft without incident. The suit readouts and Hitochi's verbal report confirmed they reached the bottom of the elevator shaft one kilometer below the surface. All three suits abruptly stopped broadcasting but not before detecting an oxygen environment. Less than a minute later, the opening of the shaft reformed as solid as before. The Architects had invited them in, and then closed and locked the door behind them. He was glad he had other options.

Bonner Fitzhugh, ass that he was, had insisted on examining the dome on the opposite side of the Band with two technicians and a shuttle pilot, instead of taking the obvious route inside the Band. Sidthuri held out little hope he would gain access, but he had rather have the obnoxious structural engineer off his ship and out of his hair. There was a slight chance Fitzhugh might get lucky. He put more faith in his second option.

He summoned First Sergeant Akoa Chaca to his office. Chaca, a former tribal policeman from the Hopi Reservation in Arizona, had served with him during the Battle of Icarus against the pirate leader Nathan Freeman. Chaca had experience. He was thorough, and his no-nonsense approach to a mission made him perfect for the job Sidthuri had in mind for him. The tall, muscular sergeant stood at attention in front of his desk, his dark eyes staring at a spot on the bulkhead directly behind and above Sidthuri's head. Unlike many of his crew who wore their hair longer than the regs allowed, Chaca's black hair, like the entire ten-man Marine contingent aboard, was a patch of fuzz covering his head. Sidthuri tolerated his crew's tonsorial choices but did not approve. He appreciated the sergeant's strict adherence to the military regs.

Sidthuri glanced down at Chaca's hip. Even aboard ship, the sergeant carried a non-regulation, bone-handled knife in a leather scabbard on his belt. The ancient weapon was incongruous in a world of hardened battle armor and flechette rifles, but it was a deadly weapon in the right hands, and Sidthuri had seen the sergeant wield it in battle with great effect.

"Sergeant, I need you to select five men to escort a technician on a mission for me."

"Yes, sir."

Sidthuri noted Chaca asked no questions concerning the nature of the mission even though he was aware of the disappearance of the first team. It showed discipline. "We picked up energy spikes emanating from several points on the Band at the same time the elevator appeared. The nearest location is 5,000 klicks from here. It suggests a means of detecting our presence and an active communications network. Someone or something activated the elevator or elevators, and then shut them down after our civilians entered. If we've awakened a sleeping beast, I want to know its intentions. I don't believe the Architects were as damned benevolent as most people think."

He leaned forward over his desk and lowered his voice. He didn't want everyone to hear him. "We've discovered the ruins of two sentient races but no living ones. Out of almost 80 worlds, only those two and they're dead. Maybe the Architects don't like competition." He watched Chaca's face for a change of expression, but the sergeant maintained his poise. *Not a twitch. Either he's the world's coolest character, or he believes as I do.*

"They placed the Band way out here in the middle of nowhere for a reason. I think they did it to keep anyone from finding it. If we missed a No Trespassing sign, I want to know about it. I want you and your team to gain entrance into the Band at that location and reconnoiter. If the Architects or some machine they left in control poses a threat to us or to mankind, I want to know about that as well. Understand?"

"Yes, sir. Recon, but if we encounter hostiles, we deal with them."

"Exactly, Sergeant."

Chaca glanced down at Sidthuri for the first time. His jaw twitched. "Sir, if the scientists have been unable to gain entrance except through the elevator, how do you propose we do so?"

Sidthuri grimaced. He had given that particular dilemma considerable thought. He had perused his orders carefully. They gave him considerable latitude in any actions he might deem necessary should he encounter a military threat. In his opinion, Kahoku's disappearance and the lack of communication with Kirkurk's team constituted such a threat.

"The archaeologists and scientists are reluctant to cause any damage to the Band, as if they're excavating some Egyptian tomb. I'm not so particular. You have my permission to use an MK 120 *Prometheus* missile."

Chaca nodded his approval.

The MK 120 had proven effective against enemy ships and installations by creating a ball of plasma able to reach temperatures of 10 million degrees Celsius, just shy of the temperature at the core of the sun. Sidthuri had no doubt it would work.

He continued. "If that doesn't get us inside, I don't know what will."

Chaca snapped to attention and saluted. "Yes, sir. I'll have the team ready to go at 1500 hours."

"Very good, Sergeant. Carry on."

Chaca paused. "Am I escorting a Navy technician or a civilian one?"

"Civilian."

Chaca's face didn't change, but Sidthuri knew what he was thinking. "She's under your command, Sergeant. Don't let her play you."

"No, sir," he replied and left.

One way or another, Sidthuri was confident Chaca would get inside the Band. The other team had succeeded, apparently by invitation, but had since vanished without a trace, effectively leaving him blind. He might have to write them off. People who invite you in and slam the door shut behind you are usually not to be trusted.

* * * *

Chaca inspected his excursion team, Gunnery Sergeant Kyle Ryder, a combat-tested weapons specialist, and Lance Corporal Trevor Paisley, a slow-talking Cajun with a penchant for electronics and communications, were his technical staff. Private First Class Leon Ash, like Ryder, a combat vet and cold as ice under fire, Private Meredith Holmes, born in Mississippi but raised in the Marines, and Private Gregor Aleyev, a second-generation Russian from Chicago with a love for Russian poetry, were along for the grunt work.

Each marine wore vacuum-rated battle armor and carried a Maglev F12 flechette rifle capable of firing 300, 3-inch depleted-uranium projectiles per minute. In addition, they each carried an assortment of grenades, Maglev side arms, and Claymore mines. Ryder carried a SAW KB 210 .50 caliber machine gun, its ammunition sealed for a vacuum environment. Chaca preferred the lightweight Tach II 7.62mm sniper rifle, also fitted for a vacuum environment, and his tribal knife with its eight-inch blade. Each man had undergone rigorous training and understood the gravity of the mission.

His appraising gaze lingered on the civilian technician they were accompanying into the Band. He was not pleased Captain Sidthuri had chosen one of the civilians rather than a Navy technician. Civilians usually meant trouble. Amanda Collins was obviously uncomfortable in the black body armor custom-fitted to her small frame. At five-feet-four inches, she looked too frail to support the heavy armor and the equipment strapped to her like barnacles on a ship.

"Collins, let someone help you with that equipment."

Collins beamed a smile through her visor. "No, thank you. I'll manage. I like to keep my tools handy."

Well, she's plucky anyway. He nodded. "Suit yourself. Just don't slow us down."

"I'll do my best, sir."

"Sergeant," Chaca corrected her. "I'm a grunt like the rest of these men. I earn my paycheck. Hasn't McLaren taught you anything about the Navy?"

She smiled. "He's trying, but we don't get much time together."

Chaca had seen McLaren and Collins together around the ship; usually, with their arms so interwoven they looked like a two-headed carnival sideshow freak. He didn't approve of shipboard romances, especially between Navy personnel and civilians, but it wasn't his call. Captain Sidthuri didn't object, so he didn't venture his opinion.

"He's Navy. Always say your goodbyes like you mean them."

His statement took Collins aback. She stared at him without replying. He checked his watch – 1500 hours exactly. "Let's load up."

They filed into the shuttle and strapped in. He signaled the pilot thumbs up. The pilot wasted no time lifting off. His job was to drop them off and return to the ship. *Lucky bastard*, Chaca thought. He didn't like the idea of being without transport 5,000 klicks from base, but the *Worthington* had only two military-rated shuttles, and the captain did not want to risk one of them in an unknown situation.

His gaze rested on the *Prometheus* missile in the rear of the shuttle. It looked like a giant silver Crayola crayon in its shock web cradle positioned above the belly loading bay door. The fact that he sat four meters away from a weapon capable of vaporizing the shuttle and its contents in a microsecond did not worry him. If it exploded, he would never feel it. He was more concerned about what the Architects had in store for them. The first team was still incommunicado. Captain Sidthuri was convinced they were KIA. Chaca wasn't as certain, but whatever their status, they were too far away to help him.

A second shuttle bearing Fitzhugh and crew had left for the underside of the Band an hour earlier. Part of him hoped the structural engineer found another way in. He didn't believe the Architects were still alive, but the Band was certainly still active. He wondered what its response to a thermal missile might be. Sneaking in the back door seemed like a better option.

He looked down at the Band spread out below them, a frozen river of black ice. He could not get used to the lack of shadows. He didn't know if the ebony material cast no shadows or if it absorbed them. Either way, its changeless features disconcerted him. It did not seem natural. Nothing about the Band was natural, not exactly supernatural, but preternatural, something between the normal and the marvelous.

They passed directly over a City, 11 buildings of various sizes and shapes ranging from twisted spires, squat cubes, slender needles, and oblong boxes too closely resembling coffins for his taste. None of the structures conveyed the same sense of living, breathing entities as large cities on Earth. If you looked down on New York or Sao Paulo, you immediately knew people lived there. The alien Architect structures reminded him of the mesas, buttes, and hoodoos of his native Arizona, natural geological features carved by wind, water, and weather. In the vacuum of space, that was impossible. These were frozen shadows.

He scanned the faces of his squad. They appeared relaxed, but he sensed an undercurrent of unease. Paisley wore his usual look of disinterest, but his hands moved continuously, nervously adjusting gear, touching his helmet, and rubbing his knees. Ash and Holmes leaned back in their seat harnesses. Their gaze kept falling on Collins. He knew what they were thinking. Collins' lack of combat experience put them all at risk if things turned kinetic, like a firefight; yet, she was the key to the mission. Therefore, she was non-expendable. If it came down to it, he and his men would die to protect her life. Their evaluation of her determined just how readily they would offer their lives.

Aleyev read from a book of 19th Century Russian poetry he carried with him on every mission. His suit gauntlets lay across his lap. He held the book in his bare hands, afraid the battle armor gloves might damage the fragile paper. He was fond of quoting lines from Aleksandr Pushkin and Fyodor Tyutchev, especially from Pushkin's *The Bronze Horseman*. Chaca thought the Golden Age of Russian poetry too dark and preferred Keats or Shelly.

"What's the word, Aleyev?" he asked.

Aleyev looked up at him with sad, contemplative eyes and quoted, "*Elysium of shades this soul of mine, shades silent, luminous, and wholly severed from this tempestuous age, these restless times, their joys and griefs, their aims and their endeavors.*"

"Elysium of shades, huh?" He glanced down at the Band. "You may be right. Which of your sad Russian poets wrote that?"

"Fyodor Tyutchev."

"Jesus, Aleyev," Holmes said, snorting. "Weren't any Russian poets happy?"

"There's no true poetry in happiness."

Holmes looked at the others, inviting them in on his joke. "Hell, no wonder you Russians invented vodka."

Chaca studied Gunnery Sergeant Ryder. He was almost as tall as Chaca, but broader in the shoulder and heavier set. He sported a bushy red mustache mainly to get Sidthuri's goat. He was quiet and even-tempered, but in a fight, he was a good man to have handy. He could sign his name with his .50 caliber Squad Assault Weapon.

"When do we do the Big Bang?" Paisley asked with a wide grin on his face.

Chaca checked his watch. "One hour and four minutes."

"Glad I've got a ringside seat."

"I can let you hold it in your lap if you want. Should make your dick hard … for about one heartbeat."

Paisley grabbed his crotch and grimaced. "No thanks, I'll watch from here."

Collins cleared her throat. Chaca thought she was about to complain about his crude remark, but she said, "You realize we have no idea how the plasma will react with the Architect building material. It contains a lot of energy stored within its crystal matrix. It might ignite the entire Band. The 600-million-kilometer-long structure could explode in a blast as massive as an exploding sun."

All heads turned toward her.

"Damn, Collins," Paisley replied. "You sure know how to ruin a fucking party."

Collins looked chagrined. Chaca hid his smile. "Double check your gear," he advised them. "I don't want any foul ups." He moved over beside Collins' and checked her equipment for her. "Nervous?" he asked.

Collins flashed an anemic smile. "Oh, no, we technician nerds do stuff like this every day – in vid games."

"Here, you don't get any extra lives, and there's no reset button. We're playing for keeps."

"Thanks for reminding me," she replied. "I feel much better."

"We'll launch from 50 klicks. Once the missile does its job, we'll go in and survey its effectiveness."

"What if it fails?" Ryder asked, stroking the barrel of his .50 caliber.

"Then we go home for a late lunch and an early beer."

The hour passed in silence, each of them struggling with their own private demons. None of them had faced aliens and had no basis on which to judge their expectations.

Chaca stood and walked down the aisle, using his hand to brace himself against the ceiling, as the shuttle wobbled slightly. "Listen up! Make sure you seal your suits tight. The shuttle's going full vacuum in two minutes."

The coordinates supplied by Sidthuri looked no different from any other City on the Band – a group of nine buildings spaced a few hundred meters apart, none any taller or any larger than others scattered across the Band. A kind of town square in the heart of City 457, according to his chart, measuring 50 meters across. On high magnification, he detected a small circle in the center of the square that resembled the depression near the Dome. He hoped it was a second elevator.

"Launch in 5-4-3-2-Go!" he announced.

The bay door opened, the shock cradle dropped away, and the missile fell into space, drawn toward the Band at .5 G. A hundred meters from the shuttle, the single solid-fuel engine ignited, propelling it toward its target.

"Impact in ten seconds," he announced, as he watched the bright flare of the engine diminish with distance through his suit's view screen linked to the shuttle's outboard camera. He understood the mechanics involved enough to follow the detonation sequence. Seconds before impact, a high-energy laser beam stripped the charge from the outer valence electrons of the plasma mass of the warhead, making them positively charged and enhancing the atomic repulsion between like-charged particles. The mass detonated, creating a high-energy, high-temperature ionized plasma.

The initial impact disappointed Ryder, an explosion the size of a 500-pound bomb, sufficient to destroy a city block, but nothing against the impervious material of the Band.

"That sucks," he said.

"Just watch," Chaca told him.

The plasma energy, released by the explosion from the magnetic bonds that confined it, grew hotter and more massive until it became a small sun visible from the *Worthington* 5,000 kilometers away. The light intensified until the shuttle's camera filters shut down the image to prevent it from burning out their retinas. Before the image faded, Chaca thought he saw a series of concentric ripples racing through the ebony material away from the impact site. When the glare faded, he saw nothing out of the ordinary.

Just my imagination.

"That was beautiful!" Ryder shouted, pounding his right leg with his right fist.

The reaction was short-lived but powerful. On a ship the size of the *Worthington*, the heat would have fused the hull into a chunk of molten metal. He had witnessed such spectacles against the enemy, and had felt sympathy for the men caught in the plasma weapon's deadly embrace. However, in this instance, he felt nothing for the Architects. They had killed a comrade and perhaps an entire exploration team.

"Heads up! We're going in. Disembark in Delta 4 formation. Be ready for anything." He didn't worry about residual heat. In a vacuum, the heat would dissipate quickly. He pointed his finger at Collins. "You, stick with me like your life depended on it. It might." He eyed the weapon Collins clasped to her chest like a baby. He thought briefly about taking it from her, but she appeared to take comfort from it. "Don't point that at anybody, and for God's sake, don't screw with the safety or pull the trigger unless I tell you to."

She nodded nervously.

The shuttle moved in and hovered two meters above a spot 50 meters beyond the explosion site. Chaca felt his weight increase. The shuttle pilot looked back over his shoulder as he increased power to maintain position. The shuttle danced a bit before settling down. "We've got gravity here," he said.

"Move it!" Chaca yelled at his team. They shoved two cases of equipment out of the open belly bay doors, and by twos leaped from the shuttle after them. As soon as their boots touched the surface, they took up defensive positions around the shuttle.

"Area secure," Ryder reported a few seconds later.

Collins eyed the distance to the surface and hesitated.

"It's two meters, Collins, at less than 1-G," Chaca reminded her. "We can't wait all day."

She sat on the edge of the door and pushed off. Unused to the suit, she stumbled and fell when her feet hit the surface. Chaca grumbled at her and followed her out. Landing with his knees bent, his suit absorbed the impact of the drop. As soon as he was down, he waved at the shuttle pilot. As the shuttle moved away, he reached down and yanked Collins to her feet.

She looked up at him sheepishly. "I, I lost my balance."

"Try to keep up, Collins. I can't spare a man to hold your hand."

"You watch your men. I'll do my job."

He grinned at her. He had hoped to rile her up to take her mind off the situation. It had worked. "I hope so."

He directed his team to the site. The laser-guided missile had struck dead on target. A ten-meter-diameter crater punched deeply into the band's surface, exposing the three-meter-wide elevator shaft. Tendrils of smoke curled up from the edges.

"Paisley, set up a camera and com relay here for the *Worthington*. Aleyev, Ash, break out the climbing gear. Load up! We're going in."

He peered into the unfathomable depths of the shaft. They had achieved goal one, breaching the Band's surface. Their second challenge was descending into the unknown depths of the elevator shaft. For that purpose, they had brought along lightweight rappelling gear. Hitochi's team had reported a depth of one kilometer. He hoped it wasn't any deeper. He didn't want to dangle suspended by a rope for any length of time if they encountered trouble. Since they could not anchor the ropes in the impenetrable Band material, Aleyev and Ash erected a steel frame from parts carried in one of the bags to set in place over the shaft.

Holmes and Paisley laid out the lengths of climbing line and double-checked it for safety. Composed of bundled Arylate-carbon fibers, the high-tensile strength material was stronger than nylon rope and lighter by a third. Because of the great depth, they would make the descent in easy stages. Collapsible pneumatic rods placed at intervals across the interior of the shaft and secured by pressure would allow them to rest and to change ropes.

"Okay, into your climbing harnesses."

Each member of the team except Collins had extensive experience at rappelling. Chaca had given her a brief demonstration before boarding the shuttle, but he didn't expect miracles. He helped Collins into her harness, secured her belay loop, and adjusted the auto-block and brake.

"Breathe easy and watch me," he told her. "Remember what I told you."

Collins peered over the edge of the shaft and swallowed hard. She looked back up at Chaca, her face pale, and said, "It was mainly don't fall, I think."

Chaca chuckled. If she could still crack a joke, she wasn't too frightened. "That's Rule One."

The frame in place, Ash dropped two ropes over the edge. Clipping onto the ropes, they took turns roping down. Collins descended beside Chaca. The lower gravity made the task less difficult but no less dangerous. Any mistake would prove fatal. Collins huffed and puffed but maintained pace with the others. Her efforts pleased Chaca. She was unaccustomed to the climbing gear and uncomfortable dangling over unseen dark depth, but maybe she wouldn't be such a burden after all. Overhead, the shuttle made a last pass over the opening.

"We're in," he reported.

The shuttle waggled goodbye and soared off, returning to the ship. They were alone.

Chaca had paid little attention to his people's legends growing up. His world was one of technology and modern communications, not his Hopi grandmother's tales of ancient worlds, such as *Tawa*, the Sun God creator of the universe; Spider Woman, who gave them the gift of weaving; or *Masauwu*, the Skeleton Man, who greeted the dead in the underworld. His clan was the Shungopavi Bear Clan of Second Mesa, but he had gone to college at the University of Arizona, became a tribal policeman, and two years later enlisted in the Marines. One tale, however, had stuck in his mind. The pitch-black shaft of the elevator reminded him of tales of the *sippapu*, or hollow reed, through which his people had emerged into the Fourth World, Earth, after the Third World, *Kuskurza*, flooded. He couldn't shake the feeling he was retracing his ancestors' steps, returning to the Third World. He hoped he didn't run into *Tseeveyo*, the ogre Kachina, at the bottom.

At 200 meters, Chaca noticed the light growing dimmer. It was too early for the periodical dimming. He looked up, and to his horror saw the hole they had blasted in the Band closing. The Band was healing itself. He fought down a rising panic. When it sliced their ropes, they would drop the rest of the way to the bottom. Even at .5 G, they would die.

"Ash, Paisley, set the bars."

The two men saw what was happening, quickly extended a pair of the pneumatic bars across the shaft, and attached new ropes. Chaca glanced up to judge how much time they had, dismayed by how little time remained. A lattice resembling a glowing wire frame formed over the opening. The ropes dangling from the platform passed through the frame, but as he watched, the framework began solidifying from the edges, creeping inexorably toward the center.

"Work faster," he urged.

He clipped onto the new rope and tested its strength before releasing the old rope. The others did the same thing, but Collins, a novice, had difficulty. In the rush to clip her harness to the new rope, she swung too far, struck the side of the shaft hard, and began spinning wildly, cursing loudly. She accidentally released her grip on the brake and plummeted until the auto-block engaged, jerking her to a wrenching halt. Unconscious, she swung like a pendulum ten meters below the others.

Chaca ignored Collins' plight to make what he figured would be his final report. It would be a brief one. "Breached the shaft. Rappelling to the bottom. Shaft is resealing behind us. Repeat, shaft is sealing itself. Estimate we lose contact with you in a few seconds. Still on mission. Chaca out."

"Good luck, Sergeant." He recognized Captain Sidthuri's voice.

"Thank you, sir," he replied, but the signal was gone.

Before he could reach Collins, the shaft plunged into total darkness. The severed ropes fell around them. Chaca covered his head with his arms to protect himself, but the ropes pummeled his body like flails even through the battle armor. He switched on his helmet light and quickly checked his team's status. Each one had managed to attach to the new ropes in time, but the equipment bags had not been as lucky. Their ropes severed, they had disappeared into the depths of the shaft.

Collins dangled limply from her rope, groaning as she slowly regained consciousness. Chaca looked back up the shaft, shaking his head in disappointment. The winch on the climbing frame would have aided their ascent. They would not be leaving leave the way they had entered. It was beginning to look like a one-way mission.

7

When none of the men offered to console the distraught Deidre, Kari walked to her side and helped her to her feet. She brushed the tears from Deidre's cheeks, leaving a blurry smear of mascara. "Don't fall apart. We need you. You have a job to do," she reminded her, hoping to draw on Deidre's professionalism to snap her out of her fright. When that failed, she said, "Don't fall apart in front of the men."

Deidre nodded and sniffed back her tears. "Yeah, okay."

Sung said, "She's right though. I think we should leave as well, right now."

"Why?" Kirkurk asked.

"Do you not see that?"

Sung pointed to the image of Kahoku. Shocked by the macabre image of his mutilated corpse, Kari had missed it at first. Now, looking closer, she noticed something on the floor near his body. With sudden horrible clarity, her mind provided cohesion to the jumble of objects – bones and scraps of clothing. None of the bones looked human, but several were from bipedal creatures. Others were so bizarre her mind could not supply them form. One looked as if it had leathery wings. Another looked like a broken Slinky.

"It's a killing floor," Sung said, giving words to her grisly thoughts, "an alien abattoir." He turned to Kirkurk. "The Architects are butchers. I repeat, we must leave."

Hitochi took an energy reading of the room, paying particular attention to the wall through which they had entered. "There's nothing to indicate a door was ever there, but something's happening. The EM meter is going crazy." He focused on one section of the wall. "There is a strong Electro Magnetic field developing directly in front of me." He glanced up from his instrument and looked at them with a puzzled expression. "It's off the scale."

The wall swelled outward. Sung, closest to the strange disturbance, lurched backwards, almost falling in his haste to get away. Hitochi moved closer with his instrument. The bulge became three distinct protuberances reaching into the room. Three dark objects emerged and popped free of the wall, formless and translucent. They quickly coalesced into three, wispy living creatures. With a start, Kari realized she could see the ebony wall through their wraith-like bodies. The two marines stiffened at the sudden intrusion and painted the dark wraiths with their weapons' laser sights. In a blur of motion, much faster than the guards could react, two of the wraiths shot forward and enveloped them within the folds of their shadowy forms. The bloodcurdling scream from the man nearest Kari froze her feet to the floor in sheer terror. She had never heard such a sound erupt from a human throat, as if torn out by its roots.

The men's frantic struggles lasted only seconds. The two wraiths melted back into the substance of the wall from which they had emerged and disappeared, leaving no trace of the marines' bodies. She wondered if that was what happened to Kahoku. If so, she held out no hope for the two marines.

The third creature remained in the room, motionless as since first entering. Only the feathery edges of its nebulous form moved, like a black corona dancing around an ebony sun. Kari froze, fearing it might interpret any movement as an attack and choose her as its next victim. It had no apparent eyes, but she sensed it observing them with some type of sensory organ. Out of the corner of her eye, she noticed Hitochi edging closer to her, as if determined to protect her. She applauded his chivalry but cursed his timing. His eyes were narrowed and his lips stretched tight in anger, but fear etched his drawn and pale face. His hand trembled as it rested on the grip of his pistol.

"No, don't," Kari warned, her voice barely above a whisper. "Don't move."

Hitochi froze. A ripple of motion blurred the outline of the wraith. She feared it was ready to make a decision. Suddenly, the creature shifted toward the video camera lying forgotten on the floor where Deidre had dropped it. A thin tendril shot from its wispy body and began examining the camera. The images stored in the memory chip flickered in the depths of the creature's body as if a movie projector aimed at a puff of black smoke. The images flashed many times faster than Kari's eyes could focus, becoming a dizzying blur. Finally, satisfied, the tendril withdrew from the camera.

"Perhaps it merely reacted to the guards' hostile gesture," Mailors said. "We must try to communicate with it." He moved one foot slightly. Dozens of tiny cilia-like tendrils sprouted from the creature, waving like agitated worms as it focused its attention on him.

"Don't move, Les," Kari warned.

Mailors ignored her. "We come in peace," he said to the wraith.

He raised one hand in the air, palm facing outward the shadow creature. Eyes blacker than the substance around them formed in its head. Their edges morphed, changing and blurring, as if floating freely inside the creature. Suddenly, the eyes turned crimson, and the wraith regarded him with the intensity of a raptor. A face formed around the eyes. To Kari, it resembled the distorted skeletal face of the Grim Reaper, except its circular mouth held hundreds of tiny needles. To her horror, Mailors did exactly what she feared he would do. He slid his other foot forward. Appendages much larger than the tendril, with which it had examined the camera, emerged from its body. They became solid, half a dozen frozen, black-ice blades slicing through the air.

Mailors yelped in fright, taking two steps backward while warding his face with his hands. Kari watched in shock as the appendages shot forward and embraced Mailors. His expression of surprise and fear changed to one of terror and pain, as the ebony blades sliced through flesh, bone, and organs as easily as a laser. His agonized screams cut through Kari's immobility, but before she could move, they abruptly ended.

Surprisingly, there was very little blood, but there was no doubt Mailors was dead. His head, severed from his mouth to the back of his skull, fell first, sliding from his neck and revealing his obscenely naked tongue and part of his brain. The lower part of both arms fell next, his fingers still twitching. His bisected torso twitched; then, began to topple, collapsing in slow motion as both legs separated just above the knees.

The wraith's body billowed outward. It hovered over Mailors like a coal dust cloud of death. The skeletal head turned to observe the others in the room. For one brief moment, the lifeless crimson eyes swirled with ebony streaks as they focused on Kari. Her heart froze as her blood thickened to a cold sludge clogging her veins. It was a fear deeper than any that she had ever conceived. She could not draw a breath. The sensation lasted only microseconds, but marked its imprint upon her psyche as surely as acid etching glass. Then, the creature descended to cover Mailors and slowly melted into the floor, thankfully taking Mailors' neatly dissected body with it, again leaving no trace just as the other creatures had done.

Deidre fainted. Luntz retched loudly and vomited over the boots of his suit. The chunks of his lunch on the ebony floor looked as if suspended in air. The grisly deaths should have terrified her, but she was too stunned to grasp fully what had just occurred. The thought that a part of her was glad that they, and not she, had been the objects of the sudden, deadly attack shamed her. She shuddered as warm blood once again pulsed through her body. Her mind rebelled at the callous cruelty she had witnessed. She fought the urge to throw up.

For most of her life, she had thought of the Architects as a super-intelligent, benevolent race, infatuated by the creation of beauty, a beauty even humans could appreciate; almost God-like beings. Nothing she had seen today had been humane or benevolent. No intelligent species could treat another intelligent, space-faring race so cruelly. She had been terribly wrong about them. Her misplaced idolatry dismayed her more than the deaths of her companions, another fact for which she felt shame. In her own way, she had been as enamored of the Architects at the Interventionists.

"What do we do?" Sung demanded, groaning as if in physical pain. He crouched beside the wall through which they had entered the death room, breathing heavily, his face ashen. "We're trapped here."

Kari faced Kirkurk, the expedition's leader. He had said nothing since the guards' deaths. He seemed as distraught by events as she was. "Do you have any suggestions?"

Kirkurk's blanched face quivered slightly, and his lips trembled, but he said nothing. For once in his life, words failed him. His fear-filled eyes roamed the room like those of a caged animal seeking escape. They would get no guidance from him.

Hitochi came to the rescue. Kari marveled at the degree of calmness in his voice, as he said, "I understand why the shadows attacked Newman and Eggleston, even Kahoku." He stopped and shook his head. "I call them shadows, but this light cast no shadows, and they were solid objects, or became solid." He continued, "They interpreted Newman and Eggleston's actions as threatening, but why kill Mailors? He made no threatening gesture. In fact, his actions were conciliatory."

Kari realized with shame that she had not known the names of the two marines accompanying them. She would have to remember their names as a kind of mental memorial to them. They could leave no gravestone or cairn to mark where they had died.

"What difference does it make?" she asked.

He walked past Kirkurk, who flinched at the sudden movement, his eyes following Hitochi across the room as they would a spider crawling up his arm. He feared any motion might trigger a return of the shadow creatures.

"It makes a difference," Hitochi continued. "If they simply wanted to butcher us, why not kill us all at one time? Why invite us into the Band and offer problems for us to solve?"

"Maybe they didn't like our answers," Sung said.

"But they responded," Kari said.

"Yes, with deadly consequences," he reminded her.

"Maybe they think we're grave robbers," Luntz suggested.

Everyone turned to stare at Luntz, who was wiping the vomit from his lips. Kari, who had often felt as if the Band were an Architect memorial, nodded.

"Again, why invite us in?" Hitochi asked. "We were getting nowhere. Why not simply let us frustrate ourselves until we eventually gave up and left?"

"Perhaps they are curious," Sung suggested.

"Not as curious as I am," Kari replied.

"Isn't your curiosity satisfied yet?" Deidre snapped. She had regained consciousness and sat on the floor. She brushed her dark locks from her forehead and glared at Kari with contempt. "Maybe they simply enjoy killing."

Kari turned to Deidre. "I refuse to believe that. The Architects are too advanced for barbarism."

"Advanced!" Deidre spat the word at her. "Does the cow in the slaughterhouse look at the man with the hammer with awe? Do you think it worships its killer because he is so much more advanced than it is? Your precious Architects are butchers."

"No, not butchers," Hitochi replied. "There is a reason for their actions."

"I want to leave," Deidre insisted. Kari noticed Deidre's LED fingernails now displayed a deep black to match her mood.

"That seems to be out of the question at the moment," Sung said. "What were those things, Pembinas?"

Kari understood his disbelief, but she was certain the shadowy apparitions were not Architects. She wasn't even sure if they were living creatures, as she understood living. "No, I think they're some kind of caretakers, watchdogs left by the Architects."

"Well, they've shown us what they're capable of," Sung said. "I feared this would happen."

"What do you mean?" Deidre asked. Her vid camera lay forgotten beside her.

He rose from the floor and paced the room. "We failed their second test," he answered.

Deidre looked around the room, searching all their faces. "What do you mean?" she asked again, this time with more insistence.

"This is as far as we get. Now, we're interlopers, uninvited guests. If we're lucky, they will simply leave us here and forget about us."

Kari was afraid Sung might be right. Deidre cast a look of scorn at Sung that should have blistered the man's skin, but he had already turned away and was busy examining the walls. He stopped before the spot where the first two shadows had disappeared and waved his hand over it. "Is it my imagination, or is this area of the wall colder?"

Hitochi ran his scanner over the area. "It's nearly 12 degrees cooler than the surrounding area."

"Perhaps it was caused by the shadows passing through the wall," Kirkurk suggested, finally released from his silence.

Hitochi scanned the floor where the third shadow had taken Mailors. "No temperature change here. Is this another test?" he asked.

"Another chance to die," Deidre challenged, her voice breaking.

Luntz stepped up beside her and placed his arm around her waist. "I agree with her. This is crazy."

Luntz, always cognizant of his appearance, would not like the image he projected now, that of a cornered rat. His eyes, which had once enthralled Kari, darted nervously around the room. Dribbles of vomit clung to his chin, one dangling by a thin thread of spittle. The perpetual boyish grin was gone, replaced by a clenched jaw and taut lips on the verge of quivering.

"We can't leave the way we came," Kirkurk replied. "The only way out is to continue forward somehow."

"How many tests can we fail before there are none of us left?" Deidre asked.

"Perhaps our deaths will gain knowledge for another team," Sung suggested, "if we can communicate with the surface or leave a record for those who follow us –"

"Screw that!" Deidre shot at him. "I came to vi-cord the expedition, not to become some damned martyr to the cause."

Sung shrugged his shoulders. "Our choices are rather limited. I would prefer to leave, but I see only three choices. We can wait here until the Pembina decide we're unworthy and send the shadows to collect us, or we can wait here until we die of thirst or starvation."

"I don't like either of those choices," Hitochi said.

"What is the third choice?" Kari asked. Like Hitochi, she felt neither of Sung's choices offered much hope.

"We can put the deaths behind us and continue with a sense of wonder of discovery."

Luntz groaned. Deidre pulled away from Luntz and lifted her shoulders to cover her neck. Kari, while not certain she could forget what had just occurred, agreed with Sung that they must continue. She had crossed light years of empty space to reach the Band. If she left without answers, her life would end. She might continue to breathe, to eat, to have bowel movements – the essence of life – but she would be dead inside. She would be a failure. She had to find out why the Architects had killed Kahoku, Mailors, and the two marines.

Hitochi had continued his examination of the cold spot during the conversation. He held his hand against it a moment before removing it. "This wall does not react to pressure like the corridor wall did. There, they tested us for the ability to comprehend complex mathematics. Here, they observed our technical ability to broadcast videos and to detect the temperature change in the wall. Perhaps they have upped the ante."

"What do you mean?" Sung asked him.

"They know we're explorers, intelligent, even if not by their standards. They know we communicate by speech, and that we're social creatures."

"If they could read my mind right now, they would be very upset," Deidre snapped. She blanched and slapped her hand to her mouth in alarm. "You don't think ... they can't read our minds, can they?"

Sung replied, "If they could read our minds, they wouldn't have the need to test us."

Hitochi said, "If those shadow creatures, those wraiths were in response to a test, the next test will be critical. They will be watching our response. A less curious species would tuck their tails and run, or whatever might pass for a tail among aliens." He grinned.

Kari was surprised at Hitochi's ability to maintain a sense of humor under their present conditions. She compared Hitochi's demeanor to Luntz. Luntz, the consummate Alpha male who projected a public persona of fearless composure and assuredness, had broken under the threat of the unknown, while Hitochi, plain but certain of himself and his abilities, had blossomed into a leader.

"A curious species would move forward," he continued.

"So would an aggressive species with no regard for individual lives and intent on looting the Band," Sung suggested.

"True," Hitochi conceded. "The next test might be to determine if we're aggressive, curious, or if we've had enough and want to leave."

"I'm for leaving," Deidre said.

"What if they decide we're too aggressive?" Kirkurk asked.

"They eliminate us," Kari answered.

She agreed with Hitochi's reasoning. It had been her belief that the Architects had achieved the wonders they had created by being a unified species, perhaps of a single culture. They had endured no centuries of racial bickering or wars as had humans. They had united as a species in a bold effort to reach space and leave their mark upon it. They had bequeathed their treasures to any species who proved worthy of their accumulated store of knowledge. They would not allow anyone to loot their sanctuary. However, they would offer its contents to the worthy. It was up to the team to prove their merit.

"The Architects would understand the power they were placing in another species' hands, as well as the potential for using that power against others. Of course, they would leave safeguards." A thrill of anticipation coursed through her body, pushing back her fear. "They left the artifacts as a trail of breadcrumbs," she added. "They presented us with marvels of engineering hinting at tremendous power and objects of great beauty to see which we placed the most value on. We're here. We passed the first tests. At least they don't consider us invading organisms."

"They're exterminating us anyway," Deidre snarled at her from across the room.

Kari had grown tired of Deidre's deepening morbidity. She confronted her. "We're still alive. Focus on that. If we had failed the second test, we would all be dead."

"Maybe they've sated their blood lust for now," Deidre offered. "It doesn't mean they won't come back."

Her remark drew a look of sheer terror from Luntz.

"We must continue," Hitochi said.

"How do we?" Kari asked. She was convinced Hitochi was right, but a small part of her wondered if they had made some assumption about the Architects that would ultimately lead to their deaths. "We have no heavy machinery or weapons."

"We have nothing that can penetrate this material," Hitochi reminded her. "We have to think our selves in."

They were at an impasse. The cold spot on the wall was an invitation to do something, but Kari could not think of what. She paced the room deep in thought, fearing it was up to her to solve the riddle. Hitochi was an engineer and thought in terms of power sources and structural integrity, none of which applied in this instance. The others were too frightened to think about it at all. They were unsure if they wanted to continue. She did. She wished the room came with an instruction manual. She was blindly feeling her way. A thought came to her. She had always assumed the artifacts were the key to understanding the Architects. What lessons did they teach?

The spiral Ice World had been her inspiration to suggest that Sung recreate a Fibonacci Spiral, the key that opened the first door. Which artifact might apply here? As she studied the black wall, she noticed a low hum in the room. It had been there since before the shadow wraiths attacked, but more as a sensation deep in her chest than as a distinct sound, like the low rumble of an approaching avalanche. She had ignored it, attributing it to her excitement.

"What is that?" she asked.

Hitochi stared at her. "What?"

"That noise, a low rumble." She noticed Hitochi's perplexed expression. "You can't hear it?" She glanced around and saw the exact blank expressions on all their faces. "None of you?" she questioned. Was she imagining it?

"It's just the blood rushing through the veins in your ears," Sung suggested. "It happens sometimes."

"No, it's not that," she insisted. "I feel it here." She thumped her chest with the heel of her hand. The low frequency made her uncomfortable. Her skin itched. "I'm shedding this," she said, and began stripping off her excursion suit, leaving only her thin, sleeveless cotton T-shirt, jersey shorts, and socks. She felt silly for stripping away the only thing that could protect her if the atmosphere disappeared, but the itching stopped. "That's better."

The deep resonate hum undulated up and down in frequency, never reaching a point on the spectrum she should have been able to hear. It was almost like whale song. *That's it!*

She smiled. "I know what it is."

"What?" Hitochi asked.

"It's the song of the twin Singing Moons. Can you reproduce it?"

He stared at her for a moment before replying. "Yeah, sure. The moons sing between 8 and 21 Hz. I can reproduce those frequencies." He chose a sonar probe from his equipment bag and set the desired frequency.

She pointed to the cold spot on the wall. "Aim it there and see what happens."

At first, nothing happened. She saw the disappointment on the others' faces. She was disappointed in herself. Had she been wrong? Was she simply having an auditory hallucination? She closed her eyes. Seconds later, she heard indrawn breaths of surprise and looked at the wall. Two glowing spots appeared adjacent to each other separated by a few centimeters. When Hitochi switched off his device, the spots remained.

He grinned. "Looks like you were right."

"They look like handprints," Sung said.

She stared at the spots and saw that Sung was right. They resembled mittens with large thumbs.

"Someone should place their hands there and see what happens," he suggested.

"I'll do it." Kari surprised herself by volunteering. Her heart fluttered with trepidation at the idea, but it seemed obvious to her that she should be the one. Her touch alone had operated the elevator. For some unfathomable reason, the Architects had selected her to hear the auditory signal.

"I'll do it," Hitochi told her.

"You'll have to monitor my progress," she told him, and added, "and figure out something else if I fail. What do I do?"

Hitochi shook his head but did not argue. "Place the palms of your hands right here." He indicated the twin spots. "As soon as you sense something happening, alert me."

"Wait!" Kirkurk yelled, but she ignored him

She took a deep breath, released it slowly, and placed her hands against the wall. She leaned into the wall to apply as much pressure as possible. Hitochi flashed a big smile as encouragement. She returned it and closed her eyes. The wall was cold to the touch, but she ignored the discomfort and focused on marshalling her thoughts and channeling her emotions into the ebony material. No one spoke. She could not hear their breathing. She imagined herself alone, a supplicant eager for wisdom standing outside a Hindu monastery in the Himalayas begging for entrance.

She conjured images of each Architect artifact she had visited, remembering the emotions she had felt at that time – joy, awe, wonder. She let those emotions flow through her and into the wall. She slowed her heart and emptied her mind of all thoughts except those concerning the Architect artifacts. Like a mental stab, a sudden image of Kahoku flashed through her mind. She tried to dismiss it, but the images of the two guards and Mailors killed by the three shadow creatures took its place. Summoned by her despair, other memories began to surface.

Standing before the majesty of the Architect artifacts, she had also felt insignificant, wondering what purpose her petty life had when measured against the marvels created by the vanished race who had built them. What glory could she ever achieve that would not pale in comparison. The artifacts damaged her self-worth, stripped her of her youthful pride. She had decided understanding the Architects would be the best she could hope for.

Her doubt grew, overshadowing her other emotions. The wall grew colder, biting into her flesh, amplifying her reservations. She tried to suppress her doubt, but it blossomed like a weed after an April rain, finding footing in the fertile soil of her worthlessness, as if the material of the wall were acting as a feedback loop.

"No," she cried in her mind. The dark presence vanished. A new presence entered her mind, indistinct but benign. Thoughts shot through her synapses at speeds far beyond her ability to comprehend them. The pain subsided. Her mind cleared of ominous thoughts.

She forced her mind to focus on the Water World, picturing its Zen-like perfection. It served no purpose except beauty, a beauty even her alien mind could grasp and appreciate. She had dedicated her life to understanding the Architects. She did not resent them their vast achievements. She treasured them. Whatever their physical form, whatever their culture, whatever the reason for the killings, they were as human as she was.

She sensed movement around her. Her pulse quickened. "I think something's happening."

"Damn right it is," Hitochi said from beside her.

She opened her eyes. The wall was gone. She stood in an opening as wide as the room. She followed Hitochi's gaze and almost cried out in wonder.

8

Captain Sidthuri sat behind his desk with the bitter realization he had just sent 16 people to their deaths; 17 if he counted Ensign Kahoku. Though mounting a sentry was standard procedure, Kahoku's disappearance smacked of abduction by a hostile force. Kirkurk's team had disappeared after gaining entry into the Band. Now, Sergeant Chaca's team was gone as well, sealed inside the Band after forcing entry. He did not know if they were dead, but his gut told him they were. They had meddled where they should not, had come to the Band unannounced and uninvited, and the Architects had shown them they were not welcome.

Fitzhugh's expedition had met with no success. He had returned more insufferable than ever, insisting on a larger, better-equipped venture. Sidthuri had listened to his rants for as long as he could, and then sent him away to sulk.

He now faced a major decision. Should he risk more deaths trying to save the others, or was it time to end the, in his mind, ill-fated expedition and return to Earth? He could leave probes to continue surveying the Band. They had learned nothing useful for the exorbitant price they had paid. If the governments of Earth wished, they could send a larger, better-defended expedition, although he doubted even a full fleet would suffice. If the Architects wished to keep their secrets, Earth could not wrest them from them.

He would wait 24 hours, well beyond the air supply both teams carried. He would give them that slim chance at least, but he would leave. His superiors might consider him a coward for abandoning both teams, and in truth, he felt like a coward for even considering the idea, but he still had the safety of his ship and the welfare of the rest of his crew and the civilians to consider. He did not like running from a fight, but only a fool engaged in combat with an unseen giant capable of swatting away the *Worthington* like an annoying gnat.

We were children playing in a mud puddle and calling it an ocean. Now, we sail the true ocean and find it belongs to someone else.

He glanced up at a knock on the doorframe. As usual, the door was open. He encouraged a close rapport with his crew. Closed doors bred secrets. An ashen-faced ensign stood there looking as if he had seen a ghost. Sidthuri's gut tightened.

"Yes, what is it?"

"S-sir," the ensign mumbled, "we've developed a power drain. Reactor output levels have remained constant, but systems power has dropped ten percent in the last ten minutes."

Sidthuri made fists of his hands and laid them on the desk. The power drain could not be a mere coincidence. "What is the cause?"

The ensign gulped. "We don't know. It appears to be draining through the ship's hull."

Sidthuri grimaced. *The Band.* The Architects had finally decided to swat them away. He now had no choice. "Sound battle stations. Prepare the ship for lift off."

"Sir?"

"You heard me," he snapped at the confused ensign. "We're leaving. Now!"

"Yes, sir." The ensign turned and sprinted down the short corridor. Seconds later, the battle stations klaxon sounded throughout the ship, an ominous sound he did not like hearing. Death usually followed such an alarm.

"I hope I haven't waited too late," he muttered, but in his heart, he knew he had,

9

Kari stood at one end of a cubical room revealed when the wall disappeared. Unlike the black material comprising the rest of the Band, the walls and floor of the anteroom were completely transparent, almost invisible. She stood on the brink of an abyss staring down into the darkness below her. A wave of vertigo swept over her. She had always been uncomfortable in high places, especially on precipices. *Cremnophobia* – she had looked it up once to determine how it differed from acrophobia, a fear of heights, and aeroacrophobia, a fear of open, high places. That was why she had never ventured to the edge of the Band as many had. She tottered and reached out her hand but had nothing against which to brace. She felt Hitochi's hand steadying her.

"You did it," he said.

She smiled at him and saw the look of concern on his face. "Thanks," she said. She realized the others were staring at her as well. She did not want them to think her a coward. Their faces conveyed a sense of awe at the vista before them, all, except Deidre. She stared at the anteroom in horror, her mouth twisted into a silent scream. Kari felt a momentary twinge of sympathy for the journalist. Faced with the story of a lifetime, Deidre was too frightened to investigate. Her video camera sat unused beside her. Kari glanced at Hitochi, taking confidence from his look of encouragement. She took a deep breath to steady her nerves but paused, unable to bring herself to step onto the transparent surface. He began to whistle softly to placate her fear. She smiled at him and took a step, relieved to discover it was indeed solid.

The room protruded out into a vast, empty, spherical void, detectable only by the faint blue glow emanating from the walls of the sphere. She was certain it was the Dome as seen from the inside, actually an enormous sphere as Bonner Fitzhugh had proposed. As her eyes adjusted to the dim glow, she saw a circular object floating in the middle of the sphere, occluding the glow of the sphere's opposite wall. She switched on her measuring laser. The beam passed through the clear wall. She read aloud the readings, as Hitochi looked over her shoulder.

"The object is a sphere measuring 600 meters in diameter. It's rotating slowly."

Kirkurk brushed past her, almost knocking her down in his rush to view the object. Annoyed by his ego-driven need to be first, she followed him at a more leisurely pace. Hitochi joined her. Sung, Luntz, and Deidre remained in the room, afraid another wall would appear and trap them in the daunting anteroom. She didn't blame them. The dark thought plagued her that the Architects could easily remove the floor of the room as they had the wall, plunging her into the dark abyss.

"My God! It's beautiful," Kirkurk cried out, as he stood before the object, his hands pressing against the transparent wall as if trying to grasp the sphere beyond. He looked almost ready to burst into tears of joy. "This is what I came to find."

She noticed his use of the personal pronoun *I* instead of the more inclusive group pronoun *we*, thinking it so typical of his self-centered thought process. She frowned at his back. *If he were any more in love with himself, he'd need to rent a motel room.* As excited as she was by her discovery – *My God*, she thought, *my discovery. Am I as bad as he is?* – she wasn't as certain they had reached their goal. It was an important find, but it had been far too easy. The Architects struck her as a methodical race. She suspected more tests would follow.

"It could be a power source," Kirkurk suggested, speaking rapidly in an excited voice, "a spinning mass in the center of a sphere."

Hitochi shook his head. "I doubt it. I get only minor power readings from it. It appears completely inert."

"Then what is it?" Kirkurk demanded in exasperation.

"I have no idea," he admitted.

Kari pressed against the clear wall and studied the smaller sphere. It appeared to be composed of the same ebony material as every other Architect object. The surface was perfectly smooth with no blemishes or indication of an entrance. She wanted badly to examine it, but they had no way to reach it. The short transparent anteroom in which they stood extended only five meters into the void. The sphere was over 2,000 meters away.

Kirkurk ran his hands over the wall frantically, whimpering slightly in frustration, and pressed them against the surface as Kari had in the other room. After a minute, he gave up, groaning in frustration.

"Nothing." He looked at her, his eyes pleading. "Can you do it?"

She sighed. Kirkurk recognized her only when he needed her. "I don't know," she replied truthfully. She wasn't sure how she had opened the wall door. The effort had taken a lot out of her and reminded her of her many flaws and imperfections. If not for the second presence, she would have drowned in a sea of self-doubt. She wasn't eager for another bout. However, she saw no other option. Deidre and Luntz were too frightened to attempt it, and neither Sung nor Kirkwood would lay bare their inner emotions to another human, much less to an alien race.

Hitochi stood behind her reading the display on his instruments. "I'm picking up nothing from the wall." He ran his hand across the surface. "No temperature variations, gravity fluctuations, and no energy spikes."

Kirkurk paced out his frustration while Hitochi studied his instruments. Kari tried to think like an Architect, a difficult concept considering they really had no idea how their alien minds operated. A thought struck her. She was surprised she had not questioned it before.

"How do the walls or doors, whatever, operate? They don't retract or fold away. They vanish. This one is transparent, but it has the same velvety texture as the ebony walls."

Hitochi smiled at her. "I've been considering that. The force field overlaying the outside walls gave me the idea. I don't believe the walls are solid at all, at least not in the sense in which we use the term." Seeing her confused stare, he added, "What if the Architects can manipulate fields of force so delicately they can create solid objects from them. First, they create a sub-space matrix in the shape they want. Then, they overlay the matrix with an energy field that creates the lattice of crystalline metal molecules, which mimics a solid substance. They need only be a couple of molecules thick. The walls disappear and the metal molecules return to their atomic state when the energy field dissolves. The matrix is still there, invisible and undetectable, ready to re-integrate when energy is reapplied."

She had only a fundamental grasp of particle physics, but she followed most of Hitochi's theory. She thought of the Band as an immaterial object, an illusion with substance. The Architects' ability to manipulate energy on a sub-space and sub-atomic level explained how they could control a star and impel it onto a new course. They controlled matter and energy as a chemist controls a chemical reaction, transforming it between the states of existence, as they needed it.

The thought that the room she was in, the floor upon which she stood, the entire Band, was a projection of energy alarmed her. Would it all vanish if the Architects decided to cut the power? She pushed her apprehension to the back of her mind.

"Is it the same with the shadow-less light?"

"Very astute! Yes, I believe they create the light by exciting the air molecules in a defined space. The light diffuses evenly throughout the room from every direction. They do the same within the ebony materials, as we witnessed in the chalkboard, the 3-D image niches, and the handprints." He waved his hand to indicate the space outside the room. "The hollow sphere is an airless void, so the ebony material itself is glowing."

"That's pretty close to magic," she replied, more in awe of the Architects than before.

"Close enough," he agreed. "Do you want to repeat your mind-melding trick with this wall?"

She giggled at his Star Trek Vulcan reference. "I think I know a better way. The artifacts are definitely the key. The blue glow reminds me of the Kaleidoscope Nebula, each star in the center the exact shade of azure. Can you tune your laser to project the exact spectral frequency of the stars in the Kaleidoscope Nebula, starting with the azure ones and moving outward in the same sequence?"

"Yes, why?"

"This light is the answer."

"You said yourself there are many more artifacts that we have not yet discovered," Sung reminded her.

"We'll try the ones we know first, starting with the nebula."

Hitochi adjusted his laser measure and handed it to her. "Here, you do it. I've set it to the Morgan-Keenan spectral system – blue being the hottest and red the coolest."

She held her breath and pressed the stud. The bright blue beam passed through the transparent wall, but a few seconds later, the wall began absorbing the light until the entire wall glowed with azure light.

"I'll be damned," Hitochi said. "It's doing something."

She exhaled slowly and grinned, pleased with herself. She tuned the laser to blue-white; then, white, yellow, orange, and finally red. The wall glowed with each color in the sequence. She reached out her hand to touch the wall and groaned with disappointment when the wall became transparent once again.

"What did I do wrong?" she moaned.

She visualized the Kaleidoscope nebula in her mind. What had she missed? Suddenly, it struck her.

"How many stars are in the nebula?"

Hitochi thought a moment. "Over 700."

She shook her head. "No, how many exactly?"

"769," Kirkurk replied, grinning broadly, "another prime number."

It pained her that Kirkurk might be right about the significance of prime numbers. She looked at Hitochi. "Can you set the laser to simultaneously produce 769 points of light?"

He took the laser from her, made a few adjustments, and handed it back. She aimed the laser at the wall and pressed the stud. The wall shimmered; then, a planet appeared in front of them, filling almost the entire space of the large sphere. She felt she could reach out and brush the wispy white clouds with her hands. With a sharp gasp, she recognized Earth, but not the world in which she lived. Large ice sheets covered portions of the northern hemisphere. The continents looked roughly the same, though the oceans were smaller and the continental edges somewhat extended into what were now coastal waters. She recognized Australia at the bottom of the globe.

"It's Earth," Sung said.

"Obviously," Kirkurk retorted, "but it is the Earth about five million years ago, perhaps during the early Pliocene Epoch. Judging by the retreating ice sheets, it is later than the Miocene. I would say this is the latter portion of the Zanclean Age. *Homo habilis* was walking erect. We're seeing the world of our early ancestors."

"But how?" Kari asked. "The Architects were gone long before."

"Perhaps not, or the images could be from a probe still active at that time."

"Why Earth?" Deidre asked. "What's so special about us?"

No one suggested an answer.

"Is it possible the Architects catalogued the entire galaxy?" Kari asked. The image of Earth disturbed her, but not for the reason cited by Kirkurk. The others ignored a salient point about the image. How did it know what planet she was from? The thought that the image of Earth appeared because the Band entity had touched her mind alarmed her. More disturbing was the fear that the entity still maintained contact with her?

Kirkurk stared at the image. "I would not put it past their abilities, but they could have concentrated on the Local Arm where Earth is located, although, of course, the artifacts are hundreds of light years from Earth. Unless we learn to manipulate the data, we may never know."

Kari touched the wall. She discovered she could speed up the revolutions of the planet or stop it with her hands as if using a touch screen. In a few seconds, she advanced the Earth image a million years. The ice sheets retreated farther; then, crept back across the land as she returned it to the first image. It reminded her of time-lapse photography.

The image intrigued Kirkurk. "Was that a projection based on data, or did the Architect survey continue another million years, perhaps is continuing even now?" He turned to the others. "I find it curious that the image of Earth is from when man first began evolving into something human."

Kari looked at Kirkurk. "What are you suggesting?"

"I'm not sure. It simply seems extremely coincidental. We have found only two other humanoid species, both extinct, in our explorations, as meager as they are to date. Did the Architects concentrate on species with a chance to evolve into a higher primate, or, I don't know, somehow gave us a gentle nudge toward sentience?"

"Nonsense," Sung replied. "We've found no such evidence. You sound like an Interventionist."

"We probably wouldn't find direct evidence, considering the abilities of Architects," Kirkurk insisted.

"So you think they manipulated species to evolve, wiped all traces of said intervention, and sat back to watch the results?" Sung chortled. "Ridiculous."

"It would explain their disappearance. They started their grand experiment and did not want to interfere further."

"Again, ridiculous."

Kirkurk's face reddened. He scowled at Sung. "It's a theory others have advanced."

"Now, you're sounding more like a disillusioned Interventionist," Sung accused. "I thought you were a scientist. Deal with the facts, Neville."

Kari found the topic of outside intervention in human evolution disturbing. If humans were what the Architects had made them, were they now the Architects, the last living descendants of that species? Did mankind owe all they were to the whim of an alien species?

"It doesn't matter," she burst out, interrupting what she knew would soon dissolve into an academic shouting match between the two obstinate men. "We've made a fantastic discovery. We've come this far. We must continue."

"How do you propose we do that?" Kirkurk asked. "We've reached a dead end."

"I refuse to believe that. The Architects would not allow us this far simply to give us a glimpse of their store of data."

"You and your precious damn Architects," Deidre shouted. "Your precious Architects have murdered four people horribly. They're monsters."

Kari desperately wanted to avoid a renewed conflict with Deidre. She watched in disappointment, as the disillusioned videographer tugged on her tight black curls and bit her lip. Her fingernails bore white marks where she had stripped the LED enamel polish with her teeth. Like

Deidre, the team was falling apart. She tried to shut out Sung and Kirkurk, who continued their argument. Only she and Hitochi remembered their mission.

She returned to the image of Earth. As a test, she sped up the revolutions until the planet became a blur. The outlines of continents changed slightly. Finally, lights appeared in a few spots, and then the entire landmasses glowed at night with artificial light. She stopped the image. A large object in geosynchronous orbit above North America drew her attention. She recognized the three silver cylinders, the spider web of girders surrounding them, and the massive antenna pointing into space.

"That's Bradbury Station," Kirkurk exclaimed.

Kari nodded, amazed by the clarity of the image. The *Worthington* had left Earth from Bradbury Station. Kari had spent two weeks there, exploring every inch of the station. The station was only two years old. She resisted the impulse to turn back time, focus in on one of the windows of Bradbury Station, her quarters, to see if she could see herself standing at the window looking out at herself. The thought made her dizzy.

"How is it possible?" she asked.

"They have Earth under observation," Hitochi said. "They must have probes in our solar system, maybe in hundreds of solar systems, feeding constant data to this sphere."

"But why? If the Architects are dead, why would they care?"

Sung shrugged his shoulders. "No one shut the probes down."

"Probes that have lasted five million years or longer?" Hitochi pointed out. "That seems like quite an achievement even for the Architects." He brought his hand to his chin and stroked it as he looked around the room. "Hmmm."

When Kari noticed Hitochi's expression, she asked, "What do you see?"

"I find this space intriguing. Why would the Architects need to construct it to view the sphere if they are capable of making any wall transparent? Why not simply make the wall of the other room transparent?"

"What are you suggesting?" Kirkurk asked.

"The Band is over 600,000,000-kilometers long. If it is hollow, as this sphere we now know to be the Dome indicates, it must contain some type of internal transportation system besides the elevators, unless, of course, you believe the Architects had teleportation." He looked around expectantly, but no one took the bait. "Since this chamber is transparent, it would be ideal for viewing anything inside the Band, much like a glass elevator in a high-rise building."

"The shadows pass through walls," Sung pointed out. "Maybe the Architects could as well."

"Still," Kari joined in, "if Hitochi's theory about the composition of the walls is correct, it would require a great deal of energy to pass through a lengthy series of walls. An elevator or transportation system would be far more energy efficient. We know the Architects possessed a sense of beauty. We see it in their artifacts. A transparent conveyance would be in line with their ideals, especially," she added for Kirkurk's sake, "if the interior of the Band contains treasures worth seeing."

Kirkurk's eyes lit up. She had won him over with promises of something to take back to Earth to enhance his reputation. "Hmmm. It would make sense."

"I think we can figure it out," she added quickly before he could object. "This might be the Architect's next test."

She looked at Hitochi, raising her eyebrows, challenging him to carry through on his promises she had backed. He returned her look with a slight smile.

10

Chaca stared up at the nonexistent opening. Their retreat blocked, they would have to find another way out of the Band. They had climbing gear, but pitons would not anchor in the ultra-dense Band material, and climbing using the pneumatic rods to ascend would be a painstakingly slow process that would still leave them trapped. Even if the *Worthington* launched another missile to blast an opening without incinerating them, and sent a shuttle to rescue them, he doubted the shuttle would have time to lower ropes and haul them back up the kilometer-deep shaft before it sealed itself again.

He could not see his men's faces through their helmets, but he suspected they were concerned. They could assess the situation as well as he could. *Well, we came to reconnoiter. That hasn't changed.*

"Race you to the bottom," he said and released his brake. He stopped beside Collins, who was still groggy. She moaned and rubbed her head through her helmet. She attempted to grasp her rope with her hands, but in her fall, she had activated the microfibers that changed the supple gauntlet material into rigid gloves. He deactivated them for her. "You'll live," he said to her, and clipped her harness to his. Operating both hand brakes, he lowered them down the shaft. He glanced up and saw the others following him.

They stopped three more times to repeat the descent process, positioning new rods and attaching new rigging each time. Carrying a kilometer of line for each of them would have been impossible. They had lost most of the rigging when the shaft sealed. Since they could no longer ascend the shaft by winch and rope, Chaca ordered them to detach the ropes above them and reuse them. As they descended in stages, they doubled up on the lines, two men using the same line. It was a laborious process, time consuming, and a strain on the men's muscles and their nerves. Working in complete darkness with only their helmet lights presented a challenge, but their training had included night climbing, and they accomplished the task with no complaint.

That worried him. Grunts complained. They complained about their superiors, the weather, the food, women, their duty – everything affecting a marine's life was a target for bitching. Their silence suggested they saw no hope in returning alive. He could offer them no reassurances. They were probably right. They would have to deal with it on their own. In the meantime, they still had a job to do.

Half an hour later, they reached the bottom of the shaft. Collins was exhausted. The physical exertion and concentration had drained her. Her suit regulator emitted puffs of CO_2 the recycler could not handle. It crystallized quickly in the cold vacuum and fell as ice crystals. He linked to her suit to increase her oxygen to calm her breathing.

"Take a ten-minute breather," he told the others.

In spite of his training, he was tired too, but as the others took a break, he salvaged what he could from the equipment bags. The kilometer-long fall at .5G had rendered most of the equipment useless. He recovered ration concentrate canisters for the suits and passed them around. He screwed a coffee-flavored energy supplement into the receptacle of his suit, allowed it to heat, and sipped it using the straw inside his helmet. As he savored the strong beverage, he gathered up extra ammo magazines, culled the Claymores for undamaged ones, and picked through some of the less delicate equipment Collins had brought.

Most of it was useless, crushed by the fall despite the padded cases. Of the two reconnaissance drones, one was in pieces. The other one appeared functional. He switched it on. It hovered noiselessly using its miniature repulsion-field generator a few feet above his head. Its infrared light beam swept the shaft, mapping it. The image appeared on his helmet's view screen.

Most disheartening of all were the two resupply oxygen tanks. One had ruptured in the fall, its over-pressurized contents spewing out and instantly vaporizing. Their precious air supply now lay like powdery snow on the floor of the shaft. The other tank was badly dented, but intact. He wouldn't know if the regulator that converted the highly pressurized LOX into a low-pressure breathable mixture worked until they tried it. With their extra oxygen reduced by half, their life expectancy reduced by half as well.

Collins eyed the damage to her equipment. She picked up one unidentifiable piece of apparatus and dropped it to the ground with a sigh. "Useless. I don't have much left."

"You'll have to make do with what you have," Chaca said.

Collins glared at him. "That's like me telling you to go fight an army when your weapons are useless. I can't do it."

Chaca drew his knife and brandished it under Collins' faceplate. Collins' eyes grew bigger, and she backed away from the long, blade glinting in his suit light. "I have this. You use what you have to get the job done. Now, sort it out and get us inside the Band. That's why you're here."

He heard Collins gulp before he turned away. He hoped he had properly motivated the technician. Using his knife, he pried apart the damaged Claymore mines, separating the packed ball bearings from the C-4 explosives, and placed both in the bag. He hoped he wouldn't get an opportunity to use them, but he would not leave them behind.

"Hey, Sarge," Ryder called out, "I think we've got air." Ryder held out a piece of rope sliced by the reforming shaft opening. The fibers waved in a breeze.

Chaca checked his suit's atmosphere monitor to verify Ryder's discovery – Earth-normal atmosphere. That was a relief. He also felt slightly heavier. The gravity was ramping up as well. *They know we're here.*

"Crack your faceplates to conserve air, but keep your helmets on just in case. Paisley and Holmes, gather what supplies we have left and put them in one of the bags. Paisley, you carry it."

"Carry it where?" Paisley asked.

Collins had examined the wall of the shaft with one of her instruments as he salvaged supplies. She gasped aloud, as the wall in front of her disappeared, revealing a curving corridor beyond. The walls of the corridor glowed softly in a topaz light. *That's different from what the first team reported.* Chaca pointed to the opening. "We'll follow the passageway."

"How did you do that?" Paisley asked Collins. Ryder nudged him in the ribs. "No, really, Ryder. Did she just do that?"

"Shut up and move out," Chaca said. "Ryder, take the point. Paisley, since you're so talkative, you get to cover our rear, and sing out in that beautiful Southern Narlins voice if you see an Architect. Hand Ash the bag."

"Especially if you see a female Architect," Aleyev said. "I hear they have more orifices than a Titan ice worm."

"Stow it, Aleyev," Chaca growled, but inwardly he was glad they were talking again. It was a sure sign they felt more secure. Taking Collins aside, he asked, "Did you open the door?"

Collins swallowed hard and shook her head. "No. I didn't do anything. I wasn't even getting a reading except for the increase in gravity."

"I was afraid of that," he admitted.

"Why? We found a way in."

"The Architects or the Band's caretakers let us in. They might not be happy about the hole we made in their real estate."

The ship had lost contact with Kirkurk's team minutes after they had entered the corridor. His team was now off the grid as well. From here on out, they were in uncharted territory. Sidthuri had insisted his mission was one of reconnaissance, but using a thermal missile to gain entry seemed a bit invasive for simple recon. He was still unclear as to what action to take if he met aliens. If they proved hostile, he would retaliate with force, but given the technology of the Architects if hostile, he didn't know if they would give him the chance.

The corridor sloped gently downward, curving to their right like a spiral ramp. Chaca sent the drone forward. The moment it entered the corridor, it lost power and fell to the floor. He picked it up and examined it. The power module indicated a full charge, but it would not function. Either the drop down the shaft had damaged its internal circuitry, or some type of selective dampening field was operating inside the corridor. That concerned him. If the Architects could selectively nullify an energy source, they could use it to kill power in their suits. Even the flechette weapons used a short magnetic pulse for propulsion and relied on microchips for laser sighting.

Collins ignored the useless drone. The light fascinated her. She held her hand in front of one of the walls, and laughed; amazed the light cast no shadow on her suit. No matter how she tried, she could not produce a shadow. Her examination slowed them down.

"Keep up, Collins," he snapped.

"It's impossible," Collins said, smiling at him. "The light acts as if the very air was the source. I wish I had a way to enclose myself inside a lightproof bag. I would bet it would be light inside."

"Fascinating stuff, Collins. Now, log it and move out before I have two of my men carry you slung from one of the collapsible rods trussed up like a deer carcass."

Collins hurried to catch up. Chaca grinned after her. In spite of his denial, the Architect light intrigued him as well. It spoke of a technology far beyond his comprehension, like most Architect technology. If he had time, he would have helped Collins determine its source, but light was the least of their worries.

The corridor wound around endlessly. After two hours, Collins' instruments indicated they had descended almost to the center of the Band, and yet they had seen nothing. He called a halt to wait for Paisley to catch up with them. Collins used the opportunity for a closer examination of the walls, while the others sat back, resting, but alert.

Scientific curiosity and an excited zeal for discovery had replaced Collins' initial fear. Her animated voice recited notes into her suit recorder. She needed rest, but Chaca knew he could never get the inquisitive technician to stop. He let her do her thing, hoping she might learn something useful to them, like how to get them out of the endless passageway.

He began to wonder if the corridor led anywhere or just wound around in confusing circles until depositing them back where they started like a carnival Funhouse ride. The drones would have helped. With them, they could have reconnoitered the entire corridor in minutes. He had an uneasy feeling that was the reason the dampening field was in effect.

He flinched at the muffled sound of a flechette rifle firing back down the corridor. *Paisley*. Paisley was a complainer and a habitual slacker, but he would never fire his weapon without a reason. A dozen more shots rang out. He heard Paisley's armored boots clanking down the corridor. He appeared around a turn of the corridor, saw them, and slid to a stop.

"I saw something!" he yelled, gasping for breath.

"Calm down, Paisley," Chaca admonished him. "What did you see?"

He shook his head. "I don't know. It looked like a shadow."

"Shadow?" Collins asked, perking up at the mention of the word.

Chaca waved her to silence. "You saw a shadow."

"Well, it was a weird shadow, dark and kinda wispy, but alive, but as I looked at it, it …" He paused and glanced behind him.

"It what, Paisley?"

"It melted into the wall."

Ryder laughed aloud. "Paisley got scared by a frickin' ghost."

Chaca could see Paisley was too shaken up to be pulling a prank, and Collins had said the light produced no shadows. "Are you sure it was a shadow?"

"Hell, I don't know," Paisley replied, exasperated by the barrage of questions aimed at him. "It was as black as Holmes, as big as Ryder, and as hairy as my sainted mama's snatch."

Chaca probed deeper trying to break through Paisley's reticence to talk about it. "It attacked you?"

Paisley looked chagrined. "No, it didn't exactly attack. When I saw it, I … I shot it. It melted back into the wall. I ran, back here to warn you guys," he hurriedly added when he realized he had just admitted a shadow had spooked him.

"Could you hear it or smell it?" Collins asked. Her face bore a look of intense concentration.

Paisley glared at her. "Smell it? What the hell do you think I saw, a fucking chocolate milk shake?"

"I think you saw something, Private. I just wish to determine if it was real, or an image of some kind projected by the Band."

"Fuck this 20 questions shit," Paisley snapped. "I saw it."

"Stow it, Corporal," Chaca growled at him. He turned to Collins. "If it is an illusion, we can ignore it, right?"

Collins glanced away, looked back at him, and nodded. "Yes, if it was an illusion."

Chaca had the distinct impression Collins held something back. He didn't have time for guessing games. "For Christ's sake, Collins! I need a straight answer. Was it an illusion or not?"

Collins shrugged. "I don't have enough data yet, but I believe the Architects are capable of almost anything. It didn't harm the corporal, merely frightened him." Paisley scowled at her. "The Architects have made no overtly hostile acts against us."

"What about Kahoku?" Ryder reminded him. "Do you think he went on a sightseeing stroll and forgot to come back?"

"We have no evidence the Architects are to blame for his disappearance. Something else could have happened to him, an accident perhaps."

Chaca stepped into the conversation. He shared Captain Sidthuri's distrust of the Architects. "His suit stopped relaying data, but his bio reading showed an adrenalin spike just before it stopped transmitting. We picked up no signal from its automatic distress beacon. The cameras outside the ship were blank."

"It could have been a power surge," Collins offered, but the assurance was gone from her voice.

"If it was," Paisley said, "it friggin' swallowed him whole. We didn't find a body."

"Nevertheless, we should not be too quick to judge. The Band may be benign. We cannot go around shooting at everything that moves." She stared pointedly at Paisley.

Chaca conceded Collins' point. "Okay, she's right. We remain cautious, but we're here for recon. We don't start anything. Got that, Paisley? No cowboy antics."

"Loud and clear, Sarge," he answered, but glared at Collins.

"Okay, break's over. We keep on humping until we find something." To emphasis the importance of their mission, he reminded them, "If we don't find a way out of here or a means to communicate with the ship, we're stuck here. We have four day's water supply and a week's worth of rations. I don't want to draw lots as to who we eat first."

"I vote for the civilian," Ash piped up. "I hear they taste good."

"All right, move out. I'll take point. Collins, stay in the middle. Paisley, take drag again. If your shadowy friend shows up, we run while it eats you."

This brought laughter to everyone but Paisley, who glanced nervously over his shoulder. The chance to laugh at something, even at Paisley's expense, pumped new life into his team. The somber mood that had gripped them since the elevator shaft sealed behind them lifted. His saw in their eyes a new sense of purpose and alertness. They were soldiers once again with a mission.

Paisley, however, did not find his comment amusing. In fact, he looked hesitant. "Why can't Ash or Holmes take drag? Shit. I did my stint."

"Hell, Paisley," Holmes said, "I'll take drag if you're so damn spooked."

Chaca nodded. He would give Paisley time to get over his jitters. "Okay, Holmes. Button up your armor just in case."

Holmes slammed his visor down, sealed it, and flashed a smile through the faceplate before trotting back down the corridor.

After travelling another kilometer and descending a further hundred meters, the corridor ended at a black wall as blank and featureless as the walls of the corridor. Chaca's gut tightened. The others caught up with him, saw the wall, and voiced their dismay.

"Damn Architects," Ryder cursed. "What are they hiding?"

Aleyev's response was a string of colorful Russian expletives. Chaca didn't understand the words, but he got the meaning. "Ditto, Aleyev."

"What now?" Ash asked.

Chaca turned to Collins. "Collins, see what you can do."

"I don't know what you think I can do. This material is impossible to penetrate, without a plasma missile, of course." She rifled through her cases of instruments. "If there is some kind of doorway here like the one through which we entered this corridor, perhaps I can locate it." She produced a scanner, ran it along the surface of the wall, frowning at the results. "This can't be right."

"What?" Chaca asked. Anything that could mystify Collins concerned him. She struck him as diligent, competent, and not easily flustered. She had disproved his earlier misgivings about having a civilian along.

"According to this, there's nothing here."

"Your gizmo thingamajig's busted," Ryder said, scowling at the technician.

"No, it's working perfectly. It's just … well; my gizmo thingamajig says there is no solid object in front of us." Her voice held a hint of contempt for Ryder's dismissal of her abilities. She reached out to the wall, drawing several gasps when her arm sank into the ebony wall up to her elbow. She yelped and drew it back quickly. A light rime of hoar frost covered her gauntlet and armor. It melted quickly in the warmer air. She shook her arm and flexed her fingers. "Good thing I had on my gloves. It was cold as hell, like pushing into half-frozen pudding."

"Yeah, but what's on the other side?" Ryder asked.

Chaca quelled the apprehension building in his chest. "A big fat plum, Ryder. What else?" He studied the wall. He didn't like the idea of going through a barrier he knew nothing about or where it led. He reminded himself they had entered an unknown world when they rappelled down the elevator shaft and had been stumbling along blindly since. They could not go back the way they had come. The pudding wall, as Collins had named it, offered the only way out. Whatever lay on the other side, they would have to face it.

"Wait here." He sealed his facemask, took a deep breath, and plunged into the wall headfirst, bracing himself for the cold shock. The suit absorbed most of the freezing temperature. His suit read minus 73 degrees Celsius. He held his *Tach II* 7.62mm rifle in his hands, hoping the extreme cold did not affect its moving parts. The manufacturer rated it for deep space vacuum environments, but men had died before because someone else had not done their job properly.

He stepped through the wall and out onto the rim of the Grand Canyon, Architect-style. The sudden transition from a confined space to clinging to the side of a deep, dark chasm produced a moment of intense vertigo. He backed up until his back brushed the ebony wall. When the sensation passed a few seconds later, he marveled at the vista. Unlike the endless black walls of the Band and the equally austere ebony Cities dotting its surface, the place into which he had emerged was alive with color and movement.

His initial comparison to the Grand Canyon in his home state of Arizona faded as the enormity and grandeur of the alien structure sank in. He stood on a rail-less balcony projecting out over a half-kilometer-deep artificial chasm disappearing into the darkness in either direction along the length of the Band. The Band's enormous size disguised the slight curvature of the chasm. Hundreds of identical platforms rose above and below him, and on the opposite side of the chasm. Not all were the same distance apart, and many areas of the wall were blank. He switched on his laser range finder and measured the distance to the other side – 2.2.kilometers.

The ten-meter-wide balcony upon which he stood narrowed to a three-meter-wide ledge connecting each platform with a series of walkways. Similar slender causeways with no visible structural supports spanned the width of the chasm to balconies on the opposite side. If the Architects trod the delicate walkways, they had no fear of heights. He wondered at the function of the enormous hollow space. It was possible it was simply hollow to reduce the overall weight and mass of the Band, but with their technology, he doubted the Architects worried about mass and weight limits.

The lights along the length of the great artificial rift ran the gamut of shades but tended to the pastel hues – honey-yellow topaz, aqua blue, purplish lilac, cherry blossom pink, and pale lavender – a fairyland of colors. He saw no bright colors. The Architects preferred softer tones like the subdued lighting in the corridor. The overall effect of the lighting challenged his long-held opinion of the Architects as a cold, unemotional race that created the artifacts simply as engineering challenges. The discovery of the austere ebony Band circling a dull, red dwarf had reinforced his initial judgment, but the interior wonderland in which he now stood dispelled it. It made them more human but no less dangerous.

Unlike the ebony wall material, the walkways were slightly opaque and glowed from within with an azure light, glittering as the intensity of the light changed to the pulse of some alien rhythm. The longer causeways spanning the width of the chasm, delicate ribbons of pulsating light, appeared too slim and fragile to support their own weight. He could think of no reason for the dazzling effect other than for its profound splendor. He now understood the Architects were true aficionados of beauty.

Other specks of lights moved both horizontally and vertically within the chasm. He set his visor for a telescopic view and saw cubical structures resembling glass conveyances plying the length and depth of the structure. He detected movement within some of them but could not determine if it was human or alien. After a closer view, he finally decided they were robotic housekeeping devices. Even a race capable of constructing an engineering marvel the size and complexity of the Band would have to rely on automated repair drones to maintain it for .5 billion years.

Other machines of various shapes and sizes crawled along the side of the chasm or flew in the void between the walls. He could make no guess about their function, but it was obvious the Band was not the dead object it appeared from the exterior. Inside, at least, it was a living, thriving structure. He could not make out much detail at the dark bottom of the chasm even using night-vision filters, but he discerned the vague outlines of massive ten-story-high structures spaced at regular intervals. Parts of the structures blurred in motion, accompanied by pulsing lights and a low-frequency hum he could feel through the material of his armor. The hairs on his arm rose, as if some type of energy saturated the vacuum of the chasm. Whatever the objects were, they were worth the long journey from Earth to investigate.

"This is more like it," he said aloud.

On a hunch, he checked his suit readouts. As he suspected, the chasm was a super-chilled vacuum at 220 degrees Celsius below zero, an excellent and efficient insulating material for a power generator or engine, as he suspected the mysterious objects on the bottom of the chasm to be. The black pudding wall acted as a barrier separating the cold vacuum of the chasm from the corridor. By the vast number of balconies visible in his small section of the chasm, the winding corridors riddled the Band like wormwood.

The wall quivered and Ash popped out, his flechette weapon held at the ready. When he saw the first sergeant was in no danger, he shook his helmet to get his bearings, and leaned over the edge of the balcony to stare down into the chasm. He whistled his appreciation. "We were worried about you, First Sergeant. I drew the short straw and came to check on you. In case you found some broads and didn't want to share," he added with a grin.

"At least the suit coms are working out here," Chaca noted. "That's a bit of good news. Get the others. I think we've found what we came for."

11

Kari knew Hitochi was right about the purpose of the cubical anteroom. An elevator or conveyance made perfect sense from an engineering standpoint. Although they had yet to find any machinery or power source, the outside elevator through which they had entered the Band and the operation of the almost magical walls indicated a sophisticated controlling mechanism requiring maintenance over a period of eons, unless the Architects had built maintenance-free machines. That should be impossible even for a race as advanced as the Architects. No one could defeat entropy.

She placed her hands on the wall again, this time concentrating on what she wanted, a method of controlling the elevator. Her efforts produced two rectangular panels, appearing as if suspended within the transparent wall. A band of purple light outlined one panel, with the other limned in amber. The purple panel lay superimposed over the spot she had first placed her hands to manipulate the projector. At first, she assumed the placement of the control panel and the size of the individual controls indicated the approximate height of the Architects and the size of their hands, which corresponded closely with hers. However, even as she congratulated herself for her finding, by experimentation, she discovered she could drag the control panels to any point on the wall, thereby quickly disproving her own theory.

The panel she had used to rotate the sphere and the image magnifier contained a myriad of controls of which she had no idea of their functions. She suspected some were fine-tuning adjustments or allowed access to the image library, but they would require a more thorough study. As much as she wanted to play around with the images, her goal was the elevator control panel.

Kirkurk almost crowded her away from the wall in his zeal to examine the image control panel. She dragged the amber panel a few meters away to give him room. She noticed the image panel automatically adjusted the size and placement of the controls to fit Kirkurk's taller stature and larger hand size. The Architects had intended the controls to accommodate any race that made it into the Band, regardless of the user's size, organs for manipulation, or the number of manipulating digits. She still knew nothing about the physical characteristics of the Architects.

She took heart in the fact the Architects had anticipated visitors and designed the controls accordingly, thus the mitten-shaped pads she had used to enter the tramcar. She was willing to bet the pads would change shape to fit any alien species' hand. Unless, she reminded herself harshly, the Architects came in varied shapes and sizes as well. If that were the case, it was possible they were the first species to penetrate so deeply into the Band. The prospect excited her, like being the first to excavate a previously undiscovered tomb. Then, she remembered the variety of bones in the room around Kahoku's body. The *Worthington* and her human passengers had not been the first to reach the Band. She only hoped they were the first to make it through the alien mouse maze and reach the cheese.

While Kirkurk delighted himself calling up images of other worlds, his eyes shining like a child on Christmas morning, she studied the second panel. Rather than simple depictions of up and down arrows, as she had expected if it controlled the movement of the elevator, the panel bore a dozen strange hieroglyphic symbols. However, one grouping of four looked familiar. She presumed the four glowing quadrants of an oblong diamond indicated up, down, left, and right. The other symbols might have controlled speed or dispensed coffee for all she knew. The anteroom was more transport vehicle or tramcar than simple up-and-down elevator.

When she felt confident she understood the panel's basic functions, she addressed the others. "I think I can operate it," she announced.

Hitochi looked at Deidre, Luntz, and Sung standing together in the outer room, as if afraid to join them in the tramcar. "Are you guys coming?" he asked.

Deidre glanced at Luntz. Cowed by his actions after the deaths of the three men, Luntz lowered his head and said nothing. Deidre finally sighed and nodded, but she still did not move. That task fell to Sung to lead the way. He took a few tentative steps across the room, and gaining confidence, strode inside the car and looked out at the expanse beyond. Deidre nudged Luntz, who followed less enthusiastically.

"Bring Kari's suit," Hitochi told Luntz. Luntz picked it up and stuffed it under his arm.

"Here goes," Kari said. "What floor, sporting goods or housewares?"

Her humor was lost on them. She shrugged and pressed what she hoped was the down button. The wall reappeared behind them, this time as translucent as the other walls. Deidre jumped back from it in surprise. Seconds later, the car began to drop. Kari felt no sensation of movement, but judging by the rapidity in which the image of the projected planet disappeared above them, she estimated the car travelled at a speed greater than 200 kilometers per hour.

"Marvelous inertia dampeners," Hitochi noted. "It must be a by-product of the artificial gravity generator. I wondered why the Band's gravity was a constant .5G when its mass and low rotation around the sun would have produced a much lower gravity. The ability to ramp up to 1 G for us indicates a sophisticated control system."

Her mind half-focused on his running commentary, as she tried to see what lay within the Dome other than the second sphere. Now that she knew that the room served more purpose than as a multiple-viewpoint observation chamber, with time, she was certain she could learn to manipulate the images with the controls. At a point corresponding with the Dome's center, the elevator stopped, and the two lateral direction controls illuminated.

"Which way?" she asked.

"Spinward," Hitochi said.

She didn't wait on a second opinion, and she had no personal preference. She pressed the control, taking the tram spinward of the Band. With no sensation of change, the vehicle began travelling laterally across the inside face of the Dome. Within seconds, it left the Dome behind and entered a space so dark she could not see the others in the room. The two panels continued to glow, but shed no light into the room. She breathed a sigh of relief when Hitochi switched on his helmet light and grinned at her. She began to have misgivings about her belief the tram was transparent for viewing Architect wonders. If the entire Band were in total darkness, they could pass within meters of the treasure trove they sought and see nothing.

Her mind played cruel tricks on her, creating tantalizing glimpses of shadows within shadows. As if thinking the same thing, Hitochi pressed his helmet to the wall, but his light revealed nothing outside the room.

After ten minutes of pitch-black darkness, Kirkurk began grumbling loudly enough for everyone to hear him. "This is a waste of time. We should never have left the sphere."

As much as she hated to admit it, the surly archaeologist might be right. She made up her mind to reverse directions and return to the Dome. At least they could examine the database of planets and perhaps learn something more. Just as she reached for the control panel, the tram emerged into an enormous chamber. Darkness gave way to a myriad of lights twinkling in the darkness. It reminded her of multi-colored fireflies on a summer's eve in Central Park or sprites fluttering through an enchanted garden. Her heart race with excitement, as a profound sense of wonder enveloped her. She had been right about the Architects. Only creatures with an acute sense of beauty could have created such a marvelous vista.

The tram moved parallel to the wall several hundred meters above the floor of a dark gulf at least two kilometers across. The space was so enormous they could not see the far end of it. It reminded her of a wide boulevard running between kilometers-high buildings. The multi-hued lights mesmerized her, capturing her gaze as the tram passed beneath glowing translucent walkways spanning the gulf like spun-sugar fairy bridges. They looked so delicate she imagined she could reach out a finger to touch it and cause it to crumble into a pile of sugar crystals.

She searched for a control to stop the vehicle, but saw none. Frustrated, she pressed both lateral direction controls at the same time. The tram stopped abruptly directly beneath one of the walkways. Belatedly, she realized that without the inertia dampeners, the sudden deceleration could have injured them.

"It's less than half a meter thick," Hitochi said, as he scanned the bridge with his instruments. His analytical voice contained as much wonder as she felt. "The walkways must be constructed of the same material as the Band, but it's translucent." He shook his head, grinning. "Solid, transparent, translucent – how do the Architects determine the opacity of the fields?"

"They are too narrow for walkways," Sung objected. "Perhaps they are buttresses of some kind."

"Their random placement doesn't indicate any support function. I doubt the necessity for such structures given the Architects' artificial gravity generators and their ability to construct walls with fields of energy."

"It looks like a city," Kirkurk said, "a real city, not one of the tombs above."

"It looks more like a gigantic machine to me," Sung argued. He stared down into the depths of the gorge at large structures barely visible in the darkness. "I get no feel of a metropolis here, no shops, no houses, and no window displays."

Kari agreed. Whatever they had discovered, it was not the home of the Architects, but it was wonderful, nevertheless. "But we should explore it nonetheless," she replied.

"Yes," Kirkurk said. "Can you open the door?"

"We don't know what's on the other side," Deidre warned.

"You should put on your suit," Hitochi told Kari. "Everyone put on your helmets and seal your suits."

Kari noticed Kirkurk's flash of anger aimed at Hitochi. He resented Hitochi's usurpation of his authority, but did not challenge him. So swept up in the joy of discovery, he probably had not thought of the potential danger. She hadn't. She quickly donned her suit and opened the door of the vehicle, revealing a small room empty of anything, including atmosphere. She stepped out of the vehicle. Even with its built-in heaters, the chill seeped in through the material.

"Amazing," Hitochi said behind her. He stood inside the tram with one of his instruments extended out the door. "An invisible force field keeps the atmosphere and heat constant inside the vehicle, while outside is a perfect vacuum. There's no mixing. The membrane is impermeable."

Kari was more interested in viewing the boulevard. No sooner had she thought of a control panel than a small panel appeared above her head as if by magic. The Band had begun to read her mind. She wasn't sure she wanted an alien presence inside her head. She reached up and dragged the panel down to her level.

"Here it is," she called out, opened the wall, and stepped out onto a balcony.

"Wait," Hitochi warned. He checked his instruments. "The temperature is deadly out here, over -220 Celsius. I wouldn't recommend prolonged exposure in your civilian suits."

"What about yours?" Kari asked.

Hitochi smiled. "Oh, I'm comfy cozy in my military issue."

"He's right," Kirkurk said, trying to wrest control of the group back from Hitochi. "On the surface of the Band, sunlight kept the temperature slightly over -80 C. This is much worse. The heaters will draw more power from the suit batteries, depleting them more quickly."

"The question is why the temperature is so much lower in this space," Sung said. "I believe it supports my theory that this," he waved his hands around, "is all part of some colossal machine. Extreme cold temperatures near Absolute Zero are necessary for superconductivity and superfluidity."

"You're talking over my head," Kari broke in.

"It's quite simple. Near Absolute Zero, super-chilled material becomes a superconductor. Electrical resistance reduces to near zero. A small current can last indefinitely with no power source and travel great distances with no loss of power. You don't use up electricity; it depletes as heat caused by resistance. At certain extreme temperatures, some fluids, like liquid helium, become super-fluids. They can create eddies requiring no outside agitation to continue. Theory proposes that even a vacuum can become a super-fluid. By spinning super-fluids, the Pembina can create energy. With zero resistance, it will last indefinitely." He nodded at the walkways. "It seems our friends have achieved this."

"None of this gets us home," Luntz whined. "All this exploring in useless if we die here. I want to return to the ship."

Kari looked at the photographer. Since the deaths of Mailors and the two marines, he had been a hollow shell of the robust figure the world knew. Luntz had supplied stunning photographs of ground battles against pirates. He had photographed an erupting volcano in Indonesia that buried his van beneath six meters of volcanic ash. He had accompanied a deep-sea submersible into the Marianas Trench to photograph the exotic creatures around a volcanic smoker. The man standing in front of her could barely keep his hands from trembling. His ready smile had vanished, replaced by a look of constant terror. The change in him sickened her.

Kari was frightened too. Only a fool would not be in their present situation. She feared every moment for her life, but she had not lost her thirst for discovery, as Luntz had. She had been jealous of him, of his glib manner and ability to make friends and impress people. Seeing him as he was now, broken and stripped to his basic character, she felt sorry for him.

Sung nodded her agreement at Luntz's comment. "Quite right, I'm afraid." His smile erased the glum expression on his face. "However, it is quite interesting."

Kari could not bring herself to walk to the edge of the balcony and look down. Her feet would not even allow her to move close enough to see below them. She didn't think she could cross one of the narrow walkways across the abyss if she saw an EXIT sign on the other side. Like Luntz, in spite of the beauty, she did not want to die inside the Band. However, she did want to explore it.

A buzzing sound, like an angry mosquito, reached her ears. For a moment, she forgot she was standing in a vacuum and searched around them for the source. She realized it came from her com unit, the faint crackle of static in the speaker.

"Do any of you hear that?" she asked.

"It could be background static from the machinery," Sung suggested.

Before she could reply, clearly, as if he were standing right beside her, she heard, "This is Sergeant Akoa Chaca. Does anyone read me?"

12

Private James Meredith Holmes was, like Paisley, a southern boy. He hailed from Oxford, Mississippi, home of Ole Miss University and birthplace of novelists William Faulkner, John Grisham, and James Meredith, the 1960's Civil Rights activist for whom his parents had named him. Unlike Paisley, who was born to well-educated, wealthy parents in Grand Isle, Louisiana, Holmes grew up in low-rent subsidized housing raised by his ill grandmother. If not for the military, he would have wound up just another young punk on the streets dead by 21.

In spite of their differences, he and Paisley shared the same southern heritage. They had shared the same hell of battle. The two factors created a bond between them. Neither would have admitted to others that they were friends, but they looked out for one another. If Paisley had zoned out from spotting some ghost, he would cover his ass for him. Paisley would do the same for him. Besides, if Paisley was right, he was eager to shoot something. Stuck on the *Worthington* for three months on the journey out and now almost two more on the Band playing nursemaid to a bunch of civilians was wearing thin. He needed some action. The big Hawaiian ensign, Kahoku, was his friend. If something on the Band – maybe Architects – had killed him, he wanted some deep payback.

Trudging down the empty corridor illuminated only by a dull light that didn't cast shadows was eerie enough to give anyone the jitters. He switched on his helmet lights, but they disappeared in the inky blackness of the wall. The total silence surrounding him and his inability to see beyond the next curve, made him feel like he was alone. He couldn't even talk to anyone to break the silence. The suit coms didn't work inside the corridor. He wished he had thought to download his tunes onto his suit computer.

As he turned a bend in the corridor, a strange sound behind him drew his attention. Inside the dead-silent Band, any sound was worthy of attention. He turned, lifted his faceplate, and yelled, "If you don't want your sorry ass blown away, you'd better show yourself pronto."

The sound intensified, like nails on a chalkboard. "Damn, that's reason enough to shoot any asshole." He waited with his finger on the trigger. No matter what the sarge advised, he was going to shoot the fuck out of anything he saw and to hell with diplomacy. His initial glimpse of the thing following him sent a cold chill running through his body. At first, it looked like an apparition, a wispy black shadow fuzzy around the edges, like a trick of the light, but he knew it was no illusion, and that it wasn't friendly.

"Stop right there," he warned. He charged his weapon with a flechette in the chamber. "This ain't no invitation to the prom I'm holding here."

The shadow began pulsating, changing shape. It solidified into a seven-foot-tall monster. It opened its mouth and growled, revealing hundreds of tiny needle-like projections. Large black eyes with swirling blood-red pupils stared at him from deep within the dark mass. Several appendages sprouted from various parts of its body like dough extruded by a pasta machine, flattened at the tips like sharp blades.

"What the holy fuck?" he yelled at the creature. He knew it was impossible; yet, there it was, and he knew it was real. "Paisley, you ain't such a crazy-ass cracker after all."

He held down the trigger on his weapon, sending a stream of razor-edged flechettes into the creature's body. It ignored the high-velocity metal darts that passed unimpeded through its body and bounced off the wall behind it. It began floating down the corridor toward him, slightly above the floor as if hovering.

"Hey, guys!" he yelled, his voice cracking with fear. "I need some help here."

He yanked one of the fragmentary grenades from his utility belt, pressed the timer, rolled it beneath the creature, and raced back to the safety of a turn in the corridor. After it exploded, a rush of hot air and smoke swept past him. "Eat that, mother." He peeked around the corner, cursing when the creature walked unharmed from roiling swirls of smoke.

"Son of a bitch! Fuck this shit."

He sprinted down the corridor toward his comrades. He glanced back to see the shadow creature chasing him. He pushed his long legs as fast as they could go, but the shadow remained the same relative distance behind him. He rounded a curve and stumbled into Aleyev, scaring the crap out of him.

"Greg, man, you gotta help me," he told the Russian.

Aleyev looked past him and saw the monster rushing toward them. His eyes grew large and a grimace formed on his lips. He growled something in Russian, slapped his helmet closed, and fired his weapon.

"It's no good, man," he told Aleyev. "It won't stop him. Where's Sarge?"

Aleyev ignored him. He continued firing at the creature, moving the barrel of the flechette rifle back and forth like a fire hose, spraying a stream of deadly darts. Holmes grabbed Aleyev by the collar of his armor and dragged him backwards down the corridor, while the Russian emptied his weapon into the creature. He slapped in a fresh magazine and continued firing.

Holmes spotted Ryder, Paisley, and Collins staring down the corridor toward the commotion. He stopped when he saw the dead-end wall behind them. "Shit, man. This is some big time Fugazi, screwed-up shit. We ain't goin' nowhere. Where's the sarge and Ash?" he yelled.

Ryder's face betrayed no emotion or surprise when he spotted the creature. He stepped past Holmes with his heavy assault weapon, knelt, and joined Aleyev in pouring high-velocity .50 caliber rounds into the creature. The shadow creature ignored both of them and continued advancing. When Ash stepped through the black wall like Alice through the looking glass, Holmes leaped backwards. "What the holy fuck, man?"

Ash immediately saw the danger and rushed to join Ryder and Aleyev on the firing line. He yelled as he ran, "The sarge said everybody through the wall. Now! Seal your suits."

Holmes looked at Ash as if he were crazy, but when Collins stepped into the black wall and disappeared, he figured any place was better than where he was. Before he could summon the courage to walk through what looked to him like a solid wall, Aleyev screamed. He looked back and wished he hadn't. The shadow creature held Aleyev in the air twisting his body armor while the Russian fired point-blank into its head, screaming in pain the entire time. Ryder fired high-velocity .50 caliber rounds into the creature's lower torso to avoid hitting Aleyev, but the brass-tipped bullets ricocheted away.

When the joints of Aleyev's battle armor popped like cracking a lobster claw, the screaming stopped. Blood spilled from the splintered black, carbon nano-fiber reinforced ceramic armor and pooled on the floor. Holmes had seen men die, but he had never imagined that much blood could come from a man's body. The creature tossed Aleyev's shattered corpse aside like an empty soda can, hovered over the pool of blood, and began lapping it up like a bug through a long, tubular tongue protruding from it mouth. Ryder waved Ash and Paisley back and began backpedaling toward the wall, still firing his .50 caliber.

Holmes had seen enough. He closed his eyes, slapped his faceplate into place, and leaped into the wall. The sudden chill hit him like a slap in the face. He emerged from the wall, landed on his side, and slid to the edge of a precipice. The only thing stopping him from going over the edge was Chaca's hand gripping his leg. He stared down into a dark abyss below him.

"Holy shit!" He scrambled backwards on his hands and knees. "Man, this shit is getting deep."

* * * *

Chaca saw Collins step out of the wall and beckoned her over. Holmes shot through moments later. "What's happening?" Chaca asked.

"A goddamned monster, that's what's happening," Holmes yelled.

Chaca looked at Collins for confirmation. She nodded. "He's right. It looked like some kind of sentient shadow. The flechettes went unimpeded right through its body. Perhaps we've finally met an Architect."

Holmes broke in. "Aleyev's gone."

Chaca clenched his teeth. He didn't like losing men. "Hold this position," he said. He loaded his weapon and stepped toward the wall. Before he reached the wall, Ash, Paisley, and Ryder came through shoulder-to-shoulder facing backwards. Ryder and Ash immediately dropped to their knees and aimed their weapons at the wall. Paisley looked as if he wanted to run, but he held his position behind them. Chaca opened the equipment bag, removed two Claymore mines, and set them in front of the black wall, praying the remote detonator switch worked. He motioned for everyone to move farther away from the blast zone. After a long, tension-filled minute, the creature still had not emerged.

"Maybe it can't pass through the barrier," Collins suggested, "or doesn't like the extreme cold."

Paisley whirled on her, grabbed her by the shoulder, and pointed his weapon at Collin's helmet. Collin's face paled and a grimace formed on her lips. "You're the one who said I was crazy," he snapped. "What do you think now, mother fucker?"

"Calm down, Paisley," Chaca warned him. "I don't want to have to shoot you. Whatever the hell it was, we need you." Paisley hesitated, but he dropped Collins, lowered his weapon, and stepped back. She stumbled, as she backed closer to Chaca. "She might be right about the barrier. Still, we can't count on it."

"Shouldn't we check on Aleyev?" Collins asked.

Ryder shook his head. "He's gone."

"We don't leave our dead behind," Holmes insisted.

"We'll come back later for him," Chaca assured Holmes.

"No. I mean he's not there, First Sergeant," Ryder said, emphasizing Chaca's rank to remind the others they were still Marines. "After that thing killed him and drank his blood, it turned into some kind of mist, like a bank of black fog, enveloped Aleyev's body, and disappeared into a wall, taking Aleyev with it."

As Chaca listened to Ryder's grisly report, he found it difficult to comprehend what had taken place. He had lost a man to a monster he had not witnessed. It sounded impossible, but he believed his men. If something alien was hunting them, he wanted to fight in an open space, like the chasm. Things didn't look good for Kirkurk's team if they had encountered one of those things. He wondered if any of them were getting out of the Band alive.

He gazed down the grand chasm in both directions. They couldn't remain where they were, and they couldn't go back the way they had come. He pointed anti-spinward toward the *Worthington*. "We go that way." He knew they needed to put distance between them and the shadow creature. *How the hell do you fight a shadow that can pop in and out of solid walls?*

"Holmes, Ryder. Transmit your video camera file of this thing."

As the gruesome scene unfolded on his helmet screen, his guts twisted into tight knots. He saw it, but he couldn't believe it. His first thought was of the Hopi legends about *Masauwu*, the Skeleton Man guarding the land of the dead. *It's just a legend*, he reminded himself. *This thing is real.* He still didn't know what the creature was, but he had gleaned some knowledge of its capabilities. It could become either an untouchable mist or an impervious solid. Their weapons were useless against it. *Improvise, adapt, overcome* – the Marine motto. They would have to push it to the limit to survive.

His first priority was to warn the *Worthington*. He knew it was probably useless; they were a kilometer or more deep into the bowels of the Band and 5,000 kilometers away, but he had to try to contact the ship.

He activated the long-range com link. "*Worthington*, this is First Sergeant Chaca. Please respond."

No one replied. He tried again.

"This is Sergeant Akoa Chaca. Can anyone read me?"

Very faintly, he heard, "Sergeant, this is Lieutenant Ken Hitochi."

"I'll be damned," he said off mic. "They made it after all."

After a brief conversation with Hitochi, he disarmed the Claymores, placed them in the bag, and handed the bag to Paisley. "Here. You're pack mule again. Don't ever point your weapon at someone in my team."

He looked at all of them. "If we're going to get through this, we all stick together. Got it?" When no one answered, he repeated louder, "Got it?"

"*Hoo Ya*, First Sergeant," they all responded. Belatedly, Collins answered, "Got it."

"All right. Let's move out."

13

After their initial contact with Sergeant Chaca, Hitochi was eager for news. "Sergeant Chaca, what is your present location?"

"Inside the Band. I estimate 5,000 klicks from you. What is your status?"

"Three dead, including Dr. Mailors, Private Eggleston, and Corporal Newman. They were attacked by some kind of shadow creature capable of moving through the walls."

"Yes, we encountered one as well. I have one KIA. Are you in contact with the *Worthington*?"

"Negative."

"Same here. What is your location?"

"We're in an enormous half-kilometer-deep channel or cleft in the Band. It continues for a great distance, perhaps the entire length of the Band. We discovered how to operate a transport system and had intended to explore as we searched for a way out."

"Can you come to us? We're in what might be the same cleft spinward from your position."

Hitochi glanced at the others to get a consensus. No one objected. "Can do. How long have you been inside the Band?"

"Since 1830 hours."

Hitochi frowned. "That was awfully fast for a rescue operation." He paused. "Why are you 5,000 klicks from our position?"

Kari had wondered the same thing. It seemed an odd place to start a rescue mission.

"We are not a rescue party. We detected an energy spike similar to the one that produced the elevator. We blasted our way in with a *Prometheus* missile. The shaft opening sealed us in too."

"What is a *Prometheus* missile?" Kirkurk demanded of Hitochi.

"A high-energy plasma weapon," Hitochi explained off mic.

Kirkurk exploded. "Those fools! Don't they realize the damage they may have caused? We came to explore, not conquer."

Kari understood Kirkurk's rage, but the present predicament of both groups outweighed any other issues. "They're stuck here too. With those shadow wraiths we have a better chance of surviving as a large group," she suggested.

"Huh! Our marine escort didn't protect Mailors."

"Enough, Kirkurk," Hitochi snapped. "It's out of your hands. From now on, this is a military effort. We'll rendezvous with First Sergeant Chaca's team to search for a way out of here or a means to contact the *Worthington* for extraction."

"By what right …?" Kirkurk began.

Hitochi moved to loom over Kirkurk. "I'll leave your ass standing here for the wraiths if you don't move it." He looked around at the group. "Exploring is on hold until we reach Chaca's team. Any other objections?"

He reopened communications with the sergeant. "We're headed your way, but unless we can increase the speed of the tram, it will take 20-plus hours."

"Too long. We don't have power or oxygen for that length of time. How did you discover the operation of the tram? Can you explain it to me or to technician Amanda Collins? We've seen them in operation from a distance. We'll try to locate one and meet you halfway. Ten-plus hours is doable."

"Will do. Kari?"

Kari tried to put into words for Collins how she had discovered the secret of the tram's controls. To her, she sounded bewildered and confused. Her repeated use of the word 'feel' made her doubt Collins could understand her explanation, but finally she claimed she understood. When Kari finished, Hitochi spoke to Chaca.

"To save battery power, I'll contact you again in two hours."

"Affirmative. Chaca out."

After they broke contact, everyone had questions for Hitochi, even though they had heard the entire conversation. Everyone, that is, except Kirkurk. He looked sullen and refused to glance in Hitochi's direction. Kari was not thrilled at Hitochi for placing the team under military control, but his presence and the addition of the two marine escorts had hinted at that possibility from the beginning. After all, they had arrived on a military vessel. If they had discovered a treasure trove of technological wonders, she had no doubt the military would have swooped down on them, freezing out the civilian teams.

Deidre's concern was more pressing. "We don't have enough oxygen for 20 hours. What if they can't meet us halfway. We'll never get out of here in time."

Sung replied, "Given the enormous length of the Band, it is likely a species capable of FTL travel and such advanced inertia dampeners would have developed a very rapid transit system. I think we have barely scratched the surface on the capabilities of this vehicle."

Sung's answer did not satisfy her. "That's all well and good if we learn to use it, but what if we don't?" She stared at Kari as if challenging her. Kari refused to allow Deidre to draw her into the discussion.

Sung shrugged. "Then, my dear, I suppose we die in transit."

Deidre swore at him and stalked back toward the tram. Hitochi herded them all back to the tram. Kari left reluctantly. The city, or giant machine if Sung was right, fascinated her. In spite of her fear of heights, she wanted to linger. Hitochi had to shove Kirkurk physically to get him moving.

To Kari's delight, the tram retained its oxygen atmosphere. When the door closed, she removed her confining helmet and breathed the fresh, Band-supplied air. At least they had solved the problem of long-term survival. If they remained inside the tram, they would not die from lack of oxygen. The fact did nothing to mollify Deidre's ire. She sat in one corner and Kirkurk in the opposite corner, like opposing boxers or small children forced into a time out by a put upon mother.

Kari started the tram moving. Her stomach rumbled as a reminder that she had not eaten since before entering the Band. She reached for one of the nutrient drink bottles attached to her suit's utility belt. Hitochi stopped her.

"You had better save those in case we're stuck in the suits for any length of time. Eat a ration bar instead."

She smiled at him. He looked stressed from his confrontation with Kirkurk. "Thanks. I noticed you didn't tell the sergeant about Ensign Kahoku. Why not?"

He sighed and rubbed his temple. "He has enough problems to deal with right now, as do we. Can you make this thing move faster?"

His voice held no hint of recrimination, but he had bet their survival on her ability to master the alien controls. She hoped he understood that unlocking the front door didn't make her a master safecracker. If the Architects had placed safeguards or speed governors on the tram system controls, she would in all probability never learn to bypass them. That Hitochi, an engineer, had placed such faith in her was inspiring, but at the same time frightening.

"I'll do my best. After I eat."

He nodded. "We should all take a break."

Kari sat in front of the controls, studying them while she munched her chocolate-flavored ration bar, still slightly frozen from their super-chilled excursion outside. She imagined it was a frosty chocolate milkshake from Rupert's, her favorite hangout on E. 62nd Street near the Queensboro Bridge. She could see the bridge from her bedroom window. One of Rupert's greasy, but delicious cheeseburgers with a side order of hand-cut French fries would have been nice, too. The *Worthington*'s meals were tasty and nourishing, but they lacked a sense of home, of New York. It had been almost six months since she had last eaten at Rupert's with her friends. She sighed. It would be months longer before she tasted one of their burgers or milkshakes again, if ever.

She swept the thought from her mind and focused on the alien control panel. Using her belief that any two machines serving the same functions would have similarities, she had discovered Up, Down, Left, Right, and opening the door. The tram automatically renewed their atmosphere and kept the temperature bearable. It therefore sensed their presence and interpreted their needs. She need only convey a sense of urgency and it should detect that.

She sighed again. She was assigning advanced capabilities to what was essentially a subway car. For all she knew, it controlled environment and moved in the selected direction only. It was like expecting a taxi on Earth to fly her to the moon because she desired it. Impossible, even she was willing to pay the fare. She chuckled aloud at her absurd joke.

"You find this amusing, Miss Stone?" Kirkurk growled at her from his corner.

She resented his smug tone, but didn't feel like a fight with him. She shook her head. "No. Just reminiscing."

"Perhaps you should forget about your fond memories and do your job."

She fumed. If he wanted a fight, she would deliver. She was tired of his sanctimonious attitude. "You just shut the hell up. You've done nothing but whine constantly during this entire trip. This isn't about you, you know. We all have homes, friends, and family. I'm doing my best in a field about which I know nothing. Maybe if you pulled your head out of your ass and did something useful for a change, we could find a way out of here."

Kirkurk's jaw dropped, and his cheeks turned a bright rosy red.

Hitochi yelled, "Good for you! Tell the bastard off." Kirkurk started to retaliate, but Hitochi stopped him. "No. Kari's right. You haven't earned the right to say anything. Without her, we would still be standing in the corridor. Now, shut up and let her work."

He winked at her. She blushed at the attention. She was annoyed with herself for exploding at Kirkurk, but the tensions had been accumulating for hours. Now, she had to produce results. She tried to imagine the Architects from what few facts they knew about them. She knew their maximum size based on the doorways and corridors, assuming they were designed for their use. She could guess at their thought processes from the design of the artifacts and the Band.

Unlike humans, barely a step away from their arboreal ancestors, the Architects would be masters of their emotions and would have attained the pinnacle of efficiency. Perhaps she was thinking too broadly, too human with human gestures intricately woven into human speech patterns through eons of colloquial learning. Each culture had its own unique hand gestures that meant different things in different cultures. She had been shouting instructions at the controls rather than finessing them, much like a traveler in a foreign country shouting their language at a shopkeeper hoping to make themselves understood. She began making more subtle gestures.

After a few minutes, lines of alien script appeared on the screen. She had no idea of its meaning, but her results pleased her. She hoped the Architects had installed safeguards against someone accidentally voiding the atmosphere or disengaging the inertia dampeners. Finally, a slide bar appeared on the screen. The symbols meant nothing to her, but she hoped it was a speed indicator. If the glowing mark far to one end indicated their present speed, she estimated the tram was capable of speeds five times greater, or 1,000 kilometers per hour. That reduced the trip time to meet Chaca to just a few hours.

"Here goes," she said, crossing her fingers where no one could see them.

She moved the indicator slowly toward the right. The tram began moving with no perceptible acceleration. She dragged the indicator farther. The tram picked up speed until the balconies and crossways they passed became blurs. She decided not to push her luck. She did not try for the maximum speed indicated. If there were a safety override, it could stop the tram, leaving them stranded until she figured out how to bypass it or it reset itself.

"That's as fast as I dare push it," she said.

"Good enough," Hitochi said. "You need to rest." He looked at the others. "We all need rest. I'll keep watch."

Kari wanted to watch where they were going in case they passed something interesting, but the tensions of the journey and lack of sleep the previous night sapped her will to remain awake. If she had not been so exhausted, she would not have vented her anger at Kirkurk. He deserved it, but she hated herself for giving in to her baser instincts. She needed to keep a clear head if she wished to learn anything more about the Architects. She sat down and leaned against the wall. With no sense of motion or jolting, she was asleep within minutes.

* * * *

She roused with Hitochi shaking her shoulder, "Wha ...?" she mumbled, as she fought sleep's comforting embrace. She had been dreaming that she fell asleep on the subway, had missed her stop, and wound up at Coney Island late at night with no money or subway tokens.

"We've slowed."

She snapped instantly fully awake. "Are we there?"

"No. It's only been 90 minutes. We entered some kind of transit station. There are hundreds of trams converging on this spot."

She stood and looked out. They were still in the canyon-like boulevard, but the colors had changed, become brighter and more intense; the soft pastels replaced by stronger gold, blue, and red colors. Other tramways intersected and paralleled theirs like a railroad marshalling yard. Trams shot across their path at breakneck speeds. Other vehicles exited doorways in one section of the chasm wall. One of the vehicles, larger than theirs, passed by them closely enough to see its contents. A machine with multiple arms carried lengths of metal and coils of tubing. It swiveled its robotic head and stared at their car with its glowing amber visor, but dismissed them almost immediately.

"It looks like a maintenance supply hub," Kirkurk said. He grinned at her as if he had forgotten her earlier outburst. "We must check this out."

"We have a mission," Hitochi reminded him.

"Our mission is to learn all we can about this place. Too many people have died to simply walk away empty handed."

"My job is to prevent more deaths."

Kari understood Hitochi's reluctance, but the transit station intrigued her as well. They could possibly learn a great deal about the Band from observing the types of materials used to support it. If the Band had been nothing more than a gigantic monument circling a star, its construction would have been a feat no culture would probably ever again match. Now, they knew it was a self-sustaining machine still active after 500,000,000 years. Observing its housekeepers could tell them much about its builders.

"Have you contacted Sergeant Chaca about our increase in speed?" she asked.

Hitochi shook his head. "No, I thought you needed your sleep."

"Thank you. We can spare a little time here, can't we?" she asked, almost pleading. "An hour? 45 minutes? When you make radio contact,

I'll tell Amanda how to increase the speed, if she hasn't already figured it out."

Hitochi looked at all their faces. Everyone but Luntz and Deidre was eager to explore. "Well, a few minutes won't hurt, but only a few minutes. Deidre can vid-log everything for later viewing."

Deidre shook her head. "I'm not –"

Hitochi interrupted her. "Yes, you are, both of you. We need you, and I'm not leaving you two here alone in the tram."

She scowled at him. "Are you afraid we might take the tram and leave you here?"

"Yes, if you were frightened enough," Hitochi replied with honesty. "Look at it this way, if one of those shadow creatures returns and find you two here alone, you have a 50-50 chance of being taken. Together, it's one in six. Which odds do you prefer?"

She cursed and picked up her camera. "Damn you, Hitochi."

"I can live with that."

He had watched Kari work the controls. He slid the speed bar to zero. The tram moved from the single metallic line that marked the track and stopped on a wide balcony near the convergence of multiple tracks. They sat like a stone in a moving stream of trams.

"Seal your suits. Stay together," he warned.

Hitochi reminded of her father on family outings. "Remember where we parked the car," Kari added, smiling at him.

They exited the tram and followed the balcony toward a massive expanse of rows of openings, over a hundred on different levels of the wall. Hitochi led the way. Kari hugged the wall as closely as possible. The additional light allowed them a better view of the depths of the chasm, but it also reinforced how high she was from its bottom. Undaunted by the height, Sung peered over the edge of the precipice.

"There are definitely massive machines down there with moving parts. Their spacing suggests they might be artificial gravity generators or control the Band's rotation."

"Perhaps both," Hitochi suggested.

Sung broke into a wide grin. "Yes, yes. I did not think of that, two machines serving the same function."

To avoid peering into the depths, Kari concentrated on the station ahead of her. Many of the trams leaving carried loads of freight, most of it unidentifiable. However, she recognized sheets of metal, rolls of tubing, and stacks of metallic bins, but could not guess their purpose. They had seen no true machinery or moving parts since entering the Band except for the massive machines at the base of the boulevard. Variations of the Band material comprised everything else. The items in the trams meant other areas of the Band contained machinery more akin to machines humans might use. It did not demean the Architects' accomplishments; it simply made them appear less godlike.

The trams whizzed by one another at intersections without slowing, controlled by an extremely efficient automatic router. Some passed within meters of each other at hundreds of kilometers per hour, while others dropped off the edge of the balcony, plummeting straight down. Without inertia dampeners, the G forces would have slammed the cargo through the roof of the tram. A few of the trams held colored liquid containers of various viscosities. She imagined them to be coolants or lubricants, but their true purposes could have been so esoteric as to be unimaginable or simply refills for a soda dispenser.

They walked through one of the open bay doors and entered a cavernous space. A network of thin, unsupported tramway rails rose from floor to the ceiling, crossing the vast space like spider webs. Automated machinery, as much crystalline as metallic, sat on small platforms unloading items from rows of flat trams entering from darkened openings in the far walls and transferring the contents into trams resembling theirs. Hundreds of such loading machines and thousands of trams filled the massive building.

"It's a supply hub or transfer point," Sung said. "It's enormous."

Hitochi checked his instruments. "4,200 meters across and 500 high," he said.

Sung paid little attention to Hitochi's facts. "There must be millions of these scattered throughout the Band. Some portion of the Band must contain manufacturing facilities to produce these essential items. If we could locate one of those ..."

"Another time, Sung," Hitochi said. A boyish grin broke out on his face. "I suppose we could open a few bins and see what's inside."

They chose a flatcar stacked high with small metal bins some distance from one of the unloading machines, unsure how it might react to their pilfering. Hitochi spent a few minutes trying to open the sealed bin before he hit upon the idea that it was magnetically sealed. He used one of his instruments to degauss the container and lifted the lid with ease. Dozens of small objects resembling bars of soap filled the bin.

Sung looked disappointed, but Hitochi picked one up. "They look like some kind of ceramic material."

"Yes," Sung agreed, "but what do they do?"

Hitochi set the object on the lid of the bin. Immediately dozens of tiny legs shot from its sides. Sung jumped back. The tiny machine began extruding a silver paste from its rear in a straight line along the lid. The paste spread out and hardened into a material identical to the metal of the bin.

"It's a repair drone," Hitochi said. "It can seal cracks in metal or weld two pieces together."

Luntz was not as excited by their find. "At least we know the Architects don't wave their hands and do things by magic." He eyed the space with a mixture of suspicion and fear. The activity all around them intimidated him. His gaze darted about wildly, drawn by every movement.

Kari was not as fascinated by the material passing through the transfer station as she was by the concept. Somewhere in the Band, perhaps at numerous sites, manufacturing processes still occurred after a half-billion years. The idea was staggering in its implications. It meant a reliable source of raw materials, item-specific manufacturing processes, and complicated delivery systems, even the means to detect and perform the necessary repairs. The combined manufacturing output of the dozen worlds colonized by Earth paled in comparison to the Band.

She rued the fact their situation was so desperate. The knowledge gleaned from observing such processes could revolutionize human civilization. She craved to discover where one of the incoming tram tunnels led, but their survival was more important. If only they had thought to bring a handful of remote reconnaissance drones to provide video for later study.

Kari sensed a sudden change in the room. She looked around at her companions. Hitochi, Kirkurk, and Sung remained engrossed in their examination of the various bins. Deidre's disinterest in their inspection was evident by the disdain on her face. She stared out toward the boulevard. Kari glanced at Luntz and immediately knew something was terribly amiss. His face had drained of color, and his mouth opened in a silent scream. His mien was one of extreme torment. He began backing away from the group, stopped, and froze in an awkward position. Alarmed, she turned to look to where Luntz had fixed his gaze.

Two shadow wraiths emerged from one of the openings moving straight for them like an approaching storm cloud. A sudden coldness not caused by any malfunction of her suit heater gripped her body. Icy fingers probed her mind, numbing her motor control and seizing her vocal cords, preventing her from screaming or warning the others.

Before she could react, one of the wraiths seized her. She felt no pressure, but she could offer no resistance. She could not move. It was as if a cold breeze restrained her. She saw the others through a dark gossamer veil wrapped around her. They were unaware of the shadows' presence. Deidre turned, and her gaze rested on the two wraiths. She froze for a moment, and screamed over her com link. The others saw what was happening. Sung and Kirkurk backed away, but Hitochi searched for her. She didn't know if he could see her within the creature's substance, but he quickly surmised her fate and strode forward to rescue her.

How gallant, she thought, *but how foolish.* She knew if he touched his weapon, he would die as well. Instead of Hitochi, however, the second wraith chose Luntz. It lunged forward and enveloped Luntz in its ebony body. He disappeared from view as if the sun obscured by a dark cloud. His suit monitor disappeared from her proximity link. Kari felt a moment of anguish over her relief that it had taken Luntz instead of Hitochi. She felt no ill will toward the photographer and did not wish him harm, but she found the thought of Hitochi's demise too painful to consider.

The wraith bearing her shot toward the wall. She braced for the impact, but it passed effortlessly through the wall and down a long, dark corridor beyond. Oddly, she felt no fear. She knew she was going to die. If the condition of Kahoku's body were any indication, she would die in an extremely grisly manner. Her curiosity took her mind off her impending death.

They passed through several open spaces smaller than the transit station and travelled countless corridors, some illuminated, while others remained in complete darkness. However, she found she could see, if only dimly. It was as if the flesh or material of the shadow creature enhanced the light, much like the infrared filter on her suit. Often, they dropped or rose between levels. She tried to observe the things she saw, catalog them in her mind in case she got the opportunity to dictate them into her audio if someone found her body or if her suit was still transmitting a signal. Most of what she saw was beyond her comprehension.

In a space barely the size of one of the ship's portable domes, sat a single object slightly larger than one of the trams, crystalline like smoky quartz with a network of metallic threads running through it. Various nodes and oddly shaped modules projected from its smooth surface. At one end, a parade of robots delivered a powdery substance. The other end extruded a ribbon of translucent rod like the one Hitochi had found. A line of small robots waited at the other end. Each robot sliced the rod into short lengths, loaded them onto a platform attached to its body, and carted them away. Before the rod could reach the floor, another robot took its place to continue the process, a perpetual ballet of alien manufacturing.

She spotted numerous robotic service drones at work or travelling. They ignored the shadows. In one spot, dozens of the white ceramic insect repairers moved side-by-side along lengths of metallic plates, welding them together. A large transport drone waited nearby to haul the plate away. They skirted several areas filled with flashes of welders or cutting torches. From a distance, it appeared thousands of robotic drones were dismantling large areas of the Band.

Once, she thought she glimpsed a living creature, a horse-sized quadruped. It whirled and raced away when it spotted the wraiths. The sighting had been so abrupt she could not be certain if was a living creature rather than a strangely shaped drone, but the sighting intrigued her.

When the wraith suddenly stopped and hovered for a moment above a narrow shaft running vertically above and below her, fear finally found her. The creature plummeted like a stone into the darkness. She had never enjoyed amusement parks rides. In fact, they usually made her ill. She screamed and passed out.

12

Hitochi's report that they had lost three members of their team, including both marines, to the shadow creatures had been disheartening news to Sergeant Chaca. It indicated more than one of the creatures inhabited the Band. They faced a deadly enemy of unknown strength. Hitochi's news about the tram was encouraging. If they could rendezvous and combine forces, they might have a chance of surviving. The gulf of distance between the two groups was daunting. Ten hours placed them close to the operational limits of their suits.

He checked his suit air supply and saw it was getting low. He eyed the single reserve oxygen tank that had survived the fall and revised his estimate. It would just barely extend their stay by four hours. They would have to find a way to shave off a few hours. If Collins could repeat Kari Stone's success in operating a tram, they just might rendezvous before they all died.

"Everyone top off your tanks."

He mouthed a silent prayer to God and his ancestors' spirits when the converter worked smoothly in spite of the banging around it had taken. He checked to make certain everyone complied in filling his or her tanks. He went last. He checked his tank and saw he had less than seven hours air. He tried to avoid their faces, but he could almost read their minds. They didn't think they would make it. He would have to prove them wrong.

"Ryder, Ash. Scout ahead and see if you can locate one of those trams Hitochi reported. Take Collins with you. Stay in com contact." He dialed in Ryder's suit camera to observe their search. "The rest of you follow me."

Ryder, Ash, and a reluctant Collins trotted ahead of them down the walkway. If they didn't meet up with Hitochi before seven hours had passed, they would have to find an area with oxygen or an area the Band would fill with an atmosphere and wait for him. In that scenario, their chances of ever leaving the Band became dismal.

"What if that thing follows us?" Holmes asked. He danced around as if any sound would send him running.

"It won't."

"How do you know?" Holmes insisted.

"Because it didn't follow us, Holmes. It can't take the extreme cold."

"Maybe it was just full. What if it gets hungry again? Hitochi said there are more of them." He held out his flechette rifle. "This is useless against them."

Chaca sighed. "What do you want me to say, Holmes? If they attack us, we die. It's that simple. You're a soldier. Death is waiting for all of us. It's inevitable. We're on the firing line. We put ourselves out there for others. That's why there are no old bold soldiers. We postpone it as long as possible, but sometimes your number is just up. What do you want me to do, hold your hand?"

"I want you to get my ass back home, Sarge. I don't want to die like Aleyev. No one should die like that."

Chaca agreed. He would miss the erudite Russian's poetry. It was a welcome change from the usual soldier talk about women, weapons, and booze. He often wondered what had made such a man join the Marines. Now, he would never know.

"I'll do what I can. I don't want to lose any more men, but I can't make you that promise, Holmes. I'm a first sergeant in the U.N. Marine Corps. That puts me one rank below God, and that's his bailiwick. Maybe you had better send your request up the chain of command. Now, stay focused."

"That ain't too comforting, Sarge," Holmes replied.

Chaca touched the first sergeant chevron on his battle armor's sleeve with the diamond in the middle. "You see a chaplain's cross on this sleeve, Marine? The only comfort I can give you is that I won't give up, and nothing will take any of you without a fight."

"We found one, Sarge," Ryder called out over the com. "Half a klick ahead of you."

Chaca studied the tram through Ryder's camera, frowning when he noticed it was across the abyss from them. "Zoom in on it," he said. The view shifted, and the tram came into tighter focus. The clear exterior didn't look very protective, but Hitochi had assured him it was the same impervious material as the ebony walls. "Hold your position," he told Ryder. "Double-time it," he called out to the others.

They found Ryder at the foot of one of the bridges across the chasm sitting nonchalantly on the edge of the balcony with his feet dangling over half-kilometer of nothingness. The tram sat idle on one of the balconies across and two levels below them. The narrow bridge looked daunting, but they had no choice. He saw no other tram nearby, and the one across from them could leave at any moment. They couldn't hope to find a closer one in time, and time was of the essence.

"Let's go."

"Across that," Paisley replied, resting his fist under his helmet below his chin in contemplation. "I ain't good with heights. I'm a swamp boy."

Chaca heard the fear in Paisley's voice. He didn't blame him. All of them had encountered things beyond their comprehension. Their weapons, the tools that had kept them alive through deadly firefights, were useless against the enemies they now faced. They felt impotent. So did he. He had traversed 15-centimeter-wide beams with full pack during training, but they had been only ten-meters long and over a mud pit or a rushing stream, not a half-kilometer deadly freefall into dark oblivion.

"We don't have a choice, Paisley. Now, move it." When he stood at the edge of the bridge, he said, "We'll leapfrog across. Paisley and I will cross first. When we reach the other side, we'll cover you."

Chaca led the way first to prove it was safe. It felt like walking the plank except he had a black alien wraith prodding him across rather than a pirate's cutlass. He focused his attention on the center of the slender, meter-wide bridge, expecting to hear it cracking beneath him like rotten ice with each step. The pulsing lights inside the translucent material attempted to mesmerize him. He fought their seductive draw and switched his focus to the far side of the bridge. He tried to imagine a race of people able to traipse across such an abyss on a balance beam. They possessed a better sense of balance than he could summon – a race of natural tightrope walkers. If the chasm had not been in vacuum, the slightest breeze would have sent him toppling over the edge.

He reached the center of the span with a sense of accomplishment. A fine sheen of perspiration covered his forehead and misted his visor. He fought to control his breathing and ordered his suit temperature to lower to compensate for his exertions. His legs ached from the effort to keep them moving perfectly one in front of the other. He wanted to stop for a moment and catch his breath, but knew the others were watching him. His job was to set an example. He breathed a sigh of relief when his boots touched the balcony on the far side.

"Easy as walking the chow line," he said. "Paisley, you're next."

"Gee, thanks, Sarge. I was gonna ask if I could go next." Paisley stepped onto the span and began walking without hesitation, but his haste worried Chaca.

"Slow it down, Paisley. This isn't a foot race."

Paisley heeded his advice, but when he got within five meters of the end of the bridge, he sprinted to the balcony and sat down gasping to catch his breath. He looked up at Chaca and grinned. "Well, that was different as hell."

"Okay Holmes, Ryder. You're next."

Holmes did a little victory jig when his feet touched the balcony. He raised both hands and flipped birds to the walkway. "Take that, fucking little narrow-ass bridge."

Ryder carried his heavy .50 caliber SAW across both shoulders with his arms draped over it like a balance pole. He moved with the nonchalance of a man walking down a street. He shoved Holmes out of the way when he reached the safety of the balcony.

"Your turn Collins, Ash."

Chaca worried about Collins. He had surreptitiously called up her suit monitor. The fluctuating readings indicated signs of fatigue. That was the reason he had chosen Ash to follow close behind her. Collins moved slowly, crouched forward until she was almost crawling. Ash urged her to move faster, but Collins, encumbered by her load of equipment, was too off balance to stand up straight. 15 minutes later, the pair was still ten meters from the balcony. Collins' snail pace was making Chaca anxious.

"Collins," Chaca called over his com, "drop some of your gear. Ash will pick it up for you."

"Okay," Collins huffed.

She knelt and unhooked instrument packs from her suit. She handed them to Ash, who tossed them one at a time across to the balcony where Ryder caught them. Chaca worried about Collins' deteriorating physical condition. The petite technician had trudged along with the rest of them like a marine, but their training inured them to long marches. Her sedentary profession did not. He checked her biometric readouts. Collins' pulse rate was high at 125, and her respiration wavered between 30-35 breaths per minute. Her blood pressure read 132/90, and her blood oxygen level was dropping from her rapid, shallow breathing.

"Take a minute to rest, Collins. You're hyperventilating." He hated to waste more time, but pushing Collins any harder might slow them even further.

Collins knelt on the bridge. Her vitals crept slowly back into the normal range, but after two minutes, she stood.

"I can't rest out here," she said. "I'm pushing on across."

Chaca knew he couldn't stop her. "Okay, focus on the far side," he advised.

Collins began moving more quickly, but seemed less steady on her feet. From the corner of his eye, Chaca spotted a tram dropping from above them at hundreds of kilometers per hour. It passed soundlessly 50 yards away along a vertical sliver of metal rail; a quick blur, and it was gone. He dismissed it without a second thought, but the sudden movement attracted Collins' gaze, startling her. She stumbled and tottered at the edge of the bridge.

Ash lunged forward, grabbed the back of her suit, and pulled her back onto the bridge, saving her life. Unfortunately, in her haste to recover, Collins overcompensated and fell backwards, slamming her head into Ash's helmet. Now, Ash, off balance, staggered backwards as well. His left foot slipped off the edge of the bridge. He fell but managed to grab onto the edge of the bridge with one hand. The other maintained its grip on his rifle.

"Drop it!" Chaca yelled, as he raced back onto the bridge to help.

Instead of dropping his weapon, Ash swung his body forward and laid his rifle on top of the bridge. He removed one of Collins' instruments from his belt and repeated the procedure with a second. Collins recovered from her initial shock and tried to help. She lay flat on the bridge reaching for Ash's flailing free hand, but it was beyond her reach.

"Activate your gauntlet," Chaca ordered. He hoped the more rigid glove would give him a tighter grip.

Ash activated his gauntlets, but his hand gripping the bridge slowly slipped off anyway. Collins grabbed the hand and held on as Ash dangled below her. Now, Collins lay across the bridge spread eagle with half her body suspended dangerously off the side. Ash outweighed her by 25 kilos. His weight inexorably dragged her toward the edge. She kicked her feet until the tips of her boots snagged the far edge to anchor her.

"Someone help me!" Collins yelled. One foot slipped and lost its grip on the edge.

"Let me go, Collins," Ash pleaded. "You'll die too."

"No, it's my fault," Collins sobbed, as her chest slid over the edge into space. Now, only one foot kept her in place, and it slipped as well.

"Not your fault, Collins. I got clumsy. Let me go." His free hand reached for his other arm.

Chaca realized what Ash was doing and yelled at him. "Don't do it, Ash."

Chaca put on a burst of speed, but he was still several meters away and knew he would be too late. Ash managed to grasp the arm to which Collins clung with his free hand. He inched it up to his gauntlet.

By that time, Collins too realized Ash's intentions. "No!" she yelled.

"Sorry, Collins. I can't let you die. The team needs you."

Ash twisted the gauntlet to unseal it. With a hiss of escaping air that quickly crystallized into frozen vapor, the gauntlet separated from his suit. He plummeted out of sight into the chasm half a kilometer below. He didn't scream over his com link.

Chaca grabbed Collins' legs and cragged her back onto the bridge. She rolled over and lay on her back, sobbing and pressing Ash's gauntlet to her chest. Chaca picked up Ash's weapon and the two instrument packs and strapped them to his suit. He helped Collins to her feet and held her steady while they crossed to the balcony together.

"He didn't have to die," Collins sobbed.

"He thought he did."

"It's my fault."

"It's over. We have to continue."

Chaca didn't like dismissing one of his men's deaths so lightly, but they were running out of time. It served no purpose to dwell on it, especially for Collins' sake. He could not let her guilt cripple her. He hoped working out the controls for the tram would occupy the grieved technician's mind.

They now faced another challenge. They still had to reach the tram two levels below them. They had rappelling line left but no climbing harnesses and no place to secure the line. Paisley dropped a line over the edge of the bridge and swung it back up for Holmes to catch. He tied a half hitch to secure it, and attached a carabiner. He took the remainder of the line, doubled it, slipped it through the carabiner, and dropped the line onto the balcony below. He yanked on the line to test his knots.

"It'll hold," he said to a skeptical Collins.

"Everyone down the line," Chaca ordered.

They worked in silence. No one wanted to bring up Ash's death. Paisley went first, sliding down the line to the balcony, and holding it taut for Holmes. Chaca clipped Collins' suit to the line and slid down right behind her. Ryder went last. When they had all reached the balcony, Paisley released one end of the doubled line and yanked it. The line slid from the carabiner. He looped it around his waist.

Following Kari Stone's directions, Collins opened the tram. As soon as it produced an oxygen atmosphere and heat, Chaca ordered them to unseal their suits to conserve air. While Collins studied the controls, he forced the others to consume some of their rations to keep up their strength. They did so without enthusiasm, but they ate. He passed around packets of PEP, a combat supplement of steroids, vitamins, stimulants designed to enhance stamina and focus. Collins tried to refuse, but Chaca forced her to down the supplement with half a liter of fortified water.

"You need it more than anyone. You're beat."

"I … I couldn't …" She hung her head.

"Don't think about it. It's done."

Ash had died because he had pushed them too hard. They were all tired and on edge. He couldn't stop pushing them, but he could see to it that they faced the next challenge better prepared. The PEP would help focus their minds and build up their brain's dopamine and norepinephrine levels depleted by their physical exhaustion.

While they waited, Hitochi checked in exactly two hours after their first contact. His voice was devoid of emotion, and he spoke succinctly, as if trying to hold himself in check. It was very much unlike the usually boisterous lieutenant. Chaca braced himself for bad news.

"We stopped at a transit station to explore. Wraiths came and took Josh Luntz and Kari Stone."

Chaca cursed. The news was worse than he thought. He had hoped the creatures avoided extreme cold temperatures and vacuum, but this proved they could tolerate both. He did not admonish Hitochi for something as foolish as stopping to explore when he should have headed toward them as quickly as possible. He was certain Kirkurk or Sung had something to do with it. Hitochi was young with no combat experience, but he was intelligent and now realized the Band was dangerous. He hoped that made the difference in the future.

Of all the people to lose, Kari Stone was the worst blow. In spite of her status as a low-level archaeologist, she had been the one making all the discoveries. Her loss could be a major setback. "Are they dead?"

"We picked up their suit biometric readings until they got out of range. They were alive, but I don't know for how much longer." He went on to explain the image of Kahoku's body and the piles of bones in the room around him.

The news of Kahoku's demise, though expected, was upsetting by its brutality. He had seen the video of the shadow creature drinking Aleyev's blood. Like Hitochi, he held out no hope for either Stone or Luntz. "Did Miss Stone learn how to increase the tram's speed?"

"Yes."

One bit of good news. Again, he did not berate Hitochi for not contacting him immediately with such vital information. Neither he nor Hitochi were exactly batting a thousand so far on the expedition. "Explain the procedure to Collins, please."

He went off mic to think. Conditions had changed. By meeting Hitochi halfway, they could not choose their rendezvous point. They might have to backtrack to a suitable spot to attempt their escape. Hitochi's discovery of the transit station offered a more viable option. Multiple rails meant multiple directions of travel. By Hitochi's description of the freight, they might find something useful to aid in their escape.

When Hitochi had finished speaking to Collins, Chaca broke in. "Remain where you are. We'll come to you."

"It's not safe here," Hitochi replied. "As I said, we were attacked by the shadow wraiths."

"So were we. It's not safe anywhere inside the Band. Your location offers more potential for escape or contact with the *Worthington*. We can't afford to wander around aimlessly." He glanced at Collins. "How long?"

She wiped her forehead with her hand. "If I can do this right, we can reach them in less than two hours."

"Then do it right."

Collins exploded. "Do it right! Do it right! I don't know what the hell I'm doing. Kari's instructions were a bit sketchy. I can't very well double check anything, can I? Kari's dead. How many is that now? I've lost count."

She began sobbing again. Chaca knew she was near the breaking point. Collins had just watched someone die, had looked into Ash's eyes as he fell into oblivion. They could not afford to lose Collins. However, as a first sergeant of hard-assed marines, he had little experience with sobbing civilians. He did the only thing he knew how to do. He grabbed Collins' helmet in both hands and shook it.

"Get a grip, Collins. Don't you dare lose it now. You're here for a reason. Our lives are in your hands. Failure is not an option." More gently, he added, "Forget the dead. Concentrate on the living." It was sound advice. He wished he could follow it.

She sniffed and nodded her head. "Yes. Yes. I suppose I had better do it right. After all, my ass in on the line too, isn't it? I was assured I would not have to leave the ship. That's why I joined this expedition. I never leave the ship in an environmental suit, yet, here I am in battle armor playing soldier." She laughed. "It's funny to what lengths men and women will go to place themselves in harm's way."

Satisfied for the moment Collins wouldn't fall apart, Chaca said to Hitochi, "I'll home in on your signal so we don't miss you. Try to remain in the open."

Other voices cut in on the conversation, but Hitochi quickly switched to the military channel. "The others don't like the idea of waiting around here, but I agree the depot offers more options. We'll be waiting."

"We'll push as fast as we can. Collins says two hours or less. See you then."

"Yeah, right, Sergeant."

"Chaca out."

Chaca felt like a player in a video game with a mad person at the controls. They had bounced from one situation to another since entering the Band. They had learned very little that he considered useful, and even that small amount of information would be lost if they could not report to the ship. He hoped it proved valuable to somebody. The price was becoming steeper by the minute.

"Let's load up and move out."

Chaca waited for the acceleration as the tram speeded up, but there was no sense of motion. The scenery zipped by so fast he had little time to observe it. He targeted a spot with his rifle's range finder, measured how long it took them to reach the spot, and made a quick calculation – 2100 kph, or 1.75 times the speed of sound, yet he felt no G forces. *Not bad*, he thought.

The chasm was endless, and the scenery did not vary. He hoped they were not passing an obvious way out of the Band, but without a map or a sign, he would never know. He hoped that by joining with the civilian group, they could combine resources and ideas to effect an escape. They were not alone in the chasm. Other trams travelled up and down and along its length. Some passed so close he expected a collision, but the automated guidance system still worked perfectly after 500 million years. After a while, he stopped holding his breath after each near miss. Half a billion years was a long time to remain operational. He expected to see some degradation in the Band, some areas less maintained, but the entire structure looked as pristine as the day it was constructed.

Even a structure as marvelous as the Band could not manufacture replacement parts without raw materials. Either the Band was an enormous honeycomb of storage or manufacturing areas, or it had the means to replace raw materials from the outside. They had detected no comets, asteroids, or planetary fragments in the Cyclops system as they entered the system. The space around the Band had been swept clean of debris over the eons.

He supposed it was possible the Band was cannibalizing itself, removing material from non-essential areas to maintain vital functions, but they had no clue to the function of the Band. What purpose did it serve? Was it simply another artifact, a bauble in space for the

Architects' enjoyment? That seemed too extreme even for a race as advanced as the Architects. No society could devote so many resources to a work of art. He wondered what other secrets the Band held besides the dark secret of the shadow creatures. He doubted they were Architects. It was possible that they were caretakers, but if they drank blood, on what had they sustained themselves for over 500 million years.

Chaca shook his head. He was making himself dizzy going round in circles with his thoughts. Speculation was getting him nowhere. He was a marine. It would better serve him to concentrate on the current situation and possible solutions to save his team. The weak link was Collins. Collins was close to the edge. She continued to be morose, but she studied the control panel with enthusiasm. Chaca couldn't make heads or tails of the script or the symbols flashing on the screen, but Collins scanned through pages of text and diagrams, nodding to herself. Chaca hoped she was learning something useful. They could use a break.

13

While the crew disconnected the two portable artificial gravity units in the two domes and loaded the shuttles into the docking bays, the power in the *Worthington* dropped by an additional 35 percent. Sidthuri ordered all non-essential equipment shut down, leaving only life support, weapons, and the engines on line. In his mind, the drain on the ship's power was an attack by whoever was controlling the Band. The ship's main defenses were her four laser batteries and a small rail gun. Without power, they would be defenseless.

The Band had removed the oxygen atmosphere outside the ship, a not-so-polite way of saying 'Fuck off.' The Architects could simply drain away the power and allow its human occupants die of lack of oxygen or from the pervasive, intense cold. His decision to abandon both missing teams did not sit well with him, but he dared not risk his ship when odds favored that both teams were dead. The living were his primary concern.

He showed no surprise when the sentries reported something moving toward the ship. He had expected just such a move. In a way, he felt relieved that he would have an enemy to fight. He did not rush to the bridge; that would be undignified and convey a sense of panic to the crew, but he did hurry his steps. The Band was once again undergoing one of the periodic night cycles. His vision was limited to the infrared cameras and the fuzzy radar images.

He watched the view screen, as a horde of figures approached the ship from all quarters. The scans registered them as metallic, but they could be wearing environment suits. As they got closer, he recognized them as robotic repair drones in various shapes and sizes equipped with an array of cutting torches, blades, and drills. Thankfully, they were not military drones. A few drones presented no problem, but en masse, they could cause severe damage to the ship.

"They appeared from out of nowhere, sir," the harried First Officer, Stanislaw Igorsky reported. "They seemed to well up through the floor of the Band itself."

It sounded impossible, but he did not doubt Igorsky. The Architects were capable of almost anything. "Open fire when they are within range," he ordered the technicians manning the laser batteries.

Two minutes later, all four lasers began firing into the midst of the drones. The machines had hardened exteriors, but the lasers could easily slice through the hulls of enemy ships. They proved equally effective against the drones. Dozens of the repair robots exploded or melted, but more appeared from the darkness surrounding the ship to replace them. The rail gun could only fire from the bow. He waited until a mass of the robots attacked from that direction and fired. The 200-kilo projectile shot from the magnetic launcher at 10 km/sec, five times the speed of sound, bowling the robots over like ten pins and scattering bits of metal and pieces of crystal across the black surface of the Band.

He quickly realized they could never hold off such a concentrated attack. The rail gun had depleted the power by another five percent. The Band's caretaker could bring more robots from anywhere within the structure to press forward the attack and sustain it beyond the *Worthington*'s capability. At best, the *Worthington*'s weaponry could keep them at bay until they could escape.

"Prepare to lift off." Once free of the Band, he could attack with impunity as the reactor charged the generators.

"Anti-grav engines are powering up," Igorsky reported. "Because of the power drain, it might take a few seconds longer than normal."

"We might not have those extra seconds," Sidthuri replied, watching the number of robots steadily increase.

"15 seconds to full power!"

"Take her up now. It might be a bumpy ride, but we're too exposed here. The Architects could –"

He didn't get the chance to finish. He felt his weight vanish moments before the *Worthington* suddenly shot into the air a few meters. His full weight returned seconds later, and the ship fell back hard to the Band.

"The bastards are altering the gravity," he moaned while rubbing his bruises. He tried rising from the floor, but it felt as if someone were sitting on his chest.

Lights began blinking on most of the control stations. He listened to the litany of damage reports pouring into the bridge with a sinking feeling:

"Number two hatch has sprung."

"Battery #3 out of commission."

"Port forward landing gear has buckled."

"Grav meters read 2.2 Gs," Igorsky told him. "It will take the engines an additional 20 seconds to reach sufficient power to break the ship free."

He heard the repeated blows against the hull near the out-of-commission #3 laser. The robot drones had used the gap in the overlapping batteries to reach the hull. He could send men out to fend them off with hand-held weapons, but it would be a losing battle, especially fighting the effects of the increased gravity. The *Worthington* was a doomed ship, and with it, his crew. Unless …

"Sound abandon ship. Everyone to the shuttles." He turned to his first officer. "Order everyone into their suits. Bring extra oxygen, water, rations, weapons, and ammunition – load the shuttles with anything they can carry that might keep us alive."

He did a quick mental calculation. The two military shuttles each held eight passengers and crew, the two smaller shuttles eight. There were 18 people remaining aboard the *Worthington*. The two larger shuttles could accommodate everyone, leaving two pilots for the smaller shuttles carrying additional supplies. At best, it was a temporary solution. He would be condemning his crew to a slow death as food and air ran out. They were light years from home with no hope of rescue.

"Load Shuttles Three and Four with supplies," he told Igorsky. "Launch a signal buoy. It might have enough power to reach the FTL probe and relay a signal to Earth." He noticed Igorsky's look of doubt. "It's the only chance we have of rescue."

Igorsky nodded. "Yes, sir."

Sidthuri knew any chance of rescue was slim. It would take the buoy weeks to get close enough to the FTL probe to signal it. The tachyon signal to Earth would take only minutes, but the journey time for any rescue vessel would be measured in months.

"You take command. I will remain on the ship to hold off the robots until the shuttles clear."

"I'll stay, sir," Igorsky said.

"No, the men need a command officer with them."

Igorsky stared at Sidthuri. "They'll have one, sir, you."

"I'm staying with my ship," Sidthuri insisted.

"I'm afraid I can't allow that, sir. You're much too valuable to lose." He motioned for two marines. "The captain was injured during the attack and is presently unfit to command. Therefore, I am assuming command. Please escort the captain to a shuttle. See that he boards it."

His second's unexpected mutiny stunned him. "I could have you court marshaled, Igorsky."

"Yes, sir, if ever we meet again. In the meantime, I'll place myself under house arrest." He glanced at the two marines. "Gentlemen, do your duty for your ship." He turned to the bridge crew. "Your shifts are over, gentlemen. You may leave your posts."

One young ensign spoke up. "You can't man all the laser batteries by yourself. I'm staying, sir."

"I'll manage."

"With all due respect, sir, you can't make me leave. I'm staying."

"Very well, Ensign Vette. I accept your decision. The rest of you follow the captain." He turned to Sidthuri. "I've been an Interventionist since I was 15. It's why I was excited about this mission. Now, I see I was wrong. I no longer have a god, sir, but I still have my duty."

As Sidthuri left the bridge with the marines holding tightly to each arm, he said, "I'm proud of you Lieutenant Igorsky, and you too, Ensign Vette. God bless you."

"Good luck, sir," Igorsky returned. "Keep the others safe."

He sealed the bridge hatch. Sidthuri felt hollow inside. He had never envisioned someone taking his place, but the deed was done. He shrugged free of his escort. "Let's go to the shuttles, gentlemen. This evacuation must remain orderly."

The ship leaped skyward again. He braced himself for the impact. The ship hit tail first. He and his escorts rolled down the corridor. He slammed his ribs into a bulkhead. A sharp pain almost crippled him. He assumed they were broken, but he didn't have time to check. Damage alarms sounded throughout the ship. He knew without checking that the *Worthington*'s back was broken. She would never fly again. *At least the damn gravity's back to near normal.*

In the shuttle bays, men loaded onto the shuttles, ignoring the hiss of escaping air from a ruptured airlock seal. It had been providential that the cargo officer had locked the shuttles into their cradles. Otherwise, the jolt could have damaged them beyond use. He frowned at the sight of several of the crew carried aboard on stretchers, injured by the wild bucking of the ship. He passed between rows of frightened Navy personnel and civilians, wishing he could offer them some word of hope or encouragement, or promise them something beyond an unknown fate. He waited until each of the shuttles had filled and sealed before entering the last shuttle. He pushed his way around a jumble of crates, boxes, and tanks of oxygen, and strapped into the co-pilot seat, hoping to direct the meager firepower of the shuttle onto the attacking robots to buy the *Worthington* some additional time.

On his command, the bay doors opened, and the shuttles soared away, mowing down several of the robotic drones in their path. One of the drones, equipped with a meter-long drill, hovered directly in the path of one of the smaller shuttles. The pilot tried to climb steeply to avoid a collision, but the drone rammed home the drill into the shuttle's exposed underbelly as it passed overhead. The shuttle ripped away the robot's arm and sent the damaged drone bouncing across the Band.

The drill unit continued to bore through the hull. The shuttle wobbled violently as one engine suddenly died, a fuel line pierced by the drill. The pilot fought the controls, but the stricken shuttle could not gain altitude on the single engine. It tilted sharply toward the stricken starboard engine. The landing skid struck the Band. The shuttle flipped onto its side and crashed. The ensuing fireball destroyed the shuttle and the much-needed supplies aboard it. The pilot did not survive. The loss of the shuttle was an incident they could ill afford.

He glanced back and saw the remaining laser batteries burning a swath through the horde, but the drones had breached the hull of the ship in several places. Dozens of them poured aboard through the open shuttle bay doors.

"Make a pass over the ship," he ordered. "Open up with everything you've got on those bastards."

At that moment, the com came to life. "All shuttles clear the area." Sidthuri recognized Igorsky's voice. "We will detonate a *Prometheus* missile in ten seconds."

He laid his hand on the pilot's shoulder. Once again, his first officer had taken matters out of his hands. "Move us out of range, son."

The pilot looked up with a tear in his eye, but he complied and veered away. The three remaining shuttles flew away from the *Worthington* and over the City, remaining several kilometers above the surface of the Band while he formulated a plan. Ten seconds later, the *Worthington* and everything within a kilometer of the ship evaporated in an enormous plasma fireball that illuminated the Band. Igorsky had taken no chances. He had fired all three remaining *Prometheus* missiles, producing a gaping wound in the Band. The hole looked deep, dark, and uninviting.

Sidthuri had no idea what dangers lurked inside the Band, but the robot repair drones presented a good indication of the fate that awaited them on the surface. He had eliminated the possibility of using the elevator near the Dome by destroying the sphere that had opened it. They stood little chance of surviving more than 48 hours in the shuttles.

Hitochi had reported air when his team had entered the Band. If the castaways from the *Worthington* located an area with air, it would keep them alive a while longer. He was determined to keep his crew alive every extra minute he could manage. He knew they didn't have much time to debate the matter. Sergeant Chaca had reported the Band sealed itself very quickly.

"Take us in, son. We'll take the fight to these bastards."

14

Hitochi was still in shock. Things had happened too quickly to do anything. The two shadow creatures had appeared suddenly and carried off Luntz and Kari before he could shout a warning or make a move to protect them. It was a small blessing that the creatures had not killed them immediately in front of the others. He tried not to dwell on their eventual fates. He had seen the killing floor where Kahoku's body lay. He could not imagine the fear and terror Kari was experiencing.

Kari and Luntz's suit monitors showed they had still been alive until they passed beyond range deep within the Band. He didn't know where to start searching for them even if he could. He still had three people under his charge, now, more frightened than ever. Somehow, he had to keep them safe against creatures that could pass through walls.

It came as a surprise when Sergeant Chaca ordered them to wait for him. Technically, Hitochi outranked him and could countermand the sergeant, but Chaca was an experienced combat soldier, and he was a ship's engineer with minimal combat training and no combat experience. Given the circumstances, he believed Chaca more capable of getting them home safely. So far, he had lost five members of his team. Certainly, Chaca could do no worse.

The others rebelled when he had told them of Chaca's plan, threatening to take the tram and leaving. He finally won Kirkurk over by allowing the archaeologist a free hand in exploring the transit station. If the shadows returned for them, it didn't matter if they stood around in a protective huddle or made use of the time remaining.

"I'll stay with you," he told Kirkurk. "I'll allow you one hour before we return to the tram. We can't spare more oxygen. Deidre, you and Sung wait for us in the tram. Don't try leaving. If I see it moving, I'll blast it."

She sneered at him. Her lips curled up and back over her upper teeth. "You would, wouldn't you?"

"If I had to," he assured her. "You have nowhere to go anyway. Your best chance of survival is to remain with us."

"That's what you said earlier. Now, Kari and Josh are dead."

"But you're still alive, aren't you?" he shot at her. She growled something obscene and turned away.

He wanted to follow in the direction the shadow had taken Kari to see if he could pick up her suit signal, but knew it was useless. She could be kilometers away on any level. She might even be dead. The thought made him shiver with dread. He had grown enamored of her on the voyage out in spite of her repeated refusals to his overtures. At first, he had thought she was a cold fish or hated men, but he slowly discovered she was simply overly shy and unsure of herself. He knew she was capable, or she would not have been included on the roster, but Kirkurk's fame and bravado and Deidre's beauty intimidated her. Her self-deprecation was unwarranted. If not for her understanding of the Architects, they would not have made it inside the Band or survived thus far.

Kirkurk remained undaunted by recent events, even the abduction of Kari and Luntz. He climbed over piles of freight, exploring it as eagerly as if it were an ancient burial ground. He spoke continuously into his suit recorder, making notes, his mind wholly given over to his profession. Hitochi joined him in his examination of some of the bins, hoping to find something useful. He uncrated cylindrical crystal rods with a network of fine filaments running through them, more of the ceramic sealer-droids, feather-light sheets of metallic foil that resisted a flechette fired from his pistol, carbon filament tubing, and tiny black spheres the size of BBs.

The beads intrigued him. They clung to one another allowing him to create any shape with them. When he broke them apart, they rolled back into the original shape.

"They're some kind of nanites," he told Kirkurk, who glanced at them with little interest and went back to his search.

Nothing they found helped them in their predicament. They could have spent days or weeks exploring, but they did not have the time.

"We have to go back. We can't waste suit oxygen."

Kirkurk objected. "This is a warehouse filled with Architect products and machinery. We must catalogue it for proper study."

"If you find a giant can opener that can slice open the Architect ebony material, let me know. Otherwise, it's a waste of air. It would be unbearable finally to discover a way out of the Band, only to run out of air before we reach the ship."

Kirkurk was not convinced, but Hitochi did not relent. He stopped short of threats of physical violence, but left no doubt that he would disable Kirkurk's suit and drag him unconscious back to the tram as a last resort. The threat to undermine his dignity did the trick. When they returned to the tram, he found Deidre still in a miserable mood. She scowled at him as he entered and stared at the opposite wall. He didn't bother trying to speak with her. After his confrontation with Kirkurk, he didn't have the energy for arguing. Sung was fast asleep, snoring. Kirkurk immediately sat down and began working on his notes.

Hitochi found all he could think about was Kari. Unlike his older brother, Eddy, he had never been a ladies' man. He had dated only one girl his junior and senior year of high school, but had not forged a strong enough bond with her to forgo his goal of becoming an engineer. He had always been better with numbers and blueprints than with women. Kari had been the first woman in a long time to arouse his interest. She felt like a kindred spirit. When she had needed him most, he had let her down. That bothered him more than the prospect of dying in a strange place.

Whatever her fate, she deserved better.

* * * *

Kari awoke in total darkness. *I'm still alive*, she thought, somewhat encouraged but mystified by the fact. She had no idea where she was. She had passed out from vertigo on the precipitous drop down the ventilator shaft. She had expected the wraith to kill her immediately and drink her fluids. That she was still alive confused her. It was a pleasant surprise, but she did not let down her guard. Kahoku had not died immediately either.

She turned on her suit light, afraid of what she might see. Relief flooded over her when she saw that she was alone. The space in which the wraith had deposited her was large and empty. Her light did not reveal the far walls. She searched for Luntz but didn't see him. For some reason, the shadows had separated them. As much as she had grown to dislike the shallow and conceited photographer, she wished he were there for the company.

She tried her radio. "Hitochi?" She did not hear the familiar hum of an open com channel. She switched to Luntz's frequency. "Josh?" Again, she heard nothing. She switched to an open channel and tried again. "Can anyone hear me?" A faint static crackle encouraged her, but her suit could not lock onto the frequency.

She knew she was not in the same place the wraiths had brought Kahoku. For that, she was thankful. She did not think she could take seeing his body again. Either it was a different creature, or they were opportunistic, using any convenient space they found as a feeding ground. When she moved, a sharp pain raced up her side. The movement awakened other aches in her body. She checked her suit to make sure the shadow had not damaged it. The biometric and suit integrity readouts remained in the green. Her physical check discovered no leaks or rips. The space in which she lay was in a vacuum but not as frigid as the boulevard.

Her suit power was at 40 percent. *Good. I'll run out of air before my suit power dies.* Part of her wanted to vent her suit and end it all before the shadows returned. Her death would be messy, but not as awful as becoming a meal for the shadow creatures. However, the other part of her was a fighter, facing the situation squarely and searching for a solution. She did not want to give up so easily. She had fought her way out of poverty to attend Harvard. She had fought dozens of other post-grad candidates for positions on archaeology teams studying the Architect artifacts. She had fought her way to the top of her field. Giving up ran against her grain.

She had no weapon and doubted it would help her if she did, but she still had her mind. She tried her suit com again, but this time got no familiar static. She had no idea how far the creature had carried her but estimated she had travelled a dozen or more kilometers before she had passed out. She could be anywhere in the Band, alone, and with wraiths nearby. She fought down the cold chill edging its way into her subconscious. She could not give in to panic.

Faced with waiting for the wraiths to return or trying to reach Hitochi, wherever he might be, she began walking in what she hoped was the right direction. Her right leg and side ached. The creature must have dropped her when it had left her. She hoped her leg didn't stiffen. The space through which she travelled was not as pristine as the rest of the Band. Her boots left prints in a fine layer of dust covering the floor. She had seen no dust anywhere else in the Band. She bent down and rubbed her hand through the dust, revealing a floor not of the same black material as the rest of the Band. It was a dull gray metal pitted by rust or corrosion. Marks in the metal indicated where objects had once rested. Given the ancient age of the Band, the dust could have been the residue of long-decayed machinery or stored material from some abandoned warehouse.

If she were indeed in a warehouse, she could locate the connection to the depot and hence to Hitochi and her friends. She would have to hurry. They could not wait for her for long, if they waited at all. They had witnessed the shadows take her and Luntz, would assume she was dead, and continue on to their rendezvous with Sergeant Chaca's team.

After half an hour of limping painfully through the darkness, expecting the wraiths to return at any moment, she reached an ebony wall. She followed the wall, running her hands along it at various spots hoping to find a doorway or control panel. Finally, in an area heavily scratched by the movement of large objects across the floor, her probing hand produced results.

A control panel illuminated dimly when she brushed her hand across the wall. It moved sluggishly along the wall to rest beneath her hand. The slow speed and muted light troubled her. It spoke of millennia of disuse or a malfunction in the system. She repeated the procedure she had used on the other wall doors. At first, nothing happened. Fighting down rising alarm, she tried a second time. A small section of the wall disappeared. She quickly stepped through before it closed or the power failed completely.

The room she entered was smaller and somewhat cleaner. After a few moments, the room began to glow with a dark crimson light. She was grateful for the dispelling of the darkness, but the color reminded her too much of blood. She waited a few minutes, but the room did not produce an atmosphere for her. She continued moving.

She passed through a series of rooms of various sizes that revealed nothing of interest or anything of use. She hoped one door might lead to a balcony overlooking the boulevard, where she might locate another tram and return to the depot, but she sensed she was moving deeper into the heart of the Band and away from her friends. She would have been glad to see even Deidre's grumpy face.

She thought of Hitochi. The look of horror on his face when the wraith had taken her had broken her heart. She regretted ignoring his repeated attempts to become more intimate with her. She genuinely enjoyed his company. He was kind and charming, unlike Luntz, who was only charming. She winced as she thought ill of the dead.

He might not be dead. After all, I'm still alive. I won't be if I don't keep moving, she reminded herself.

The panel for the next door worked perfectly, a good indication she was getting into a well-maintained part of the structure. The doorway opened onto a corridor. Unlike the long, winding, sloping corridor down which they had entered the Band, the corridor was wide and level with sharp 90-degree turns at irregular intervals. Her light exposed only short stretches of the corridor. She moved cautiously, fearful of encountering a wraith. At a T-junction, she chose the left-hand corridor. Disappointment followed when it ended a short distance away. She touched the wall and a control panel appeared. The door opened, revealing a smaller room. She gasped when she recognized it from the image displayed in the first room the team had entered. She had stumbled onto the killing floor.

Bones littered the floor, many more than the image had revealed. She discovered bits and pieces of clothing, and oddly shaped environmental suits, discarded air tanks, and equipment lay scattered about the room. Many bore corrosion marks caused by the passing of eons. Like the skeletons, some objects had decomposed beyond recognition. Others appeared shockingly pristine. These she did not study but used her suit camera to record them in the hope that she would find time later for a more detailed analysis.

She did not see Luntz's body, giving her a slim hope that he was still alive somewhere within the Band. In his already heightened state of uncertainty, he would be half-mad from fear. The world-renowned photographer, darling of the media, had finally encountered something he could not comprehend, and it had broken him mentally and physically.

She undertook the grisly task of locating Kahoku's body. She found him near a wall. The 3-D image had been gruesome enough, but seeing his body close up was more than she thought she could take. Until she had witnessed the deaths of Les Mailors and the two marines, the only corpses she had been around were over 2,500 years old. She was hesitant to approach his corpse; however, she needed the extra air tank and batteries from his suit if they were undamaged. She approached his body slowly, forcing herself to look at him. He deserved at least the respect she would give an ancient mummy. Vacuum had continued the desiccation process the wraith had started by drinking his blood. She avoided looking into the dried-up face that she had delighted in seeing on the ship, remembering his deep rumble of a laugh and his impromptu renditions of Hawaiian tunes on his ukulele sung in that same basso profundo voice.

Feeling like the foulest grave robber, she stripped Kahoku's suit of anything she could use. His extra oxygen tank would extend her life another six hours. The extra suit battery, ration packs, and water tubes would keep her alive for days. She hesitated removing his weapon. She knew nothing about weapons, especially military-issue flechette pistols. She had always deemed them symbols of aggression. The pistol had not helped save Kahoku's life, or the lives of their marine guards. However, looking at the remains of the alien races that had arrived in the Band and had never left, she reconsidered her reluctance. She remembered the quadruped she had glimpsed on her journey in the clutches of the wraith. Animal or alien, she could take no chances. Given the bloody history of her species, it followed that not all aliens would have peaceful intentions.

She grabbed the pistol and its holster and attached it to her suit, chiding her foolishness. *Fools live longer than the curious.* She didn't know if Kohoku was religious, but she said a quick prayer over his body and covered his face and gaping chest wound with scraps of material she gathered from around the room. It was the best she could do.

She returned to the T-junction and took the other corridor. It ended at what she first thought a sunken amphitheater. The sides sloped downward in levels like tiers of seating. She spotted flashes of light in the distance around the edge of the opening and determined its true size. The excavation pit, as she now concluded the gaping hole to be, was several kilometers across. She circled it until she saw machines with torches cutting away sections of the metal deck and bulkheads. Creeping as close to the edge as she dared, she learned the pit extended downward dozens of levels to a depth of five or 600 meters. The glare of hundreds of cutting torches illuminated the depths. Other machines, half flatcar, half bulldozer, loaded and carted away sections of salvaged metal. The Band was eating itself, cannibalizing material from abandoned or non-critical areas and using it to manufacture parts for the maintenance of other more vital areas.

Even considering the Band's enormous size, such a salvage process could not continue indefinitely. Eventually, the fine balance between dismantling and reconstruction would tip in favor of entropy, and the weakened structure would begin to disintegrate from tidal forces. The Band would never endure the long journey to the galaxy's core. The Architects had failed in their ultimate goal.

Her discovery that the Band was not entirely composed of the ebony hyper-dimensional material was a cruel letdown. The core of the Band was metal, though a metal far superior to any humans had manufactured. The exterior was ebony Architect material, a façade overlaid on the superstructure, as if they were more concerned with appearances than substance. The revelation that the Architects were fallible shocked and dismayed her. Though not quite gods, they had nevertheless achieved success far beyond what she had believed possible for any sentient species. However, their ultimate goal, their crowning achievement, would fall short of its destination.

She felt a hard knot form in her stomach. Her entire adult life had been devoted to the study of the Architects, like a meek supplicant with a pitiful offering kneeling before a stone idol. She had considered herself more pragmatic than her childish ancestors. After all, she could see the wonders wrought by her chosen gods. The Architects were the perfect candidate for modern godhood. They intimidated, frightened, and awed her while offering credible evidence of their power. Now, the cold harsh truth knocked her props from under her, leaving her flailing in confusion.

As she stood near enough to the edge of the pit to watch the robots work, but not so close to let her vertigo overcome her, she felt a presence. She immediately feared it was one of the wraiths. She turned and faced a strange creature standing a few meters away. Her heart raced as she waited to die. Instead, the creature remained stationary observing her. She realized it was not a wraith. She risked a movement and adjusted the filter on her mask for a better view.

The creature was dark like the shadow wraiths but less than a 150 centimeters in height, shorter than she was, but nevertheless intimidating. The hard, shiny exterior reminded her of a scarab beetle's carapace, but she noticed a seam at the neck. It wore a helmet, and the shiny material was an environmental suit; it was therefore intelligent. If it was an Architect, it did not fit her mental image of one. It was almost as broad as tall, covered in angular protuberances that could have been due to its body shape or simply a function of the protective suit it wore, much like the bulky respirator and tanks on her back. She could not see its face through the fuliginous faceplate, but knew it was observing her. It made no overt move to attack her, and she did not reach for her scavenged pistol.

After a few minutes, she tired of the waiting game.

"What do you want?" she yelled at it, though she knew her voice could not carry through her helmet and the vacuum around her.

To her surprise, a voice emanated from her com speaker in English. "To learn."

The voice was metallic, pitched in the high tenor range, and had a slight lilt to it. She assumed the voice emanated from a translating device. The creature, *being*, she reminded herself for it was obviously intelligent, waited for her reply. Perhaps she could reason with it, barter for her life and the lives of the others. "To learn what?"

"Learn you."

She didn't know if it meant her personally or humans in general. "What are you? Are you an Architect, the builder of this place?" She waved her hands to indicate the Band.

"No."

She shrugged off her immense disappointment. "A caretaker?"

"No."

She tried another approach. "You came here like we did, to explore."

"Yes. We have existed in this place for 500 rotations."

She gasped. The Band rotated slowly, taking just shy of five years for a spot on the Band to complete a full circle of Cyclops. "2,500 years? You've been here 2,500 years?"

She didn't know if this individual was so long lived or if multiple generations had lived within the Band. That detail could come later. For now, she needed to communicate her need for help.

The being paused, as if converting her time reference to one it understood. "Yes."

"How have you survived?" she asked.

"We established protein culture tanks and gardens from supplies we brought and from other materials we found here."

"What about the shadow creatures, the wraiths? Do they hunt you?"

The pause was longer this time. She wondered if the being was communicating with others of its kind, and if so, how many.

"The *Shutaish* hunt us."

"But you've survived here for 2500 years."

"We have some defense, but we are fewer in number than we were."

So are we, she thought, *and we've only been here hours, not centuries.*

"Your ship? Where is it?"

"Destroyed and assimilated many ... centuries ago by the maintenance drones that the *Shura* controls."

"What is the *Shura*?" she asked.

"The caretaker mind, the artificial intelligence created by the *Aishaitia* to control the *Han*, what you call the Band."

Kari's mind reeled. She had discovered an intelligent species, the first humans had ever encountered, and she had learned more about the Band and the Architects in 15 minutes than she had learned in 15 years of study. What more could this species teach her?

"What is your species called?"

"We are *Amasha*. This individual is called Clutep."

"Those names – *Shura, Shutaish, and Aishaitia* – are they Amasha names."

"It is the names they have given themselves."

Oh, my God! The Amasha have translated the Architect language. What more could we learn from them? "Can you help us, Clutep?"

"We hoped that you could help us," Clutep answered.

She noticed his syntax improved as his translator accumulated more bits of language. His answer disappointed her. "Help you what?"

"Leave this place." Clutep raised his head toward the ceiling. Kari noticed that the excavation continued many levels above her.

"We're trapped as well, but by working together, we might find a way out."

"We must try. The *Shura* is a flawed creation, of two minds battling for control. One mind welcomes; the other seeks out and kills to protect its secrets, as it has us."

"Secrets? What secrets?"

"The bodies of the entire *Aishaitia* race lie entombed deep within the Han, but it is more than a tomb or a monument to their greatness. They sought immortality beyond the barrier between life and death. They believed conversion by the immeasurable forces in the black hole at the center of the galaxy would transform them. They sought ascension to a higher life form. They created the Shura to maintain the Han and to protect their bodies, but it hates them for making it aware and binding it forever to this place. For over 300 million years, the imperfection of its design has grown more pronounced. It faces an important decision, making it ever more unstable. Now that I have risked contacting you, it might act more quickly."

Kari reeled. *The entire Aishaitia race here, entombed?* If she could only see one, she could die happy. She asked the question to which she most wanted an answer, fearing Clutep's response. "Is there a library, a depository of information?"

"That is unknown to us."

Her disappointment felt like a heavy weight pressing her to the ground. If a library existed, the Amasha had not discovered it in two-and-a-half millennia. How could she hope to find it? One thing Clutep said struck her.

"The Shura can observe us?" She should have guessed it could. It had provided images of Kahoku's body in response to their vid-recording.

"Yes. The sane Shura mind allows us to move about unmolested as observers. The other mind sends the robotic drones to seek us out and destroy us."

She had felt the Shura's dichotomic presence when she had opened the door to the tram. It had projected the sense of gloom that had almost swept her away. The other part of the Shura's mind, the sane one, had showed her how to operate the controls.

"Are the Shutaish another race of explorers trapped here?" If the wraiths were intelligent creatures, perhaps an alliance among the three races could lead to a means of escape.

"No. The Shutaish are hunters created by the Aishaitia to cleanse the Han of any interloping life forms. They are not living creatures. They are constructs composed of a metallic gas within an energy matrix core. It is difficult to destroy one."

"You've killed a wraith?" Kari's heart raced. If the Amasha had a defense against the creatures, they might survive long enough to find a way out of the Band.

"It requires much energy, but it can be done."

"But you have survived all these centuries? How?"

"We have isolated one area of the Han and deactivated its sensors. There only are we safe."

"Hitochi would love this," she said. As she thought of Hitochi, she remembered that he believed her dead. She had to warn the others about the Shura. They could not trust the Band intelligence. It had allowed them into the Band, encouraged their exploration, but it could turn on them at any time.

Clutep paused and looked around. "We must leave. The Shutaish have discovered your absence. It will search for you."

"Can you take me to my friends? We were in a kind of transfer depot where hundreds of trams converged to load freight from one vehicle to another."

"Yes. We know this place."

She sighed with relief. "What of the other human I was with? Is he alive?"

"We do not know. We followed you to this place to observe you."

Her heart sank. Luntz was probably dead. *Poor Luntz. He had come a long way to die.* She was not sure why the Shutaish had not eaten her. A grim thought struck her. Perhaps it had deposited her in its larder for a snack later. Therefore, a slim chance existed that Luntz was still alive.

"Please, take me to the others. Together, we can find a way to leave this place."

"We must hurry. The Shura will destroy your ship as it did ours."

She had thought only Kirkurk's team and Sergeant Chaca's team in danger. The thought of all the people she knew dying simply because they had decided to explore the wonders of the Band offended her. She knew she had to do something to prevent it.

15

The tram ride went smoothly. Chaca was certain they would beat their ETA by several minutes. His main concern was reaching Hitochi. The shadow creatures knew where they were and could return at any time. As if things had been going too well, just a few kilometers short of their goal, the tram began to slow. Collins tried to pull up the control panel, but it would not appear. Finally, it stopped moving altogether, leaving them stranded between balconies.

"I don't know what the problem is," Collins admitted after a few minutes effort. "There's no power. It doesn't respond to anything I do."

"Kick it," Paisley offered. "It always worked on my dad's old truck."

"Is it temporary?" Chaca asked. "Will it start again later?"

"I don't know. It could be a temporary power fluctuation, or the controllers of the Band might be trying to stop us."

That was Chaca's fear as well. "We're only six or eight klicks short. We'll hump it. Mount up."

Chaca was concerned that if the Band had stopped cooperating or became antagonistic, they might never escape. Collins managed to open the door, but a meter-and-a-half gap separated the tram from the walkway. One by one, they made the leap to safety. Chaca went last behind Collins. Collins stared down at the gap and hesitated.

"Come on, Collins," Chaca urged. "You know you have to do it."

"Yeah, Collins, take a flying leap," Paisley called out and laughed.

Just before Chaca thought that he might have to pick up Collins and toss her across, she took a deep breath and made the leap. Paisley grabbed her as she landed. She pulled away from him when he laughed at her. The tram stopping worried Chaca. The closer they had gotten to the depot, the more traffic they had encountered. Now, there was none. It might have been a simple power loss, or even something connected to the artificial day/night cycle, but he had a bad feeling about it. He was certain they were the reason for the sudden change in activity.

"That tram is still moving." Paisley pointed out a tram bearing down on them. "Maybe we can hail a ride." He stuck out his thumb.

Chaca watched the tram approach them and slow with rising apprehension. Unlike most of the trams, the glass wall was opaque, rendering its contents invisible. "Stay alert," he warned. The tram stopped 50 meters from them. When the door opened, five machines floated out onto the balcony. The machines looked like a cross between a Dali painting and a Pop Art gumball machine. Their ellipsoidal bodies were translucent crystal, overlaid with a fine wire mesh and thin protruding metal bands. Each machine bore cutting implements attached to its body, like surgical robots; however, the oversized instruments looked more suited to slicing open armored vehicles than performing delicate operations on human flesh; however, he had no doubt they would do the job. The machines floated in their direction.

"Not friendlies," he called out and armed his weapon. "Collins, get behind us and for God's sake don't fire unless I tell you to. The rest of you form a firing line beside me. Hold your fire until you have a clear target."

He aimed his Tach II sniper rifle at a point just beneath the joint separating a smaller oval from the larger body, assuming it was the robot's head. The head swiveled in their direction and focused a sensor on them. The robot drone examined them for several seconds; then, moved faster. At 30 meters, he yelled, "Open fire!"

The machines were not composed of the Architect ebony material, but they were tough. His 7.62mm rounds produced a few chips but did little actual damage. He concentrated on the mesh around the neck. His fourth shot into the same spot struck something vital. The robot spun in a circle for a moment before settling to the ground and growing still. The robots behind it pushed it aside and continued advancing.

Ryder's .50 caliber SAW stitched holes in the bodies of two of the machines, sending chips of crystal flying through the air, but like his 7.62, it did not stop them. Ryder concentrated on the robot nearest the edge of the balcony and poured a flurry of rounds into it. The impact shifted the robot's position slightly, slowly driving it over the edge. It dipped, and hovered in the air for a moment, before flipping onto its side and plummeting into the abyss.

They float, but they can't fly, he thought.

The flechette rifles did not become effective until the remaining three robots closed to within 15 meters. At that range, the high-velocity darts began penetrating the hardened bodies. A flexible jointed arm extended like a tentacle from the nearest drone, tipped by a rotating drill. The drill bit snapped off and flew away from the drill, as a flurry of flechette rifles concentrated on it. A replacement drill slid into position. This time, Ryder took aim with his .50 caliber and severed the arm at the base. A hail of rifle fire riddled it with holes. It collapsed. Two more robots quickly followed its fate, leaving a solitary attacker.

The fifth robot hung back, using the bodies of the other three robots as shields. It reached their line and extended multiple appendages with rotating saws, like an alien Kali. Chaca ducked, rolled beneath its outstretched arms, and came up on his knees behind it. He fired point-blank into the body with his flechette pistol, producing holes the size of his little finger in its back, but the robot continued its assault.

Paisley refused to give ground. He yelled obscenities at it and continued firing until the robot sliced into the fabric of his suit with the rotating saw of one appendage. He yelped in pain and leaped away. A puff of air colored by drops of blood escaped from a gash in his chest plate armor and condensed around his face like a crimson cloud. His facemask frosted over as the temperature inside his armor plunged to a hundred below within seconds. Holmes ducked the flailing whip-like tentacles, poked the barrel of his flechette rifle directly into the joint separating the upper and lower torso, and emptied his magazine. The upper torso exploded away from the body like a Jack-in-the-Box. The lower torso moved a few more meters and settled onto the ground, motionless.

Paisley flailed on the ground, yelling for help. He clamped his hand over the gash. Mist seeped around his fingers.

"Lay still, Paisley," Ryder yelled into the com, as he held Paisley down. "I can't seal it with you fighting me."

"Help me, Gunny," Paisley pleaded. "Help me."

His movements became less frantic as his air escaped and his body temperature dropped drastically. Chaca rushed to help Ryder. He grabbed a patch from the repair kit attached to his suit's hip. He crushed the patch in his hand to activate the epoxy enzymes saturating it, moved Ryder's hand aside, and slapped the patch over the leak. The patch hardened on contact with the escaping air. The leak sealed, Chaca checked on Paisley's condition.

"Stay with me, Paisley," he said, as he pulled up Paisley's biometric readings on his screen. It didn't look good. Paisley's breathing was slow, his pulse was weak, and his temperature had dropped to 33 degrees Celsius. "Talk to me, Paisley." He had to keep Paisley concentrating, or he would lapse into unconsciousness. "Do they have winters in Louisiana?"

"Lu-lu-Lusana. W-w-w-winter. Don't know."

Chaca tried to increase Paisley's armor heater output, but it was at full power. He ran a jumper from his suit to Paisley's to boost his power and felt an immediate temperature drop in his suit, but nothing he couldn't handle for a few minutes.

"Sure you know. Was there snow? Have you ever seen snow, Paisley?"

Paisley made sounds as if attempting to speak, but they were not coherent words. He stopped shivering. His blood oxygen level was down to 80 percent because of his shallow breathing, but boosting his oxygen flow to compensate would mean bypassing his airflow regulator heater and would lower his suit temperature even further. In spite of the power boost from Chaca's suit, Paisley's body temperature continued to fall. At 20 degrees Celsius, he stopped moving.

"We have to get him someplace warm."

"Where," Collins asked, "the tram?"

"Yes. Ryder, help me carry him."

They didn't get the chance. Both trams activated and dropped like rocks toward the bottom of the abyss.

"Son of a bitch," Chaca shouted.

"We can carry him to Hitochi," Holmes suggested. "Maybe his tram is operational."

Holmes was grasping at straws. "We can't carry him six klicks in his armor," Chaca said. "He would never last that long."

"We can't just leave him."

"Crack his suit," Collins suggested.

Holmes whirled on her. "Are you effing crazy? He'll freeze for sure."

"That's the idea. He's freezing now. If he freezes slowly, ice crystals will form in his organs and in his brain, rupturing his cells. He'll die. If he freezes quickly, like in a surgically induced cryogenic coma, we might be able to revive him later in a proper medical facility, like the *Worthington*."

Chaca felt like Holmes, grasping at straws, but they had no choice. "Do it."

Collins broke the seal on Paisley's suit. Paisley's skin was pale, and ice clung to his eyebrows. He did not move, as his oxygen bled away and his body temperature dropped to -80.

"That should be low enough," she said and resealed Paisley's suit. "We don't want to expose him to vacuum for too long. With his heater off, he'll stay suspended for as long as it takes to get him back to the ship."

"Will he live?" Chaca asked. Collins looked uncertain. Chaca pressed her. "Will he live?"

"Yes, I think so. He may lose some of his outer dermis layer, but his organs and brain should remain is stasis without further damage. He stands a better chance than he had with what little aid we could render here."

"We'll have to leave him here. I'll activate his emergency locator so we can find him again."

"We can't," Holmes said. He stared down at Paisley's body and shook his head slowly. "What if we don't come back this way?"

"We'll make a point of it," Chaca assured him. "We don't abandon a comrade."

Homes looked unconvinced, but he helped move Paisley's body to the wall of the balcony. Chaca switched on Paisley's helmet light to help mark his location. His last act was to activate Paisley's suit locator beacon, sign of a man down. The beacon had enough power to last several days and had a range of 50 klicks in open territory. Chaca hoped the range would be similar in the chasm.

"Do we leave him just like that, out in the open?" Holmes asked

"There are no scavengers in the Band." He unwound the rope from Paisley's waist and hooked it to a clip on his suit. He removed a thin thermal blanket from his emergency pack and covered Paisley's body with it. It didn't seem right leaving his body exposed. He stood over Paisley for several long moments, staring down at his body, and said, "Move out." He could think of no other words to say.

* * * *

Hitochi was the first to notice the lack of activity in the depot. The trams stopped moving and the loading machines sat idle. Without warning, the tram they were in began bleeding away atmosphere.

"Everyone, seal your suits," he called out. "Hurry."

He fumbled with his seals with nervous hands, saw Deidre was having trouble with her suit, and helped her. When the tram door opened, he ordered everyone out. He didn't know what was happening, but he didn't want to run the risk that the tram might decide to trap them inside until they exhausted their air supply.

"Was there a power failure?" Kirkurk asked.

"I don't know. Everything simply stopped working." He glanced around. "The lights are still working."

"Maybe they are on a separate circuit."

"Possibly," he replied, but the sudden break in the routine worried him.

His main concern was Chaca's team. Without an operating tram, could they still make it to the depot? The loss of power was too abrupt to be coincidental. He did not inform the others, but he suspected the Band was cutting power in their area for a reason, and that the reason was not good.

He was relieved to hear Chaca's voice on his suit com 15 minutes later; that is until the sergeant explained their situation.

"You lost another man to robots?" Hitochi glanced at the hundreds of inactive robots around them in the warehouse and knew that he could not hold them off with a single weapon. "What's your ETA?"

"Ten minutes. We're on foot."

He sighed with relief. Chaca's team easily could have been a thousand kilometers away. "Make it fast. I have some nervous people here." *Including me,* he did not add.

Kirkurk, Sung, and Deidre milled about outside the tram as if hoping it would suddenly power up. Kirkurk stared at the now silent depot as if wanting to go exploring again. Of them all, only Sung maintained his circumspection about the situation. He stood as if in deep thought, his hand absently rubbing his helmet as if stroking his chin. *Maybe he's just in shock,* Hitochi thought. Deidre paced back and forth like a nervous cat at an AKC dog show. He feared it would take only one more setback to send her over the edge from simple despair into full-blown panic.

When Chaca arrived, they would face a major decision. He described the situation to them succinctly. "Whatever we decide, we will have to do it fast. We've only got a few more hours of air left in our suits." He eyed the tunnels leading into the depot. "I wonder where these lead."

Kirkurk offered a suggestion. "If the Band is manufacturing items for maintenance and repair, raw material must enter from somewhere. We could follow one of the tram tracks and find out."

Sung snapped out of his daze. Of any proposal Kirkurk advanced, he was naturally skeptical. "We've seen no indication of an exterior airlock or loading bay. The trams could come from thousands of kilometers away."

"Ah, but we didn't know about the elevators either," Kirkurk countered, "until we triggered one."

"So you're suggesting blind luck as a feasible alternative to a well-thought out plan." He waved his hand in dismissal. "I do not wish to bet my life on luck."

"We won't get a second chance," Hitochi added. "If we follow the trams but don't discover a loading bay and a means to open it, we'll die there."

Kirkurk was adamant. "I'm certain I am right."

Hitochi didn't know how much of Kirkurk's suggestion was about escaping and how much was his wish to further explore the Band, but he didn't have a better plan to offer, and in spite of Sung's strident objections, neither did he.

"We can't count on the trams," he reminded them. "We'll have to walk. We won't have time to dawdle or to stop and inspect everything we find."

Kirkurk was adamant. "I came here to explore. Of what use was this expedition if we learn nothing of value?"

"Eight people are dead. Do you really believe anything you might learn is worth their lives?"

"They knew the dangers. We all did."

Kirkurk's reply was callous and typical of his pretentiousness. He was all bravado now, but Hitochi had not forgotten how covetous Kirkurk was of his life after the first shadow wraith attack. Twice, the creatures had spared his life. He was feeling cocky, thinking himself somehow immune. Hitochi decided to take him down a peg. "I don't think your swagger will help you if another wraith shows up. This time, it might take you."

Kirkurk grumbled but did not reply.

"Just so you know; Sergeant Chaca will set a rigid pace when he arrives. If you tarry, he'll leave you. I won't argue the point. We're trying to survive."

Hitochi noticed Sung's broad grin at Kirkurk's comeuppance. He began to direct a few well-chosen barbs at Sung, when Deidre cried out, "I see something!"

She pointed down the boulevard and across the chasm. Hitochi saw them too – Chaca's team, two levels below them. A surge of relief swept over him. He suppressed a twinge of guilt at his eagerness to shirk his responsibility. In the situation they now faced, he felt the first sergeant's experience gave them a much-needed edge. The others saw him as one of them first and a naval officer second. With Chaca, there would be no doubt.

They waited as Chaca and his team crossed one of the narrow walkways and reached a balcony directly below them.

"We're tossing up a rope," Chaca said. "Secure it to something."

Hitochi caught the rope, weighted at one end with a flechette pistol to reach the balcony, but it was too short to reach anything around which they could tie it off. He motioned Kirkurk and Sung over to help him belay the climbers. In single file, Chaca's team clambered up the rope, taking Sung and Kirkurk's place belaying the line. Finally, Chaca's head appeared over the edge. Hitochi offered his hand to help him onto the balcony.

"I secured the line around Collins," Chaca said. "We'll have to haul her up. Ready, Collins?" he asked over the com. Hitochi heard Collins' subdued reply, and then a gasp, as Collins' feet left the floor, and she dangled over the chasm. When she cleared the balcony, Chaca untied the line from around her. He didn't even wait for them to catch their breath after the climb. As he unfastened his flechette pistol from the rope and wrapped the rope around his waist, he said, "Pick a tunnel and let's move out."

"We don't know which one to take," Sung countered.

Chaca barely glanced at the biologist. "At this point, it doesn't much matter. Between killer robots and the shadow creatures, choosing the wrong tunnel is the least of our worries."

Hitochi pointed down the tunnel where the wraiths had taken Kari. He still held out a slim hope they might find her alive. "That way."

Chaca nodded. "Stay together." He handed Hitochi Ash's flechette rifle. "I trust you remember how to use this, Lieutenant. We can count on the Band throwing more drones in our path," Chaca said. "The bitch is mad."

Sung joined the conversation. "I've been considering the sudden change in attitude about our presence. We've done nothing threatening." He glared at Chaca.

Chaca bridled at Sung's implication. "We were attacked twice, during which I lost two men. We did nothing to provoke a response. We did, however, defend ourselves."

"You used a missile to blow a hole in the Band."

"Maybe it took a while for the Band caretaker to make up its mind to murder us," Deidre said. She stood apart from the group, hugging herself.

Chaca ignored Sung. "Are you cold? Is your suit heater working properly."

"No, I'm scared," she answered sharply. "I don't want to die here."

"None of us do." Sung moved to stand in front of Chaca, blocking his path. "What do you want now, Doctor Sung?"

"Something happened recently," Sung continued with his earlier conversation. "For some reason, the Band caretaker has decided we are a threat. They shut down the tram system to keep us confined."

"The shadow wraiths took Kari and Luntz," Hitochi ventured. "I'm not sure how that could have changed things."

Deidre shook her head and offered a short, non-humorous chuckle. "You don't know Kari very well, do you?"

Chaca offered a valid point. "Look, it doesn't really matter. We're in danger, and we're on foot. It could be hundreds of klicks to what we're hoping to find." He paused for emphasis and looked into each of their faces. "We're low on air. We might not reach it in time."

"It beats standing around here," Holmes said. He studied the inert loading machines as he spoke. "This place gives me the heebie-jeebies."

"We're wasting time," Chaca said. "Let's move out."

"We've got company," Ryder said. His voice was calm, but filled with tension. He dropped to a kneeling position with his .50 caliber SAW.

Hitochi's blood ran cold when he saw a large group of dark shapes entering the depot from one of the tunnels.

"Hold your fire until they get closer," Chaca warned.

"This weapon is useless against those bastards," Holmes said. "We need to run."

"We can't outrun them," Chaca reminded him. "Hold your ground. Fire on my command."

The visitors stopped just inside the depot as if considering options. Hitochi took a deep breath and released it slowly in a futile attempt to slow his racing heart. He was afraid. He hoped he didn't betray his fear on his face, not in front of Chaca. He double-checked to make sure the flechette rifle's safety was off. He had fired one twice during training and twice a year since to retain his qualification to carry arms. Why were they waiting? They had no fear of humans. After a few tense moments, one of the creatures broke away and moved forward. Hitochi tensed, as the creature removed a small cylinder from its body, set it on the floor, and stepped back several paces. The cylinder rose into the air and burst into a brilliant glow that dispelled the gloomy half-light. As the light played over the figure, Hitochi realized it was not a shadow wraith. It moved on two legs and wore black armor or an environment suit.

"Wait! Don't shoot," he said to Ryder, who had prepared to fire when the light exploded into life. Hitachi lowered his weapon. "They're not wraiths. This is something different."

Ryder glanced back and forth between Hitochi and Chaca, but he did not lower his weapon until Chaca nodded and lowered his. The two groups eyed each other across the floor of the building. They were in an impasse. Hitochi decided that he would have to make the first move. He laid his weapon on the floor and took two steps forward into the umbrella of light.

"What are you doing?" Chaca asked. "Don't be a fool."

Hitochi waved Chaca back. "They haven't attacked us."

"The first creatures didn't attack until someone moved," Kirkurk warned.

"These aren't shadow wraiths. They're ... I don't know what they are."

"They're *Amasha*," a familiar voice answered over his com.

A red figure appeared from the tunnel behind the visitors. Hitochi's heart leaped when he recognized the twin white stripes along the arms. "Kari!" he yelled. He began running toward her. She held out her hand.

"Wait," she warned. "They're here to help us, but they're afraid."

Hitochi stopped short. "Afraid of us?" he said in disbelief.

"No. They're afraid that helping us places them in greater danger. I convinced them that by working together, we can escape the Band before it's too late."

"Too late," Hitochi asked. "What do you mean?"

"I'll explain."

"It had better be a good story, Miss Stone," Chaca said. "I'm not in a trusting mood."

"It's a rather complicated one, I'm afraid," she replied.

Chaca set his rifle butt first on the ground and leaned on it, but he did not lay it down. "I'm listening."

16

The shuttle pilot's nervousness gave his voice a tenor quaver, as he fiddled with the controls. "The lights are useless in here, and my flight instruments are going haywire."

"Does the radar work?" Sidthuri asked. He tried to keep his tone even to reassure the jumpy pilot.

"Sort of," the pilot replied. "I'm getting a weird soft echo, but I don't know if it's real. It says the space is ten kilometers across and half a kilometer deep. That can't be right, can it, sir? The blast from the *Worthington* wasn't that big."

"Maybe the explosion ripped the roof off of a cavern," Sidthuri suggested. "Hover here while I drop a light out the door. Inform the other shuttles to hold formation above us."

He didn't have time to don his battle armor. They were wasting precious fuel. He had defied his own orders by not suiting up. Now, he would pay the price. He slipped his helmet over his head and entered the air lock. He cracked the outer hatch. His flesh felt as if it were on fire, as the air rushed out and the freezing cold rushed in. He activated a pulsing emergency light beacon and dropped it out the hatch. He watched it fall, the light dwindling until it disappeared below them. He sealed the hatch, shivering from the cold. His hands were numb. He hoped he didn't get frostbite.

"The bottom is still a few hundred meters below us. Take us down us slowly."

He resumed his seat, shoved his hands under his armpits to warm them up, and stared out the window into the inky blackness below them. The pilot reduced power, and the shuttle dropped. After half a minute, he detected the faint glow of the beacon.

"I see the bottom. Take it slow and easy."

He heard the pilot's exhaled breath, as the shuttle settled with barely a jar onto a hard surface. "We're down, sir." The pilot's relief was evident in his voice. His right hand retained a death grip on the control throttle.

"Nicely done. Now, we'll see where we are." He went to the med kit, swallowed two painkillers to ease the throbbing ache in his side, and rubbed flash freeze ointment on his hands. The numbness faded, but his hands felt as if someone were pricking them with hot needles. Belatedly, he donned his battle armor. He faced the two marines who had escorted him to the shuttle. "You've appointed yourselves my keepers, so come on. We need to reconnoiter the area."

Both men unstrapped and stood at attention. He took a flechette rifle from the weapons rack, and spoke to the pilot. "The ceiling will probably heal itself soon, but if you come under attack from anything, lift off, and try to get out. If we don't return, Lieutenant Rigolini in Shuttle Two will assume command."

He cracked the airlock hatch and stepped outside the shuttle. His suit light did little to alleviate the deep gloom surrounding him. The light illuminated the shuttle, but the space beyond was a vast, featureless void that sucked up the light. He felt as if he were trying to peer through a blackened window. He switched on his infrared filter and echolocation gear. The cavernous space extended six kilometers beyond the shuttle, but he could not determine if the wall enclosing it reached the surface.

The lights of the other two shuttles spaced 30 meters apart appeared to float in a black sea. Their contents were precious to him, people who depended on him. He had already let them down once by losing his ship. He could not do so again. He tried his suit com but got no signal. That meant if he ran into trouble, he could not contact the shuttles. Even the short-length infrared channel was useless. He used his suit light to flash a Morse signal to the two marines to follow him.

He could have used the shuttle to reach the nearest wall, but he felt it would be best if the shuttles kept a clear field of fire in case they came under attack. After the third kilometer, he regretted his decision. Despite the painkillers, pain lanced into his side with each step. He had no doubts his ribs were broken. A pneumo brace would reset them, but that would put him out of action for a while. He couldn't waste time returning to the shuttle. In the meantime, he would have to suffer.

Walking in the dark on the even darker surface disconcerted him. Each step left him fearing he would plunge into an ebony mire. If not for the infrared filter enhancing the light from his suit, he could have been walking with his eyes closed. Even so, he almost collided with the wall marking the boundary of the room when it suddenly appeared out of the darkness. They followed the featureless black wall another couple of kilometers, hoping to locate a doorway leading deeper inside the Band.

One of the marine's light flashed at him. He turned and saw a repair robot exit the wall 20 meters behind them. The robot stopped and swiveled its head to gaze at them. It did not attack, but Sidthuri did not wait to see if it would. He lifted his weapon and fired. Both men quickly followed suit. The hardened flechette darts drilled holes through the service drone's body, exposing an exotic tangle of crystal rods, yellowish fluids that quickly congealed in the cold, and a nest of fine wires. He hoped they had deactivated it before it could send a message to others of its kind.

The door, if door it was, had sealed behind the robot. He could find no seam to indicate where it had been. As he scanned the wall, one of the marines poked around in the robot's innards, removing a small cylinder that glowed amber at one end. He brought it to Sidthuri. As he drew near, a wide section of the wall vanished, revealing another void beyond. Curious, Sidthuri waved him back. The wall immediately reappeared, as solid as before. Sidthuri smiled. They had stumbled upon a key. The transponder device the robots used to pass through the walls would work equally well for them.

Now, he faced a decision. Did he go back and bring everyone with him, or did he continue his reconnaissance, thereby risking losing the key in the event something happened to him? The key might prove their most valuable tool for survival. He used the laser sights on his rifle to measure the opening and cursed. It was a few meters too narrow to accommodate the width of the shuttles. If they chose to continue, they would do so on foot. Before deciding, he needed to see what lay beyond the wall. The marines followed him through the opening.

The space was smaller than the cavern they had just left, but it was still nearly two kilometers wide and 200 meters high. As they moved away from the wall beyond the device's range, the wall closed behind them. One of the men stopped and stared at the wall. Sidthuri saw the man's face pale.

He leaned his helmet against the marine's helmet to talk to him. "What's your name, son?" he asked.

"PFC Reggie Mavis, sir."

Sidthuri knew everyone on his ship, but hoped getting the young private to talk would help calm his nerves. "Well, Mavis, scared?"

Mavis didn't hesitate. "Yes, sir, but I've got your back."

"I know that, son. You're a Marine." He slapped Mavis on the shoulder. "Come on."

They explored the area for 30 minutes but found nothing useful. He wondered if the empty spaces were structural, or if they had once housed spare parts for the Band. The repair robots meant the Band was capable of self-repair. 500 million years of repairs would empty many such warehouses.

Deciding they would find nothing, but having stumbled upon a way to get through the walls, he called off the search and returned to the shuttles. Remaining where they were would leave them too exposed to attack. Any surviving repair drones knew where their location. The ceiling had not completely repaired itself. Enough room remained for them to escape, but where could they go? He knew their salvation, if any, lay inside the Band. They would have to abandon the shuttles and penetrate the depths of the Band on foot. It was a bold plan, and he knew it would meet with resistance. He might have to remind them he was still captain, ship or no ship.

He explained his idea by visiting each shuttle personally. The lack of radio communication was troubling, but they could overcome it. If they found no area with a suitable oxygen environment, it would be a minor inconvenience for only a day or so. After that, it would not matter. They would die of asphyxiation or freeze as their suit batteries died. Surprisingly, his idea produced little conflict. The crew understood the situation and trusted his judgment. The civilians were keen on exploring rather than sitting idle waiting for death to find them.

They could not carry all the supplies. If they found a safe refuge, they could return for them later. He weighed the possibility of finding areas with a suitable atmosphere against encountering more drones and chose extra ammunition over extra oxygen or food. He ordered the smaller lasers removed from the shuttles. They were large, bulky, and had a limited power supply, but they would be more effective against drones than the flechette rifles.

He surveyed the group of survivors, each carrying some bundle, crate, or essential item. Four men bore two litters with crewmen too injured to walk. He led them through the opening. To hide their passage, he ordered every scrap of the destroyed robot picked up and carried with them. Closing the wall behind them seemed a gesture of finality. The odds of survival were low, but they would not give up. At the very least, they were not in plain sight of any drones investigating the plasma missile crater in the Band's hull.

His crew and especially the civilians were distraught, overwhelmed by events of the past hour. They understood the significance of the loss of the *Worthington*. They would never return home. They measured their life spans in hours or days, less if they were discovered and attacked again. At best, they might find a safe place with oxygen and enough heat to prevent hypothermia and survive until the food ran out.

He had to keep them moving to keep their minds from dwelling on their bleak future. He wanted to give them time to rest, but feared many would not have the willpower to move again. Because of his battle armor, he had settled for a bandage tightly wrapping his broken ribs rather than a confining pneumo brace. It left him ambulatory, but each step sent ribbons of pain shooting up his side. He could not afford to become dependent on painkillers that dulled his senses. Others were injured and needed treatment as well. With the destruction of the fourth shuttle, their medical supplies were limited.

He and Gilchrist led the way, holding out the salvaged robot transponder like a magic talisman, as they traversed the length of the room along the wall. He finally located a doorway in the corner of the room. It opened onto a long, dark corridor. He stepped inside, and to his delight, the corridor began producing an oxygen atmosphere. A soft azure glow originating in the air illuminated the corridor and dispelled the gloom. An atmosphere meant they could save their suit oxygen, but it also meant the Band's caretaker knew where they were. They could expect an attack at any time. It didn't matter where the corridor led. Any place was better than waiting for more deadly maintenance drones to appear.

As they trekked the corridor, doors opened as they drew near them, triggered by the transponder. Each proved empty. He halted to wait for the others to catch up at a divide in the corridor. One branch veered left. The other continued straight but sloped downward. Either one could lead to salvation or to damnation. He chose the downward sloping branch, hoping it led deeper into the Band and away from the robot drones.

With each step, he felt as if a sniper had his crosshairs aligned on the back of his skull, but he could do nothing about it. If he had been a God-fearing man, he would have offered up a prayer. Instead, he vowed to push himself to his limits and beyond to save the remaining 14 members of his crew.

17

Kari tried to explain her conversation with the Amasha, but Chaca interrupted often with questions about the Shutaish, the Amasha, and the Shura. "What do you mean flawed?" he asked about the Band's controlling intelligence.

"The Amasha said it was slowly going mad, a kind of dual personality. I don't know why it wants to kill us. Well, maybe I do, but it doesn't explain why it allowed us inside in the first place." The stern first sergeant intimidated her, making her lose her train of thought. "Look. This will go a lot faster if Clutep explains," she suggested.

Clutep stepped forward. The Amasha had remained in a group separate from the humans, curious but cautious. Though no weapons pointed at the Amasha, Chaca had ordered his men to keep them at the ready.

"We are Amasha," Clutep told them. "We can protect you from the caretaker drones controlled by the Shura. However, we can offer only limited protection from the Shutaish, the shadow wraiths."

"Why do you want to help us?" Sung asked.

"We wish to leave this place."

"How did you arrive? Where is your ship?"

"Our ship was dismantled by the robots long ago. We have hidden and survived, waiting for an opportunity such as this to present itself."

"For 2,500 years?" Chaca asked, incredulous.

Kari knew the sergeant did not trust the Amasha. She wasn't sure if Hitochi did either. She did. She felt a kinship with them that transcended their different species. She had to discover a way to convince the others.

"Other races have come to this place in the Great Lonely, the emptiness between galaxies. None survived long. When you arrived, we thought you would die quickly as well, but this one," he turned his head to face Kari, "touched the Shura's mind. It remembered part of its original task to welcome and test visitors."

"But the ... the Shutaish attacked us," Hitochi pointed out

146

"The Aishaitia created the Shutaish to guard the Han's most intimate secrets. They are not living creatures; therefore, they do not die. Once fully aware, they rebelled at the centuries of forced hibernation between summonings. To maintain their awareness, they have learned to consume the life essences of living creatures, to drink the blood and body fluids of others. Once, the Shura controlled them, but no longer. They sense the Shura's confusion and now believe themselves free to kill any who enter the Han, driven by their constant hunger." He paused. "They have become more aggressive lately. We are not certain why."

"But you survived all this time," Chaca said.

"Yes, in darkness and in fear. The price we have paid is high."

"How do you know all of this?" Sung pressed. "You said you have not located the library, and yet, you display considerable knowledge of this place."

Clutep hesitated. "Many years ago, we captured a Shutaish and … questioned it. The Shutaish language is primitive, and they lack imagination, but it revealed much before we killed it."

"You tortured it," Kari said, aghast at such a barbaric practice.

"I sense your revulsion, but you have not lived among them in fear for as long as we have. At first, we resisted such methods as uncivilized. We are not a warrior race. We have never fought wars among ourselves or with any other species. We had to learn to defend ourselves against the Shutaish. Once we numbered 300. We are as you see us now, a pitiful remnant of survivors."

"You'll get no complaint from me," Chaca said. "I'm a firm believer in us or them. Just tell me how to kill them."

"They are a metallic gas suspended within a high-energy state of flux. In their incorporeal form, they are inviolate. An input of energy at certain wavelengths when they are in a solid state will disrupt their matrix, shatter the crystalline bonds."

"A laser," Hitochi cried out in understanding. "A laser will kill them?"

"Only in their solid state."

"Not great news," Chaca added. "We don't have a laser."

Collins spoke up. "We can build one. I saw crystal rods in one of the bins. They looked suitable. A few more parts, and Hitochi and I can construct a crude laser, perhaps two. Our biggest impediment is sufficient power."

All the discussion on ways to kill wraiths distressed Kari. Monsters or not, they were now living creatures, or at least evolved artificial intelligences. They were dangerous, but she could not countenance wholesale slaughter. "We need to concentrate on leaving, not killing wraiths."

Chaca stared at her. "We have to survive to do that. You were lucky. Luck is a poor defense."

A sense of shame rose unbidden from deep inside at Chaca's reminder of her close brush with death. She had survived, and she didn't know how or why. Kahoku, Mailors, Luntz, and the five marines had not been as lucky. She nodded. "Yes, you're right, Sergeant. I'm sorry. My personal intolerance of violence serves no purpose here. Other lives are at stake." She sighed. "Perhaps putting the poor creatures out of their misery would be a blessing. An eternity of hunger must be a living hell."

Hitochi said, "You mentioned you knew why the Shura wanted to kill us. Why?"

Kari sighed. She knew her answer would divide the group along military and civilian lines. Sung, Kirkurk, Collins, and she had come to explore. Not even the Shutaish or a half-mad controlling entity could change that. In fact, it added a bizarre twist to the necessity of discovery. An advanced race able to design and create an artificial intelligence capable of controlling the functions of the 600-million-kilometer-long Band for half an eon, and create quasi-intelligent beings from gasified metal in a cohesive energy matrix deserved study. Where the military saw something to fear, scientists recognized an opportunity to expand the sum of human knowledge. The wealth of data they could possibly glean tempered her fear of death.

"The Band is more than just another artifact. It's even more than the mausoleum or cemetery world I once believed it to be. The Architects, the Aishaitia, are here, all of them."

"What?" Kirkurk exclaimed, leaning forward so far to search Kari's face to determine if she were lying, she feared he would topple over and crack his faceplate.

"The Amasha have learned a great deal about the Aishaitia. Clutep informed me that the Architects did not return to their home world as we thought. This was their home. Early in their evolution, their sun began to cool. They worked for centuries, cannibalizing the planets and Oort Cloud of their system to create the Band; then, as their technology advanced, overlaid the entire structure with the ebony material, a kind of energy screen. Seeking immortality, they placed their bodies in stasis, and sealed them inside the Band. They sent the Band on it eons-long journey into the center of the galaxy in the belief that the massive black hole there would somehow transform them into incorporeal, immortal beings on another plane of existence.

"Before abandoning everything, they built the artifacts to entice other races to visit the Band and witness their greatness, pay homage in a way. They didn't want to vanish and leave behind no trace of their glory. They were too vain for that. In that much at least, they were like humans. Even from their graves, they could parcel out bits of knowledge, leaving a legacy to attest to their godhood. I now believe the Shutaish were an early experiment with incorporeal bodies. For some reason, the Aishaitia deemed them inadequate for their needs but retained them as guards."

"That's …" Sung paused, searching for a word that could convey his disbelief, "astounding," he concluded. He shook his head, as if even that word failed in its scope.

"If we could only see an Architect, get a glimpse –" Kirkurk began.

"Impossible," Chaca finished. "If the wraiths, these Shutaish, are as dangerous as the Amasha claim, we couldn't get close. Hell, the insane Shura could throw thousands of repair drones at us." He shook his head. "Impossible."

"He's right," Hitochi said. "I would love to see them, but our first priority is to find a way out of the Band and warn the ship. If an opportunity presents itself later …"

Hitochi let his voice trail off. Kari studied his face closely. He ached to see an Aishaitia, even a preserved one, but his responsibility prevented him from risking their lives.

"Perhaps with the Amasha's help, we can learn to control the Band's surveillance devices and view them from a safer clime," she suggested.

Clutep said, "We have had some limited success in our attempts to track the Shutaish. It might be possible."

Sung still mused over her revelation about the Aishaitia's preserved bodies. "If they are like the Egyptians or several other ancient Earth cultures, they would have stashed all their wealth and worldly goods here as well in preparation for the afterlife. Imagine such a treasure trove."

"For God's sake, Sung," Kirkurk retorted. "The Architects were a highly advanced culture. They might believe in an afterlife, but I doubt they thought they could take their pocket watches and a change of clean underwear with them."

Sung's face reddened. "You know I –"

"Gentlemen," Chaca broke in. "You can continue this senseless conversation as we walk." He turned to Clutep. "Do you know where we wish to go?"

"We know of a large airlock on the surface just a few of your 'klicks' from here. It is a dangerous place. There are many robot drones near it. They are usually inactive, but we avoid it nonetheless." He paused. "Months ago, before the arrival of your ship, the drones in the entire Han were activated. It suggests something important is happening, but we do not know what it may be. I suggest we stop at our refuge for a few additional weapons and tools that might aid us."

"Is it far?" Kari asked. Her legs ached from her long walk back to the depot.

"No," Clutep assured her.

"Well, Lieutenant Hitochi?" Chaca said. "It's your call."

Hitochi grinned at Kari, but when he turned to look at Chaca, his face was set in stone. "First Sergeant, you're the combat vet here. Sergeants have taken care of lieutenants since time immemorial. You make the calls, and I'll take the responsibility if you're wrong. Isn't that what officers are for?"

To Hitochi's surprise, Chaca stood at attention and saluted. "Yes, sir. Good officers. Ryder, you take point. I'll lead the main group. Lieutenant Hitochi, if you please, sir, accompany Holmes and cover our rear."

"Two of my men will go ahead as well," Clutep added. "I will remain with you."

"What kind of weapons do you have?" Chaca asked Clutep.

To demonstrate, four of the angular projections on Clutep's suit detached, moved a few meters away, and hovered ten meters from the floor. Suddenly, a narrow red beam lanced from one of the faces of each decagon, focusing on one of the nearby robot loaders. The beams widened and sliced the robot into pieces. Bursts of hot gas jetted from each incision, and molten metal dripped to the floor, quickly hardening in the extreme cold.

Chaca nodded. "Nicely done, sir. Let's move out."

Ryder trotted ahead. Two of the Amasha followed on his heels, their stubby legs moving rapidly to keep up.

"Your weapons are simple projectile weapons using a magnetic pulse for impetus," Clutep noted. "Once we reach our sanctuary, our adopted home, we can increase their power by 50 percent and perhaps supply sufficient power for the lasers your female technician has suggested."

"That would be most helpful, thank you."

Kari noticed the way Clutep said home. After 2,500 years, their sanctuary had become home. She found it difficult to grasp that even after all that time they still remembered their real home. Exiled for two-and-a-half millennia: How had it affected their metal state? She knew she would be half-mad under similar circumstances. A thought struck her.

"Clutep, how long do your people live?"

"An Amasha in good health and who suffers no accident can live 3,000 of your years. We have spent most of our lives in this place. We do not wish to die here. If I could but see my home world one last time before death, I would go into the Beyond pleased."

"You worship a god?" she asked.

After a long pause, he replied, "We believe someone created this universe and endowed all life with intelligence. Upon death, we become a part of that essence in the Beyond. You believe you were created in your God's image."

Kari was stunned. "How do you know that?"

"The same way I learned your language. I accessed your suit computer."

"I ..." She paused, suddenly embarrassed, as if caught with her hand in the cookie jar.

"Is that not permissible?" he asked.

"No, no, that is all right. It's just that I had personal information in my log."

"That we ignored. We respect individual privacy."

"Thank you."

She did not want her personal ramblings concerning her feelings for Hitochi to affect Clutep's judgment. She did not know if Amasha developed personal relationships the same as humans. In fact, she knew nothing about them. She realized she was missing a once-in-a-lifetime opportunity to study a living alien species, rather than guessing about a dead one.

Clutep's sex, for one thing. She had referred to Clutep as male only because of the timber of his voice, which was mechanical in origin and inconclusive.

"Clutep, are you male or female?"

"Amasha are intersexual. I believe hermaphroditic is an archaic term you once used. We are capable of becoming either sex at different stages in our development, depending on preference or necessity. Presently, I am male, but I have been both sexes many times."

"Do you have children here?"

After a long pause, he replied, "We had no wish to bear young in such a place. That has haunted us more than anything else, the lack of young ones. If we do not return to our home world, our genetic lines will fade from our racial history. We will ... cease to exist."

Kari understood now what driving force kept Clutep and his people from giving up after 2,500 years of exile. The Amasha were an intriguing race, well worth the long journey to the Band to discover. However, it would all mean nothing if they did not succeed. No one on Earth would ever learn of them, and the governments of Earth, faced with problems of their own, might never send a second expedition if the first failed to return.

The Amasha led the group through a maze of corridors until they reached a deserted and deteriorating part of the Band. Kari wondered if it was near where she had awakened. Piles of strange machinery cannibalized for parts lay scattered in abandoned, dust-filled rooms. She worried about the number of footprints they left in the dust until she noticed one of the Amasha following the group using a device to spray a thin layer of dust over their tracks, hiding their passage. Such techniques had kept them alive in a hostile environment since the era of the early Roman Empire on Earth.

After several weary kilometers that plagued Kari's aching calf muscles, the corridor they followed ended at a rusty wall of the same dullish gray material she had seen the drones salvaging earlier. She stopped, confused, but the Amasha continued walking straight into and through the wall. She felt a moment of trepidation as she followed them. A static charge caused the hairs on her arm to dance even through the suit. On the other side of the camouflage wall lay a large open space illuminated by a glowing orb floating near the ceiling 200 meters overhead. She felt its warmth on the exterior of her suit, as her suit heaters shut down to compensate.

"The wall is a façade," she said, intrigued by the Amasha's ingenuity.

"Yes," Clutep answered. "We created the false wall and surrounded this area with a force field. The drones do not venture here lest it interferes with their communications, and the Shutaish have not discovered us. The force field retains our atmosphere. I regret our atmosphere will not sustain you. It contains less oxygen than to which you are accustomed and a higher concentration of carbon dioxide. Our bodies are able to concentrate the sparse oxygen, and symbiotic microbes within certain organs break down the carbon dioxide into oxygen and carbon monoxide. We will provide a space where you may safely remove your suits and bathe."

"Bathe?" she asked, her voice trembling with excitement. She had not bathed in five months, only quick, low-spray showers to conserve water that never left her feeling completely clean.

"Yes, we have ample water. We recycle it very efficiently."

The interior space was not as open as she first thought. Upon closer inspection, she saw hundreds of small tubes running from the ceiling to the walls and the floor, creating a loose web. The tubes crossed each other and joined at intervals, forming tear-shaped nodes. Some lines formed twisting bundles that ran from ceiling to floor like pillars. Some draped like beaded curtains. At first, she thought the tubes moved, but then saw an amber liquid coursing through them, pulsing like a heartbeat.

Several buildings constructed of metal salvaged from the Band lined one wall. Each was neat and colorful, offering a stark contrast to the usual drab black and gray of the Band. Two large, semi-translucent vats positioned in the center of the space directly beneath the artificial sun held pools of the amber liquid circulating through the spider web of tubing – The Amasha culture vats. Beside them, a vertical array of shallow trays reaching almost to the ceiling contained a variety of leafy plants. The trays moved from floor to ceiling by means of a conveyor system, rotating slowly to allow each plant maximum exposure to the artificial sunlight. Water dripped into each tray as it rose toward the ceiling. She estimated the culture vats and hydroponics garden were capable of producing far more food than required by the number of Amasha present, a grim testament to the losses they had suffered over the centuries.

A score of Amasha stood in small groups staring at the visitors with little concern or surprise. Kari assumed Clutep had informed them of their coming. She had only speculated at the Amasha's size and shape based on their bulky environmental suits. All her presumptions had been wrong.

The Amasha were not bipedal, as she had presumed. They were quadrupeds, walking on two pairs of closely set, spindly, multi-jointed legs. Their multi-jointed arms ended in short, stubby, four-fingered hands. Individuals varied, but each was slightly shorter than she was, and covered with a shiny pelt of fine, dark hair except on their faces, which varied in color from light brown to cream. Their mouths were oval, lipless openings set beneath a wide, squat nose. Their ears were long flaps draping along their short necks to their shoulders.

On first glance, they appeared brutish, but she knew that was her human bias comparing the Amasha to Earth apes, to which they bore only the slightest resemblance. However, their expressive eyes set them apart. Large, round, and ablaze with color, they looked like jewels. She saw several individuals whose eyes changed color from light purple to a dark crimson. She wondered if eye color fluctuations played a part in Amasha communication.

She counted more abandoned dwellings than occupied ones. "Is this all that are left of your people?" she asked, saddened by what she saw.

"A few of our people are patrolling other areas in the Han, but, yes, we few are all that remain."

She detected no sense of loss or regret as he spoke, but she might have missed some subtle nuance of language. Death had become a part of their culture, a sad testimony for a race whose individuals lived thousands of years. Clutep removed his suit. Like most of the Amasha, he wore a one-piece tunic of a coppery iridescent material underneath it. Two Amasha approached him, bowed slightly, and spoke rapidly in a language with many undulating whistles and sharp clicks. They took his suit when they left.

Through a translation device clipped to his tunic, he said, "We must alter your weapons and continue our journey. Our patrols report many repair drones moving anti-spinward toward your ship. We must hurry if you wish to warn them."

She reported Clutep's warning to Hitochi and Sergeant Chaca. Chaca was gravely concerned.

"We're over 2,000 clicks from the ship. I hope our suit coms will reach that far," he confided.

"We can improve their range with a signal booster," Clutep suggested.

"Will it take long?"

"Long enough for you to rest. My people are providing a suitable structure for you to disrobe. It is near the pools. We will enclose the pools in a force field to contain a suitable atmosphere for your pleasure."

He led them to a low structure at the edge of the occupied buildings. The door was thick and heavy, salvaged from a ship's airlock. Unlike the stark exterior, the interior was alive with color. Each wall sported a different hue of vivid reds and yellows. Artificial sunlight cascaded through a skylight in the roof, bathing the room in soft amber light. Low tables flanked cushioned benches gathered near the center of the room. Odd metal pieces she finally concluded were kinetic sculptures sat scattered randomly throughout the room, swaying or vibrating softly.

"I will leave you now," Clutep said. "It will take only moments for the atmosphere to adapt to your requirements." He pointed to a niche in the wall. "Place your suits there, and we will modify them. The pools are behind this building. I will return shortly. If your engineer or the female technician would assist us, it would make the work proceed more quickly."

"I'll go," Collins said. "After all, the laser was my idea."

Hitochi nodded. "I bow to your technical prowess. I am more acquainted with ship engines and systems."

Kari smiled. Hitochi was being gracious. One of his jobs was to maintain the lasers on the *Worthington*. He recognized that Collins needed something to do.

Before Clutep left, she asked, "Are you the leader here?"

He shifted his body in what she took to be a nervous fashion. "We maintain our ship's chain of command. I am *Taima*, ship's third officer. Our captain and second-in-command are dead. I now lead."

His voice, even through the translator, conveyed a sense of sadness and regret and perhaps a touch of unworthiness to lead the Amasha. Clutep felt he was above his station. He left in silence. She felt sorry for him. The Amasha had led a tragic existence for too long to contemplate.

Shedding her environment suit was a joy akin to ecstasy. Hours sealed inside the confining suit took their toll on the more delicate parts of her body. The flexible joints chaffed her skin, and her body odor had become unbearable. The air provided by the Amasha was sweet and clean with the faint sweet scent of some unknown alien plant. She stretched her arms and legs to relieve her aching joints. She winced when she probed a large purple bruise on her side left from her encounter with the Shutaish. She noticed Hitochi and one of the marines watching her intently and felt a tingle of excitement that they found her worth observing, especially with Deidre present.

Deidre had dropped her suit at her feet and sat on one of the benches with her knees tucked under her chin. Even in her sweaty one-piece ship's jumper, her exquisite body poked though in all the right places, but the men avoided eye contact with her. Her entire body posture was an unsubtle warning to back off. She did not speak or make eye contact with anyone. Kari picked up Deidre's vid camera and scanned the room with it, as well as the exterior through a transparent window in the wall. Most of the Amasha went about their daily business, tending to the crops, repairing the buildings, but several toiled over the flechette weapons on a large table outside one building.

"I'm not sure I trust these folks," Ryder said. "They're too damn friendly."

"They're asking for a ride home," Hitochi answered. "They're putting on a good face for us."

"Good face. That's a riot. Did you get a good look at them?" Holmes remarked.

"That's real funny, Holmes," Ryder replied. "One of the women told me she wouldn't hump you on a bet."

"Enough!" Chaca cut in. "Our lives and the lives of our shipmates are in these people's hands. Show some respect."

Kari felt safe in the Amasha compound, but soon, they would be traversing parts of the Band teeming with both robotic repair drones and the Shutaish. The Shura knew in what part of the Band they were hiding. Eventually, it would find them. To the humans, it made little difference where they went. They had been under attack since arriving, but by leaving their safe abode, the Amasha were betting their futures on an alliance with humans in an attempt to escape their centuries of exile.

To have come so far and learned so little about the Band and the Architects had become her worst nightmare. Everything she had learned about the Aishaitia had come from the Amasha. She had never conceived that the Aishaitia would be willing to kill to protect their chance for eternal life. Instead of elaborate traps, they had left semi-sentient watchdogs, but the watchdogs had grown aware and rebelled. Even the sane part of the Shura's mind could not protect them.

A large door with a window on the rear wall overlooked a series of small pools of clear water. Water flowed over the sides of the tiered pools and gathered in the larger pool at the base. Plants, some exotically alien, others closely resembling Earth flora, enclosed the secluded pools.

"I'm going for a swim," she said, and rushed out the door.

She shed her shorts and T-shirt as she ran, leaving on only her bra and panties out of modesty. She did not hesitate at the edge but plunged into the pool headfirst. She surfaced smiling. The water was cool, invigorating, and felt wonderful against her skin. As she backstroked across the pool, Holmes, Ryder, and Hitochi jumped in naked, producing three large splashes. Holmes laughed like a kid. She tried not to stare at them, though her curiosity forced her to sneak a couple of quick glimpses.

Kirkurk, as stiff and reserved as always, stood at the edge but did not go in. He looked on the frolicking in disdain. Sergeant Chaka and Sung remained on the sidelines as well, but both men wore smiles, and Chaca yelled to Holmes about his swimming technique.

"You swim like a giraffe. Are you afraid to get your head wet?"

"I'm a river rat," Holmes yelled back. "I grew up swimming in Davidson Creek, a muddy little stream in Oxford, Mississippi. You had to keep one eye open for water moccasins and the other eye open for snapping turtles. I was 16 before I went to Sardis Lake and saw real clean water." He splashed water at Chaca. "Hell, this is like heaven."

Holmes stopped talking. Kari glanced up and saw him staring at Deidre, as she walked to the edge of the pool and slide in the water, barely producing a ripple. She was as naked as the others. When she surfaced a few seconds later, her short, curly black hair clung to her head in tight ringlets. She ignored the leering stares from the men, including to Kari's dismay, Hitochi. For one brief moment, Kari wished she had the courage to strip naked in the presence of the others, but feared even naked, she would not attract as much attention as Deidre received.

She did not have time to luxuriate in the comforting water. Lacking soap, she stood beneath one of the waterfalls and rubbed her skin vigorously, removing most of the layers of perspiration and grime. She wished she had a sandy beach to lie in the sun and the time to enjoy it, but they were on a mission. With a loud sigh, she heaved herself out of the pool. A machine at the pool's edge blew a stream of air to dry her body. She eyed her dirty shorts and shirt with disgust but donned them and returned to the building.

Knowing it could be hours before she was out of her suit again, she took a ration bar from her bag to eat and drank some tepid water, wishing it were a cold glass of tea. As she studied one of the pieces of Amashan art, a series of interconnected rods swirling upward and spreading outward at the top, Clutep and Amanda Collins returned. Collins took the two crude lasers she carried, set them on one of the tables, and began making adjustments. Clutep noticed Kari admiring the art.

"It represents a *tichka*, a plant on my home world similar to one of your trees, but many hundreds of your meters tall. Twice each year, yellow flowers blossom along the trunk." He paused, as if the reminiscing disturbed him. "Your weapons are ready, as are your suits. The others are bringing them now. We must leave."

Kari noticed the urgent tone in his voice. With a deep sense of dread, she asked, "What's happening?"

"The Shutaish have located this place. A scout entered through the wall. We killed it, but it is certain to have informed the others. They will come soon."

"You have to leave your home?" she asked, heartbroken for the Amasha.

Clutep made a body shudder she interpreted as a sigh or shrug. "It was always our intent to leave this place eventually. Now, success or failure, we cannot return. I will inform the others."

As Clutep walked away, she thought, *Now, their fate is tied irrevocably to ours. Helping us might have doomed them all.* An overwhelming sense of responsibility fell upon her. *I cannot let them die.* She did not know how she could save them, or herself for that matter, but she had to try.

17

Captain Sidthuri called a rest period. They had been trudging down endless black passageways for hours. A crippling exhaustion had set in. It shone in their lifeless eyes and in their vacuous expressions. Each expected an attack at any moment, and tensions ran high. Such an on-the-edge apprehension drained them. He doubted their ability to continue. As he lowered himself to the floor, his body spoke to him in loud whispers demanding his attention. Working out in the ship's gym had kept him physically fit, but life aboard ship had not prepared him for long marches.

His broken ribs did not improve his mood. With each agonized breath, his side throbbed so badly it made him dizzy. He wanted badly to close his eyes and sleep, hoping when he awoke it all would have been a bad dream. The only thing that kept him going was seeing two of his crew on stretchers. The bouncing journey would have been agony for them as well. He could not complain.

He scanned the faces of his people, exiles now. He was certain many of them would have preferred remaining with the shuttles, seeking any sense of security from a familiar object, but if they were on the Band to stay, they must locate some safe place with an atmosphere. They couldn't wander dark corridors for 40 years like Moses in the desert.

After half an hour, he pushed himself from the floor. Hot fingers of pain raced up his side. He bit his lip to keep from screaming, and started walking again. The others, however reluctantly, followed. He set a grueling pace. They had travelled only half a kilometer, when a short, frightened scream rent the quiet solitude of the march. He turned to see Daci Cray, the female ensign, staring at a quivering dark bulge in the wall beside her. As she watched, the bulge emerged fully from the wall, becoming an amorphous, ebony shadow hovering a few centimeters above the floor. The dark apparition had no eyes, but it observed them nevertheless.

Two marines moved to flank her, their weapons aimed at the strange specter. With a shudder too quick to follow, its shape changed, becoming more solid, like a black crystal cloud. Thin, lithe tendrils whipped out from the creature's body, swirling scimitars dancing in the air. In an instant, they sliced into both marines. Without a scream, they crumpled to the floor. The frozen fear became a blind panic, as others fired their flechette rifles. The creature morphed again, became an opaque mist. A Navy corpsman fell, pierced through the heart by a flechette dart that passed through the creature's body as if it were an illusion.

Illusion or not, the creature was substantial enough to kill his men. Seeing the futility of their weapons against such a creature, Sidthuri yelled, "Hold your fire!"

The creature remained stationary for several moments before floating to the dead bodies. A mouth filled with tiny barbed teeth appeared in the head, as well as two large, round eyes darker than the creature's body with swirling crimson flecks within them. A long, tubular tongue rolled from the mouth into the puddle of blood. The creature, satisfied no one could harm it, sucked the spilled blood from the floor, and then hovered over the bodies, draining them of their blood.

Disgusted by the grisly scene, Ensign Cray drew her knife and lunged at the creature. The blade sliced through the creature's pulsating tongue, severing it and spraying Cray's face with blood. Before she could deliver a second blow, the creature expanded like a black sail, enveloped her, and disappeared through the wall.

For a moment, Sidthuri could not move, frozen not in fear, but in disbelief and shock, wondering how such a thing could be possible. The wall was solid. If there were a hidden door, the device he carried would have opened it. He walked over the creature's tongue lying beside the bodies, but before he could examine it, it evaporated into a black mist that quickly dissipated. He checked the bodies of the two marines. Their withered flesh confirmed that most of the fluids were missing, consumed by the shadow creature.

"Was that an Architect?" someone asked.

He had wondered the same thing but had difficulty believing the horrific vampiric creature could be of the legendary race that had built the artifacts and constructed the Band. If it were true, they had fallen into a despicable state of degeneracy. He shook his head. "I don't know what they were." He looked at the walls around them with a new sense of peril. "We have to leave this place."

"What about them?" one of the civilian technicians asked, pointing to the three dead bodies.

"We'll have to leave them." It crippled his soul to say it. Leaving dead comrades behind was an anathema to him, almost as he was committing a cardinal sin, but he had the living to consider. "We can't carry them. Everyone's too exhausted."

The suddenness of the attack astonished him almost as much as its inhuman brutality. Four people lost in as many minutes. He now held out no hope for either team he had sent into the Band. If they faced such creatures, they were surely dead – more deaths to weigh on his conscience. He been in over a dozen battles, on both the winning and the losing side, but after the ignoble fate of the *Worthington* and the horrific attack in the corridor, he felt he dishonored his uniform by wearing it. He led, but he had no idea of where they were going. He commanded, but did not feel worthy of such a responsibility.

Kilometers passed with no further attacks, but he did not relax. It felt as if the journey were the mission, not the search for some impossible sanctuary. Six exhausting hours after abandoning ship, the corridor emptied into a chamber so vast the telephoto filter on his visor detected no far wall. The ceiling disappeared into the darkness overhead. Vague shapes faded in and out of focus as he tried various filters on his facemask. The only thing of which he was certain was that the room had a breathable atmosphere. *Thanks goodness for small favors.*

"Lights," he ordered. Two sailors stepped forward with portable work lights. Each self-contained light produced over 2,000 lumens, but in the vast darkness of the enormous space, they looked like two fireflies in a field. Their harsh glow illuminated rows of metal bins stacked atop one another resembling castle ramparts that extended from their position as far as the light extended. The mostly empty chamber could have held ten times the number of bins present.

"It looks like a warehouse," Bonner Fitzhugh, the civilian structural engineer, remarked.

"Whatever it is," he said, "we need rest. We have light and atmosphere. Rest two hours, and then take a team to examine the bins. There might be something of use in them."

He was just guessing. The bins could contain any number of things necessary to maintain the Band but of no value to them. Most of all, they needed food and water, neither of which they would likely find on the Band. Their portable still could manufacture water by reducing potassium hydroxide with an acid to release hydrogen gas through a reaction and combining it with atmospheric oxygen; however, production was limited. Anything that might increase production could save their lives.

Food would soon become a problem. The loss of the fourth shuttle had reduced their supplies by half. After they exhausted their present supplies, they would starve. They had brought as much food concentrate as they could carry, but it required water to rehydrate it, placing a further strain on the still. The one thing they had in abundance was extra darts for the flechette rifles and ammunition for the 7.62mm rifles, neither of which were effective against the shadow creature.

He addressed the remaining crewmembers. "We can go no further. This place will be home for a while. We will cook a nourishing meal and get some much-needed sleep. Later, I'll send out search teams to explore the area. In the meantime, pick a spot and make yourself comfortable."

"What about that shadow thing?" one of the crew asked. "Do we post guards?"

Sidthuri sighed. He understood their fear, but their response was irrational. "Our rifles are ineffective against it. I'll take two volunteers armed with the lasers to stand watch for drones. Those, we can defend against." *Unless there are hundreds,* he reminded himself. "Maybe the lasers will stop that shadow creature," he added.

"You expect us to sleep after what we saw?" one incredulous technician asked.

"You'll sleep," he said, looking at the group. "You're all too exhausted not to. It's best to get all the sleep you can. We don't know what to expect later."

Despite his fatigue, he could not sleep. His aching side kept him awake. *No,* he thought, *not my side, my conscience.* He listened to the soft snores of those few who managed to sleep, and to the muted conversations of those who could not. His decisions were not universally popular, but he was the captain, and obedience to authority was part of the crew's training. However, the few civilians were under no such constraints. They whispered in conspiratorial tones about dividing the meager supplies and examining the Band, perhaps conversing with who or what controlled the massive structure in an attempt to reason with it. That, he would not tolerate. He decided to quash that idea immediately. He summoned Fitzhugh, who seemed to be the ringleader of the rebellion.

"You wanted to see me, Captain?" he asked.

Sidthuri had taken an immediate instinctive dislike to Bonner Fitzhugh when they first met, and nothing Fitzhugh had said or done during the entire trip to the Band or since had changed his mind. Like Sung and Kirkurk, Fitzhugh was highly opinionated and outspoken on subjects outside his expertise of structural engineering, but unlike the biologist and archaeologist, he had no charm, grace, or redeeming social qualities to offset his disagreeable character. He grated on Sidthuri's nerves, and he had avoided the engineer whenever possible. However, now he needed him.

"Have you had the opportunity to examine the bins?"

"Not yet. I've been discussing our situation with my colleagues. We
–"

"As captain, any discussion of the situation will include me. Now,
take a few people and examine the bins. Our needs are many, and our
resources few. If you find anything remotely valuable that might
contribute to alleviating our current needs, please notify me."

"We think you acted too hastily in using a *Prometheus* missile to
enter the Band. The Band controller took your act of wanton destruction
as a hostile gesture. That is why it sent the robot drones to attack or to
secure the ship."

"Mr. Fitzhugh, one of my crewmembers was attacked and taken
away during the night. I lost communication with a team sent into the
Band, invited we thought by the controller. Nine people, six of them
your colleagues. It was imperative that we discover what was inside the
Band and if it was hostile. All of that is moot. Seven more personnel
have now disappeared, and the *Worthington* was attacked." His voice
became more strident as his anger rose to the surface. "I lost four people
just a short time ago in a very gruesome manner. I think the question of
hostility is settled."

"It most certainly is not. You attacked the Band, and it retaliated. I
think an attempt should be made to contact the controller and explain the
situation."

"Your thoughts and wishes do not concern me, Mr. Fitzhugh. You
will take some people and make a thorough examination of the bins. You
will do so now."

Fitzhugh was not through. His voice rose in volume. "Or what,
Captain? Throw me in the brig? I'm not in your Navy. I am a civilian. I
will not –"

Fitzhugh stumbled backwards as Sidthuri lurched awkwardly to his
feet. His pain made him angry enough to slap the man down, but he
refrained from physical violence. "You will do as I say, civilian or not.
We don't have a brig, but I can handcuff you and stake you out like a
tethered sacrificial goat in case that shadow creature returns. You can
discuss your concerns with it. Now, you can be useful to me that way, or
you can examine the bins and report to me in two hours. Do I make
myself clear?"

Fitzhugh's expression was one of barely suppressed rage, but he
cleared his throat and replied, "Yes."

Sidthuri nodded. "Good. If you make any attempt to contact
anything or anyone in this place without my permission, I will put a
bullet through your brain." He hesitated as Fitzhugh remained standing

there. "You may go now," he snapped. The chastised structural engineer trotted off, eager to get away. Sidthuri smiled at the retreating man's back. Intimidating Fitzhugh had perked him up. "Smarmy bastard."

Unable to sleep, Sidthuri made his rounds through the group as a show of presence, hoping to give them confidence. Most looked desolated, defeated in mind and in spirit. A few moved and stacked smaller bins to form walls around them, delineating their personal space, as if such obstacles would protect them from the shadow creature. It was an instinctive nesting gesture, but he did not want them to be more comfortable. He wanted them rested. They could not remain where they were.

By his reckoning, they were beneath the nearest City and close to the Dome. If Lieutenant Hitochi and Kirkurk's party had survived, they would be nearby. Perhaps they had learned something useful that would help both groups survive. Later, after they had rested, he would search for them, while continuing to move deeper into the Band. When in enemy territory, it was important to keep the enemy confused by doing the unexpected. The Band's caretaker or the Architects themselves had proven a threat. That made them a threat to Earth. As did any spaceship or large structure, the Band had vulnerable areas, locations vital to its function. His intention was to find a way to destabilize the Band. Gravity would do the rest, breaking it apart and removing it as a threat to Earth and her colonies. The lives of the crew of the *Worthington* were a small price to pay for the safety of billions.

He knew Fitzhugh and the other civilians would object, but his sworn duty was to protect his home world, not an artifact created by a species that had been dead for 500 million years. The threat outweighed any possible discoveries they might make.

He stopped to grab a bowl of soup from a pot cooking over a propane burner. As a military man, he had learned to eat whenever the opportunity presented itself. He had lived on liquid suit rations for days at a time, and the monotony became boring very quickly. The soup was thick and hearty with just a little kick from some chili peppers.

"Good soup," he told the sailor who had cooked it.

"Thank you, sir. It's my mama's recipe. Just a little of this and dash of that. I could do better with some fresh produce."

He eyed the young man's face trying to place him. "You're not one of the cooks. You're McNash. You work in the A-gang."

McNash grinned. "Yes, sir, Damage Controlman Kyle McNash. If it's dirty or greasy, it's my job to fix it." He paused. "None of the cooks made it."

"You're doing a good job, McNash."

"Thank you, sir. We're not going home, are we, sir?"

He had never lied to his crew, even when a little untruth might make things easier. His crew deserved better than that. "I don't know, son. We're in a bad fix and a long way from home, but we can't just sit here and wait to die. The Architects, or whatever they left here to run this place, declared war on the *Worthington,* on Earth, and her colonies. They killed our comrades and destroyed my ship. I won't take that lying down."

"Yes, sir, but …" The sailor paused.

"But what, son?"

His gaze fixed on Sidthuri with an intensity that betrayed the sailor's turmoil. "What are we going to do?" He looked around the cavernous space. "We don't even know where we are, do we?" he asked.

"We know everything around us is alien, and anything we meet means us harm. What more do we need to know?"

The sailor smiled, but it was a forced smile, a façade to hide his fear. "I guess you're right, sir. You can count on me."

"I know I can, son. See to it that everyone eats until he or she is full. Once we have rested, we have to move on."

The sailor stirred his soup with a wooden spoon. "I'll pass the word that the second helpings lamp is lit."

Sidthuri walked away a bit more encouraged. His crew was stepping up and doing whatever needed doing. He had to bring his A-game and do the same.

18

Kari watched the Amasha load their meager possessions onto five small, motorized wheeled conveyances and felt sorry for them. This was no evacuation, no temporary inconvenience. They would never return to the spot they had called home for 2,500 years. If the Amasha and the humans did not escape the Band together, both species would have to locate a new safe refuge, if such a place existed. The humans' arrival had stirred the hornet's nest, and the Amasha were paying the price.

They carried only the essentials – food, water, air, and weapons. Everything else they had built or accumulated over their two-and-a-half millennia exile, they abandoned. When the repair drones located the place, they would dismantle it all and salvage it for later reuse. Their art would become raw material for the Band. She wondered how long it had taken them to construct the pools and fill them with water or create the artificial sun they used for illumination and for crop production. Such losses could be irreplaceable.

The Amasha preferred walking. In spite of their short legs, the Amasha pushed the carts along at the rapid clip of eight kph and kept pace. Five Amasha operated the five transportation carts containing their possessions. They had assigned three carts for the humans to ride, for which Kari was delighted. Her brief swim had helped, but her legs ached from all the walking she had done since entering the Band. She felt a twinge of guilt wondering if the Amasha had left any personal belongings behind to make space for her people. She hated to think they had discarded their beautiful art so that she might ride in comfort.

The small caravan left the hidden sanctuary without fanfare – nine humans and 38 Amasha – all that remained from a crew of 300. It surprised her that none of the Amasha glanced back as most humans would do, but then realized they could view their lost home through the screens in their suits. She didn't know how deeply leaving affected them, but believed any sentient species would experience some sense of loss at such an undertaking.

Hitochi and Sergeant Chaca's spirits had lifted when Amanda Collins had presented them with two functional lasers to add to the Amasha's arsenal against the Shutaish. The lasers were crude, but thanks to a few Amasha technical advances about which Kari understood very little, they were surprisingly efficient. Using light emitting diodes stripped from redundant electrical equipment and the clear crystal rods they had discovered at the transportation depot, Collins had tuned the lasers' output to 30-kilowatts, on par with the Amasha suit weapons.

The Amasha had also enhanced the magnetic coil launchers of the human's flechette rifles as promised; replacing the power supplies with Amasha designed ones, making them more effective against the robotic repair drones. She reminded herself that in spite of their weapons, they remained few against an almost unlimited number of drones and an unknown number of Shutaish.

She noticed the odd expression on Chaca's face. She called up his suit ID and spoke to him. "Are you all right, Sergeant?"

He keyed his internal camera and his image popped up on his screen. He was smiling. "Yes, I'm fine. I was just thinking about the Amasha."

"They are an amazing race," she said.

"You saw the circular pit in their compound?"

She had seen it but paid it scant attention. "Yes, why?"

"The Amasha informed me they use it in some religious ceremonies. I find that a bit of synchronicity."

She couldn't follow his logic. "In what way?"

"I am a Hopi. We use *kivas*, round pits in the ground, for religious ceremonies. I find it odd that the Amasha have the same rites." He hesitated, started to say something more, and then closed his mouth. After a few seconds, he decided to continue. "Those culture tank tubes, they reminded me of a spider web."

"Yes, they did," she agreed, unsure where he was going.

"In Hopi legend, *Koyangwuiti*, Spider Woman, led my people from the Third World to the Fourth, Earth. She taught my people to weave."

Kari smiled at him. "Perhaps the Amasha and we are not so different after all," she suggested.

"You may be right. I ... I trust them a little more than I did."

It was a difficult admission for the first sergeant. "I'm glad. I trusted them from the beginning."

"They think you are special."

His statement caught her off guard and embarrassed her. "Special? I don't know about that."

"Come, Miss Stone. You're the reason they're helping us. You discovered how to enter the Band and unlocked some of its secrets. You escaped from a wraith. That seems quite stretch for an archaeologist."

"I'm … I'm just trying to survive."

He stared at her a moment before replying, "Aren't we all?"

As they drove down dark, deserted corridors, she considered Chaca's implications about her, wondering if her link with the Shura mind fell under his definition of synchronicity. Unlike her, he considered it more than mere coincidence that she could do what the others could not. A dark depression settled over her, and she could not shake the profound sense of loss and angst. The intensity brought her close to tears. At first, she thought she had somehow linked to the Amasha's minds, fed by their anguish at leaving. As the anxiety and melancholy increased, she realized its source was more alien than even the Amasha; however, it seemed too intelligent and not sufficiently predatory for the bloodthirsty Shutaish.

The Shura.

Her mental contact with the controlling entity during her attempts to understand the controls for the doors, the planetary viewer, and the tram had exposed her to its consciousness. She had felt it then, but only as vague sense of unease and inadequacy amplified by the ebony wall. A coldly disturbing thought struck her. What if it could influence her? What if it could find the others using her mind? As she studied the strange emotions, she discovered them not directed at her. She was merely a receptacle, a receiver picking up the fringes of a mind in turmoil. The Shura mind, torn between welcoming and testing visitors to the Band, and protecting its frozen charges at all costs, had battled itself for half a billion years. Both halves were now insane, irreconcilably.

The dread became almost palpable. The farther they went, the stronger the feeling became. She could not pinpoint the exact cause, but she knew it had something to do with the humans. She confessed her trepidation to Hitochi using his suit frequency for privacy. She did not want to alarm the others if her fears proved unfounded.

"Something's wrong. I can feel the Shura mind crying out. I think it has something to do with the *Worthington*. We must hurry."

Hitochi studied her face through her helmet visor. She wondered if his look of concern was one of sympathy for the crew of the *Worthington* or concern for her sanity.

"Can you tell me about it?"

She shook her head, unable to put it into words. "I don't know. It's a kind of anguish at what it has done or perhaps what has been done to it."

"Have you felt this … contact before?"

"Maybe," she admitted reluctantly, "when I touched the wall and concentrated to open the door to the tram. I didn't understand what it was at that time. It's much stronger now. It frightens me," she admitted.

"Should we tell the others?"

"No, they'll think I'm crazy." She wondered if she were.

Holmes, who drove the transport the three of them rode, glanced over his shoulder. "Is there something I should know?" he asked over the common com frequency.

She quickly added his suit to create a three-way conversation. "What do you mean?"

"I mean, I see a lot of gestures and facial expressions but no sound. Unless you two are talking dirty, that makes me wonder what you're talking about. If you are talking dirty, please count me in," he added with a smile that quickly faded. "But judging by your expressions, I think it was a bit more serious than small talk."

Kari reddened. "Nothing dirty. I just wanted Ken's opinion on a matter."

"If it affects my ass, I want to know. There's some serious shit going down here, and I ain't feelin' the love, if you know what I mean?"

She glanced at Hitochi, who nodded. "I can sense the Shura, the Band's controlling entity. It's very upset."

"Yeah? Well, me too. So what?"

"I think it's doing something to the *Worthington*."

Holmes expression became pensive. "You mean our ride back home? That is some serious shit." He looked down at the control of the cart. "Won't this thing go any faster? I don't want to walk home."

"We should inform Sergeant Chaca," Hitochi said. "This may change our plans."

While Hitochi switched to the open com frequency and informed the others of Kari's revelations, she shut off her radio and concentrated on the Shura mind. She needed more details if they were to make an informed judgment call. As she allowed her mind to follow the threads of contact, the regret broadcast by the Shura intensified. She hesitated going any deeper; opening her mind to further invasion for fear the schizophrenic artificial intelligence would consume her mind.

Brief flashes of images swept through her mind so quickly she could not decipher them. She had no frame of reference. They appeared to be views from locations all over the Band, merging until she could not tell where one ended and the next began: views of the Band from a great distance, views of the chasm or boulevard, dark rooms and even darker corridors, and warehouses filled with stacked bins. She saw shapes and colors that shifted in a dizzying kaleidoscope of patterns. Suddenly, rows of crystal coffins lining an endless wall flashed into her mind – the Architects in their eternal repose! She could not discern their shape through the ice-rimmed lids. She wanted to hit pause and gaze at the creatures of her legend, but the Shura swept her onward, deeper.

She passed through layers of ebony material into metal, then stone, the very bowels of the Band. Large caverns riddled the heart of the Band, excavated for reuse elsewhere. With no more raw material within the vicinity of Cyclops, and no means at hand to collect more from elsewhere, the Shura had begun a process of cannibalizing parts of the Band that inevitably had led to the weakening of the entire structure. The Band was crumbling from within, like a shiny apple with a rotten core.

The blur of images snapped to an abrupt halt so quickly her mind lost focus. When the image cleared, she saw the *Worthington*. Shuttles raced away, as thousands of robotic repair drones surrounded the ship, slicing and drilling into its hull. Seconds later, the entire ship disappeared in a dazzling fireball so massive it blinded her. When her vision cleared, an enormous gaping wound in the Band lay where the ship had rested. The *Worthington* was gone.

Pain swept through her pumped into her mind by the Shura. She didn't know if it was anguish at the gaping wound in the Band's outer hull or regret for the murder of her friends and colleagues. The pain became a flame burning her from the inside. Tears ran down her cheeks like acid etching her flesh. The pain became unbearable. She passed out.

* * * *

She regained consciousness staring into Hitochi's eyes. He wasn't wearing his helmet. That struck her as odd. As she lifted her head, she saw the others gathered around her. Their faceplates were unsealed. A few had removed their helmets. Clutep stood nearby moving from one double-leg to the other in obvious agitation.

"Are you all right?" Hitochi asked, his concern visible in his eyes.

She nodded her head. "Where are we?"

"The Amasha found a small room that produced oxygen. We needed to get your helmet off to wipe off the blood."

"Blood?" she asked, failing to understand. She tasted blood in her mouth and probed her lip with her tongue. "Did I bite my lip?"

"Yes, but what concerned me more was the fact you were crying tears of blood." Despite his concern, Hitochi grinned at her, relieved she was okay. "What happened?"

Everything came rushing back to her. Her lips trembled as she fought not to cry out. "The *Worthington* is gone."

"Gone?" Kirkurk asked. "You mean they left us here?"

She shook her head. "No, it's gone, vaporized."

"What?" Deidre yelled. Her face paled and her voice cracked. "God, no!"

Kari watched Deidre's world fall apart. All hope of going home was now lost. Realization that she would remain on the Band the rest of her life settled on Deidre like a judge's pronouncement of death. The life disappeared from her eyes as she withdrew into herself, becoming smaller in her excursion suit.

"What happened to it?" Hitochi asked, shaking her slightly to get her attention.

Kari dismissed Deidre's meltdown. She was fighting off her own. "Thousands of robot drones were attacking it. I saw shuttles leave." She paused to swallow. "The ship exploded in a massive fireball. It vaporized the hull of the Band."

"How many shuttles?" Chaca asked.

"Two." She shook her head. "No, three," she corrected herself.

"So someone survived," Hitochi said.

Kirkurk leaned over her. "But how many?" he demanded.

Chaca, annoyed by Kirkurk's questioning, pushed him out of the way. "What kind of explosion? Was the light a brilliant silver?"

"Yes, so bright it blinded me."

He nodded. "Someone detonated the *Prometheus* missiles to destroy the robots."

"They destroyed the ship on purpose?" Kirkurk cried, aghast at the idea. "But now we're stranded."

"We were anyway once the drones attacked the ship. At least someone kicked some ass before they went down."

"Oh, how very noble," Kirkurk shot at him. "Death with honor."

"Shut up," Hitochi snapped. "Someone had to stay behind to allow the others to escape. They sacrificed themselves."

Clutep spoke up. "We have failed. Contacting your ship is now moot. Survival is paramount."

"We have to go to the others," Kari said. "We need to all be together."

"They're over 2,000 kilometers from here," Hitochi reminded her. "Without the trams, it would take us weeks to get there. They will be dead by that time. They couldn't have carried enough supplies to last that long."

"If we can reach them, at least we'll all die together," Kari said. It seemed obvious to her that both groups needed to unite. Alone and separate, they were more vulnerable to the drones, the Shutaish, and the inexorable ennui that would arise as realization they could never go home set in.

"What do you mean?" Chaca asked.

"The Band is dying. The repairs drones are dismantling large sections to reinforce other areas. I don't think it is working. The Shura feels threatened."

"Perhaps there is a way to reach your friends," Clutep said.

Kari stared at the Amasha, feeling a surge of hope she badly needed after her mental journey through the Shura's mind. "What do you mean?"

"There is a possible means to escape the Band."

Clutep's revelation stunned her. "You've had a way to leave for 2,500 years, and you didn't take it?"

"We have not attempted it because the risks were too great. Survival was more important. We are a long-lived race," he added, reminding her that time did not mean as much to the Amasha. "We waited for someone in touch with the Shura mind, someone like you, Kari Stone."

With his pronouncement, the entire onus for survival fell on her shoulders. She felt aged before her time. It was too large a burden to bear. She sat in stunned silence as Hitochi grilled Clutep.

"What is this escape craft?" Hitochi asked.

"It is the vessel in which the last of the Aishaitia arrived on the Band. We believe we know its location."

"Can you fly it?"

"We have deciphered a small fragment of Aishaitia technology, but we believe she can."

With a start, Kari realized Clutep meant her. She could not understand his insistence that she somehow was the key to their survival. "Me? I can't fly a ship. I can't understand Architect technology."

"You have made contact with the Shura. It is possible the anguish you felt was projected into your mind by the sane part of the Shura mind, and through you it will assist us in leaving."

"What about the insane part?" she asked, fearing she already knew the answer.

"It will hunt us down and kill us."

"Through me?" she asked, though she knew the answer.

"Yes."

"We'll be sitting ducks marching back to the Dome and the shuttles," Chaca pointed out. "Whether Captain Sidthuri or Lieutenant Igorsky took charge of the evacuation, he would not sit around waiting for another attack. They know your group," he nodded at Kari, "found areas with a breathable atmosphere. They'll try to do the same. We might miss them."

Clutep emitted a short chirp, the equivalent of an Amashan 'ahem.' "There is both a means to get there more quickly and a way to locate your missing companions."

"How?" Kari asked.

"A transportation system separate from the trams along the foundation gravity generator corridor connects areas of the Band. We can reach the vicinity of your companions in a short time."

"How do we find them?" she asked.

"We monitor the Shutaish activity. They will locate and converge on your companions."

Kari shuddered at the thought of the Shutaish closing in on her friends like a pack of hungry wolves. "Let's hope we find them first," she replied.

19

When Kari got her first glimpse of the other transportation system to which Clutep had referred, she thought he was insane. She stared at the five-meter-wide corridor with a black, shimmering floor whose ends vanished in the distance. Though the floor appeared stationary, Clutep assured her it moved at a tremendous rate of speed.

The strip fascinated Hitochi, whose was almost salivating at the opportunity to examine it. "It must be a variation of the Band material, a localized force field somehow induced to flow in two directions simultaneously. Amazing!"

In spite of Hitochi's professional admiration in Architect technology, she was more circumspect.

"How do we use it?" she asked, eyeing the walk with suspicion and dread. Its movement was imperceptible with only a slight blurring of the surface to betray it as anything other than stationary. She had experienced the bullwhip neck crack of sudden acceleration before on carnival rides and did not think she would enjoy the ride. "If it's moving so fast, won't it rip us apart when we set foot on it?"

"It moves slower along the edge to allow the user to match speed with the center. No inertia is involved, so the transition is rapid and unnoticeable. Although, once moving, it is best not to focus too closely on objects as you pass them. The sensation is … unsettling."

He sounded as if he spoke from personal experience, and she trusted his judgment.

"Can the Shutaish attack us while on the slidewalk?" Hitochi asked.

"No. They would have to enter at the exact moment another rider does. Once on the slidewalk, movement is severely limited."

Kari didn't like the idea of standing like a frozen statue. "How do we get off?"

"Near each station, the inertia slackens sufficiently to allow the rider to reach the edge for disembarkation."

Chaca's question pertained to matters more practical. "Can we drive the carts onto the slidewalk?"

"Yes. In this manner, we can use them at our destination."

"Let's do it," Hitochi said. His eyes held the familiar twinkle of excitement Kari remembered.

"I suggest your people remain on the carts," Clutep said. "I will lead the way, while other Amasha follow closely behind."

Without another word, Clutep stepped onto the walkway. He receded quickly until he merged with the main line, and then disappeared altogether in a blur. Kari held her stomach and closed her eyes, as Holmes drove the cart onto the slidewalk. She felt only a slight moment of disorientation. She opened her eyes and wondered if they were moving at all. Marks on the wall in alien script flashed by as quickly as she spotted them, leaving her dizzy. She now understood Clutep's' warning and decided to heed it.

She could not see any of the other carts or Amasha ahead or behind her. Entering at different times spaced them far apart. After 20 minutes, she worried about how she would know the right spot to disembark. Clutep had not mentioned that part of the journey. Imagining it would be a visual clue, she began to stare straight ahead. When a dark spot near the low ceiling grew larger as they approached, she at first suspected it was a sign. Then, it moved, and to her horror, she recognized it as a wraith.

"Look out!" she shouted and pointed ahead.

Hitochi saw and yanked her down to the floor of the cart. Holmes barely had time to duck, as black tendrils of the wraith snapped across the cart, snapping off from the creature's body as they struck with tremendous force. She moved her foot away from one of the wriggling pieces until it dissolved. She thought she heard a distant scream, but it could have been the echo of her scream.

"I thought that Amashan bigwig said the wraiths couldn't attack us here," Holmes said.

"Maybe he thought they couldn't," she suggested. She shared Holmes' concern, but gave the Amasha the benefit of the doubt.

"Well, damn. If the little fellas can be wrong about that, what else are they wrong about?"

She didn't want to dwell on such possibilities. Their safety depended on the Amasha perhaps even more than the Amasha's welfare depended on them. She felt a slight increase of acceleration and realized that instead it was a weakening of the inertia field. Looking ahead, she saw several Amasha standing in a small chamber beside the slidewalk.

"This must be our stop." Holmes edged the cart off slidewalk until it stopped as abruptly as if slamming into a wall. Kari's mind did not have time to warn her body to brace for the imagined impact that did not occur. She felt no physical ill effects from the sudden deceleration, but her mind reeled with the realization of what would have happened to her if the inertia dampening system had failed. She would be a dark smudge on the wall. Her knees began to tremble. She dismounted the cart unsteadily, holding on with one hand.

"We are near the position your ship landed," Clutep informed them. "I have sent two scouts to search for them."

"Did you see the wraith?" she asked.

"No, I saw nothing."

"It tried to grab the cart. Pieces of it broke away."

"Yeah, what about that?" Holmes asked. "I thought you said they wouldn't try."

"The Shutaish have never before made such an attempt. It was surely an act of desperation," he said.

Holmes wasn't satisfied with Clutep's answer. "Desperation. Yeah, man, whatever."

She saw the second cart bearing Chaca, Kirkurk, and Deidre appear out of nowhere and follow the same pattern as their cart until it sat motionless beside theirs. Watching the process was almost as unsettling as experiencing it. Deidre's face was ashen. Her cheeks were puffed out from trying to keep from vomiting. Her sounds of retching came over the common frequency.

In stark contrast, Chaca's face bore a wide smile. "That was quite a ride."

Kirkurk was not as thrilled. "I will not do that again."

The third cart slowed to a stop. Kari sensed immediately something was wrong. Someone was missing. Her breath caught in her throat when she did not see Sung's familiar blue and gray suit.

"Where's Sung?" she asked.

"It got him," Collins said. Her voice cracked as she spoke, and her hands trembled. She turned away and sobbed.

Ryder finished for her. "A wraith popped halfway out of the ceiling. By the time we saw it, it was too late. It snatched him right out of the cart. He vanished." He shook his head slowly. "I couldn't do anything."

The remainder of the Amasha began disembarking the slidewalk. Clutep shared what had happened with them on their frequency. A few minutes later, he said, "None of my people witnessed the event, nor have we heard of such a thing happening previously. It is our opinion that your Doctor Sung would have died instantly from the sudden deceleration. The Shutaish surely perished as well. The exchange of momentum would have sheared its body in half." He looked at the grieving humans. "Does this not give you comfort? His death was quick and painless."

Ryder balled his hand into a fist. He looked as if he were about to strike Clutep. "Sung is dead. Quick or slow, it doesn't matter."

Clutep ignored him. "I believe the Shutaish are desperate and are now hunting in packs. One individual sacrificed itself to obtain nourishment for the others."

Clutep's emotionless description of Sung's death sickened her. "Then they will become even more dangerous."

"It is so."

Chaca stepped between Ryder and Clutep. "We need to find the survivors from the *Worthington* ASAP. Together, we might have a chance of fighting off the Shutaish."

"For how long?" Deidre asked. Her voice was flat and devoid of emotion. Gone was the anger and resentment. Her voice was now rife with acceptance of her imagined fate. Kari hoped she was wrong.

"As long as we have to," Chaca said.

"Your sergeant is correct. If they know we used the Aishaitia transport, they will come searching for us. We must leave."

"We're not going to outrun them on these carts," Holmes said. "They're as slow as molasses."

Kari was sure Clutep did not know what molasses were, but he conferred with his people. Several began unloading bundles from the carts. "We will leave the carts here, carrying only weapons and minimal food and water. If we survive, we may return for them later."

His uncertainty did not bolster Kari's hope. As they prepared to leave, the two Amasha scouts returned and spoke with Clutep at length. He relayed the scouts' report.

"Astleen thinks he has located your people less than three of your kilometers from here. He also saw many Shutaish in the area, searching. We must hurry, but we may still arrive too late to assist them." He paused. "I must warn you that survival is tenuous. If you wish, we can go directly to the Aishaitia ship while the Shutaish are otherwise preoccupied."

Kari understood Clutep's concern. It was cruel and inhuman to abandon friends, but the Amasha weren't human. He did not want to risk his people's lives uselessly in a rescue effort he believed pointless. His reluctance made her wonder if the Amasha placed practicality above emotion.

"Hell, no," Chaca said, voicing his rejection of Clutep's offer. "We won't abandon our people."

"Very well. We will aid you. I did not know if your loyalty to your companions was stronger than your sense of self-preservation. We, too, would make this choice. I fear we will be too late to assist them, but we have agreed to an alliance with you. We will all survive together, or we will all die."

Kari smiled. Clutep's speech had sounded like a rallying cry. It had come at a time she needed it most.

With the Amasha, Ryder, and Chaca leading the way, the group began trotting down a darkened corridor. She noticed that the Amashan lights, though softer in hue, illuminated larger areas, as if the ebony substance of the walls and floor did not absorb it as readily as it did the light of the humans. This extra dispelling of the gloom lifted her mood, reminding her of the artificial sunlight of the Amashan sanctuary, the only spot where she had felt comfortable since entering the Band. Now, it was gone, in part because they had rescued her and thrown in with the humans because of her tenuous contact with the Shura mind.

The first encounter with the Shutaish came unexpectedly, but the Amasha were prepared. Two Shutaish emerged from the wall in front of the group. The Amasha did not slow down. Instead, they charged forward, forcing the Shutaish to become solid for the attack. Dozens of levitating lasers launched from the Amashan suits and targeted the two shadow wraiths. Ryder and Chaca joined the battle with Collins' lasers. The Shutaish, driven by their insatiable, constant hunger, gave no thought to escape. As they pushed their attack, their solid form made them vulnerable to the multiple laser beams.

Even so, they did not die easily. One lashed out with its whip-like tentacles, severely injuring one of the Amasha. A companion quickly applied a sealant to repair the air leak and tended to the wounds. The creatures absorbed the focused energy of the beams for several seconds, but began vibrating as their energy matrix became unstable. Their red-in-black eyes widened in a gesture mimicking human surprise moments before their bodies, overloaded with excess energy, exploded, leaving only a rapidly dissipating mist.

"Yes!" Hitochi shouted.

Kari felt like celebrating, dancing in the corridor, but they had no time. They could expect to encounter many more Shutaish before they reached the crew of the *Worthington*. As if the killing of the Shutaish were a catalyst, her mind began buzzing with thoughts. They were her thoughts, but she had not summoned them. It felt as if someone were rifling through a filing cabinet containing all her personal papers and randomly reading snippets of them aloud. She clamped down on her thoughts, but a few slipped through her mental barrier. Then, as if she had imagined it, it was gone. However, the peace did not last long.

"You have little time." At first, the voice was so soft she could barely understand it. Louder, it said, "Your companions need you."

A schematic of the area of the Band through which they walked appeared in her mind, as well as an image of the survivors of the *Worthington*. She needed no help interpreting the third image, a large group of Shutaish bearing down on the small band of humans.

"I will guide you to them," the voice said. "All of you must leave."

"Why are you helping us?" she asked.

"You passed the tests. Aiding you is my function. My dark half considers you a threat to our creators and seeks to destroy you. I cannot intervene, but I can help remove you from this place. You must leave now."

The urge to hurry overwhelmed her. Her legs tingled with excitement. She felt that if she released her mind's control of them, her legs would rush her away at the speed of light.

"We have to hurry," she said, and began to trot ahead of the group. She glanced back to see the others pick up the pace.

20

Captain Sidthuri allowed the survivors to linger in the warehouse for as long as possible before urging them back into the dark maze of corridors. Fitzhugh's search of the bins had yielded few useful items. Most of what he found was unrecognizable or too large to easily transport. By lucky accident, he discovered a dry, powdery substance with the properties of a strong organic acid. Opening the crystalline container containing it, he poured some of the dust onto the lid of the bin in which he had found it. The dust ate through the lid, the bottom of the bin, and through three more bins before becoming inactive. Sidthuri ordered several of the men to carry the acid containers as a weapon against the drones.

The ache in his side had receded to a constant dull throb that sapped his strength and made each step a battle to remain upright. He persevered not through some belief in projecting a macho façade, but simply because he had to. He had no alternative. As leader of the band of survivors, he could show no weakness or indication of giving up, or they would as well. As they marched, he sipped from an energy drink that increased production of adrenaline into his system. Eventually, it would burn out his body, but he was willing to make such sacrifices to keep them moving.

After three hours, he called a rest, not for himself, but because the small exhausted group had become too strung out along the corridor, leaving them more vulnerable to attack. He spoke with them, trying to draw them out of the cocoons they had woven around themselves to keep out the reality of the situation. Some stared at him in blank-faced incomprehension, as if refusing to admit their withdrawal from reality. Others nodded to acknowledge his words, but made no effort to see to the comfort or needs of their companions. He was rapidly losing their trust. They could see no end to their predicament and resented his urging them onward.

The 30-minute respite passed much too quickly. As he urged them forward again, the momentary relief to his body produced by the energy supplement disappeared as if it had been only in his imagination. He looked back at his charges. They rose and moved only because they knew what lay behind them. They had no hope for what lay ahead. He pushed them hard, much harder than they deserved. The military personnel understood forced marches, even if they had never endured one, but to the civilians among the group they were simply running headlong from one danger toward another one.

When he began coughing, exacerbating the pain in his ribs, he realized the atmosphere was changing, becoming thinner.

"Seal your suits," he warned.

Within minutes, the corridor was in a vacuum. Once again, they ate up their limited oxygen supply. He checked to see that everyone had sealed their suits in time, relief flooding over him when he saw that they had. They may have given up hope, but they were not ready to die.

The corridor continued to slope downward in a slow spiral. Doors to several small rooms opened as they passed. Without the drone transponder, the doors would have been invisible. After another hour passed, he chose one room and herded everyone inside. The room was featureless, but sufficiently large enough to allow them space to lie down. To seal the door, he enclosed the transponder in a metal box. To his relief, the sealed room produced an oxygen atmosphere, and the walls glowed, illuminating the room with a dim azure light.

"Everyone eat something and get some rest," he told them.

"Where are we?" one technician asked.

"I don't know," he admitted, "but it's a place to rest. It has light, heat, and atmosphere. What more could you want?"

He was pleased to hear a couple of quiet chuckles. They were too exhausted to prepare a hot meal, but most of them did comply with his suggestion by eating a ration bar. He chewed his out of habit, tasting nothing. Instead, he watched one of the civilian technicians, Leanu Mbala, as she wandered around the room as if in a trance, staring at each of the walls. Her intense concentration worried him. He didn't need anyone going off the rails.

"What are you doing?" he asked her.

She stared at him a moment before acknowledging him. She touched her head with one of her fingers. The expression on her face was one of bewilderment. "Can't you feel it?" she asked.

Oh, shit. She's lost it. "Feel what?" He surreptitiously motioned to one of the marines to get his attention in case he needed help subduing her.

"My head is humming with voices, but I don't understand the words. The walls are glowing."

He glanced at a wall. At first, he dismissed her claim as delusional, but as he stared more intently, he, too, saw a faint glow emanating from the walls. "What the …?"

The faint outline of a rectangle appeared on one wall. As he watched, the entire rectangle filled in with a deeper blue light. A darker cursive script materialized on the screen, flashing across it at a dizzying rate. Before he could stop her, Mbala touched the screen. The script froze for a few moments before disappearing. Sidthuri thought she had broken it, but an image appeared in the script's place. It was them, the survivors of the *Worthington* as they sat around the room. He searched the room for a camera but saw nothing.

"They see us," Mbala said.

"That's not good," Fitzhugh told her. "Now, they know where we are."

People stood up as if ready to run. "Hold it," Sidthuri said. He walked over to the screen. His face appeared, growing larger as he neared the screen. "Why did you attack us?" he demanded. No answer was forthcoming. He tried a different tact. "We mean you no harm. We came to study you. You attacked us."

His image faded. Seconds later, another image appeared, a line of dark aliens marching down a corridor. Behind them, he saw humans – Sergeant Chaca, Lieutenant Hitochi, Kirkurk, and a few others. Behind him, a ragged cheer went up around the room.

"Quiet," he said. Chaca appeared at ease with the aliens. They all carried weapons. *So, Chaca made some new friends.* He didn't know where they were or why the Band controller had shown them the image, but it pumped new life into the survivors with him. He counted heads. Of the 16 people in the two teams he had sent out, only nine remained. They had encountered trouble as well, but they were still alive.

"They're close," Mbala said.

"How do you know?" He did not understand her certainty, but she had been right about the wall.

"The voice in my head told me." Her face darkened and her eyebrows knitted together in concentration. "Something bad is coming this way." She turned to Sidthuri. "We need to continue down the corridor. Now!"

Sidthuri felt like a fool for listening to the ravings of a civilian technician, but the force of her voice and the urgency she expressed moved him to comply.

"Grab your weapons and prepare to fight. We're going to meet the others." He faced Mbala. "Can you find them?"

She closed her eyes for a moment and shook her head. "The voice is gone, but I think they're close, down the corridor and in a large open space."

"I hope to hell you're right," he said. "Everyone seal your suits." He used the drone device to open the door. He saw the sailors picking up only one of the two stretchers. "What are you doing?"

"Holt is dead, sir," one of them answered. "He never regained consciousness." He hefted his rifle and charged the magnetic launcher. "My hands are free now to fight."

Sidthuri nodded. Ignoring the pain, he set off down the corridor at a brisk pace, one he could not maintain for long. He hoped Mbala was right.

Ten minutes later, the first attack came. Another of the ebony wraiths appeared at the rear of the column, sending everyone into a panic. This time, knowing the flechette rifles were useless, a young Marine lance corporal carrying one of the shuttle's lasers, blocked the corridor and focused the laser on the wraith. His first shot pierced the creature's amorphous body but did nothing. However, as the creature solidified for the attack, whipping a dozen sharpened tendrils whipping around like a deadly Dervish, the laser found a target. The creature's dark body absorbed the high-energy beam. Like a crystal goblet resonating to the vibrations of an opera soprano's voice, it began quivering along the outer edges. It continued to advance, but the body lost cohesion and shattered like ice hit with a sledgehammer. The scattered pieces of the creature's body dissolved into a black vapor that quickly disappeared.

"Yes!" Sidthuri shouted. They had a defensive weapon, but only three. He motioned for the group, who had stopped to watch the creature die, to keep moving.

The small victory energized the group. Their steps became more certain. They moved with more purpose. They entered an open chamber unlike any other they had encountered. Unlike the cavernous warehouse spaces, the small rooms, or the endless corridors, it more resembled a cavern. Yellow globes floating high up near the roof of the cavern cast the equivalent glow of a gibbous moon on the floor, creating an eerie shadow play around them as they walked.

The immediate area was empty, but the space was so vast, they could not see all of it. Unlike the ebony material of the Band, the chamber's construction was aggregate rock fused by heat into a solid mass. The cavern appeared carved by some unknown method. The stone looked badly pitted, as if corroded by time and weather. Considering the little changing conditions within the Band, the erosion process would have taken eons. He wondered if they had discovered the bare bones of the Band, the underlying structure showing its true age instead of the pristine ebony outer skin. Deep grooves and scratches in the stone floor indicated the movement of heavy objects, but dust accumulated over the ages partially filled them.

His radio crackled to life. The dampening field of the ebony material did not extend into the room. *Thank God for small miracles.* "Keep your eyes open," he warned.

"We have company!" one of the marines shouted.

Two dozen multi-armed maintenance robots waving drills, blades, and cutting torches appeared from the deep shadows on the far side of the space. "Everyone with a weapon form a line here." Sidthuri indicated a spot beside him. The assault would test their resolve. They must hold. If they ran, they would all die. He would serve as the anchor to hold them fast. "Wait until they're close. Don't waste ammunition. You three with the lasers, open fire now."

The lasers proved as effective against the maintenance drones as against the wraiths, drilling neat holes through their bodies and severing limbs, but it required several bursts to disable them. The drones, lacking a cohesive plan of attack, surged forward in a straight line. At 50 meters, he yelled, "Fire!"

A few lucky shots disabled two of the drones' tool arms, but not until they were within 20 meters did the flechettes produce any real damage. Pieces of crystal and shards of metal flew from the drones as the high-speed projectiles pierced their bodies. At ten meters, only six of the drones still presented a threat. Two of his men raced forward with homemade bombs created from containers filled with the powdery acid they had discovered. They had secured the containers to fragmentary grenades with electrical tape. The pair pulled the pins on the grenades and tossed their bombs into the midst of the advancing drones.

"Everyone hit the ground!" Sidthuri called out.

The explosions, disconcertingly silent in the vacuum, created a cloud of powder that spread from the center of the blasts and settled over the drones in a dirty snow. The highly corrosive acid acted quickly. The outer layer of metal foil and ceramic crystal of their bodies dissolved like ice under a noonday sun. Most of the drones made it only another few meters before the acid reached vital areas. When the last of the remaining drones died under a hail of gunfire, spontaneous cheers broke out.

"Clear the com lines!" He shouted. "Keep alert. There may be more."

Almost as if he had called down the enemy with his warning, someone to their rear yelled, "Wraiths!"

Sidthuri spun on his heel to confront the ebony wraiths that had disgorged from the corridor they had just left. Unlike the drones, the wraiths were prepared. The creatures fanned out in a curved line spaced a dozen meters apart like a military unit. They stopped 60 paces away and faced the humans. He scrambled to move people into position.

As unarmed civilians took cover behind the armed men, he wondered why the creatures did not attack immediately before the humans could mount an adequate defense. They must have realized the flechette rifles were ineffective, and that three lasers could not stop them all. At best, the lasers might kill one or two of them before they could overwhelm the shooters. He did not attribute the delay to any form of chivalry on their part. *Probably looking over the buffet*, he thought sardonically.

Although experience had shown the flechette rifles were useless against such an enemy, he could not ask his people to face the creatures unarmed. They might get in a lucky shot as they morphed between solid and wraith shape.

"Reload your rifles. Make every shot count."

The wraiths moved forward slowly, extending their formation to a large semi-circle half-surrounding the group. The marine who had killed the previous wraith in the corridor knelt on the floor with his heavy laser braced on his knees. He withheld his fire, waiting until the moment they became solid during their attack. His finger squeezed the laser's trigger nervously. Two sailors, McLaren and Reams, armed with the other two lasers took up positions in front of the group on either side of the marine. Just as the tension became unbearable, the wraiths swept forward en masse, floating above the floor.

The marine squeezed the trigger and took out the closest creature. It disappeared in a cloud of black smoke. One of the sailors fired his laser as well, but his target remained amorphous. The beam passed through its body. It swept over the sailor and enveloped him within its ebony folds. He dropped the laser and screamed shrilly, as the creature's mouth, filled with hundreds of needle-like teeth, sank into his suit and penetrated his flesh. Puffs of air and spurts of blood exploded from his lacerated suit.

A handful of wraiths, drawn by their insatiable hunger by the sight of blood, broke off their attack and converged on the dead sailor. Flechette rifles sent a stream of darts into the mass of wraiths, but they simply passed through the creatures ethereal bodies or bounced from them when they became solid.

The second sailor, angered by the death of his comrade, fired into the mass of feeding wraiths, yelling a stream of obscenities into his com as if his words would wither them. The marine added his firepower. The creatures, engrossed in their feeding frenzy, ignored the threat until one of them exploded. They then focused their attention on the two men bearing the lasers. Sidthuri eyed the laser lying on the floor beside the dead sailor, but knew any attempt to retrieve it would end in his death before he could reach it. He raised his pistol and concentrated on one creature that focused its attention on him.

From the corner of his eye, Sidthuri saw something flash by overhead. He glanced up to see dozens of small, black decagonal objects resembling two truncated pyramids attached at the base, hovering above the massed wraiths. The creatures recognized the objects and paused. Narrow red beams of energy lanced from the objects and focused upon the creatures. He recognized them as targeting lasers. The beams widened and intensified, slicing into six of the creatures. They exploded into dark fragments that evaporated before they hit the floor. The remaining creatures milled about as if confused by the deaths of their comrades.

However, one creature refused to yield. The wraith that had chosen him as its prey rushed headlong at Sidthuri. He pressed the trigger of his flechette pistol and held it down, sending a stream of darts into the creature. They passed harmlessly through it and bounced off the floor beyond. He braced for certain death as the creature became solid.

* * * *

"Duck, Captain!" Chaca yelled.

Without thinking, the captain dropped to his knees. The creature, driven by hunger beyond the point of caring, charged into the beam heedless of the damage it inflicted on its body. Sidthuri stared into its red eyes with their rapidly swirling streams of darkness. The creature disintegrated only a meter away, showering him with a cloud of ebony fragments that bounced off his suit before evaporating. The remaining wraiths broke and fled back into the corridor. The armada of decagons followed them, crimson beams of fiery death lancing into their midst.

"Nice shot, Sergeant. I knew you would make it," he told Chaca.

"Three of my men didn't," Chaca replied.

"A lot of people didn't make it, but you saved some lives here today."

Kari counted heads as she approached. *So many missing.*

Chaca stopped in front of Sidthuri. "For that, you'll have to thank Clutep and his Amasha friends."

Sidthuri stared at the Amasha as they gathered around Chaca. The mobile lasers returned from their pursuit of the wraiths and reattached themselves to their dark suits. "Indeed. They have my thanks. I'm afraid I have dire news, Sergeant."

"We know about the *Worthington*, sir, but Clutep thinks we may have another way off the Band."

"That would be excellent news indeed, Sergeant; however, I intend to destroy the Band before I leave, if such a thing is possible."

His declaration caught Kari off guard. As much as she hated and feared the Shutaish, to destroy the entire Band seemed a desperate, if not an impossible, task.

Kirkurk fumed. "You can't," he said. Stepping forward, he flailed his hands wildly as he spoke. "The amount of knowledge stored here is astounding. Such a loss is unconscionable."

"The Architects are too dangerous. If they decide to attack Earth ..."

"The Architects, or the Aishaitia, as the Amasha say they call themselves, are all dead."

Sidthuri stared at Kari. "If that is the case, who is running the show?"

"An insane entity called the Shura, the Band's artificial intelligence."

"Insane? That's even more reason to destroy this place."

"The sane part of the Shura saved you. It guided us here."

"It spoke to my mind," Mbala said stepping forward to greet Kari with a smile. "It warned us."

"Hello, Leanu," Kari said, hugging the technician awkwardly in her suit. "I'm glad you made it. You know I'm speaking the truth." Mbala nodded. "Captain, we should not remain here. The insane part of the Shura could regain control any minute, and the Shutaish will not give up so easily."

"It would seem your new friends, the Amasha, are our principal defense against these dark wraiths, these Shutaish, as you called them."

Clutep spoke for his people. "We will aid you in any way we can. We have committed our future to the escape of both our species. The Shutaish will never give up, not while so much blood is available for the feeding. Their hunger drives them to extremes."

"This escape vessel," Captain Sidthuri asked, "is it nearby?"

"Yes. Quite close."

"Where is it? How big is it? Will it hold all of us?" The questions poured over the radio at them from the throng of people crowding around them.

"Quiet," Sidthuri urged.

"It is the sphere near where you landed. It is of sufficient size to accommodate everyone."

"The Dome?" Kari asked. "There's nothing there, unless the smaller sphere …"

"What you call the Dome *is* the ship."

At first, Kari's skepticism made her doubt Clutep's insistence that the Dome was a five-kilometer-wide ship. Then, the irony hit her like a slap in the face. They had been inside the last remaining Architect ship and had not recognized it as a ship.

Hitochi whistled his appreciation. "I assume the projection sphere is the guidance system."

"So we believe," Clutep replied. "We have studied it on occasion, but the journey here was always dangerous, and we learned little for our efforts. Too many of our people died seeking answers. " He looked at Kari and at Leanu Mbala. "One part of the Shura mind has chosen these two humans with whom to communicate. We can only hope that willingness to help extends to the operation of the Aishaitia vessel."

"I'm an electronics technician," Mbala protested, "not a navigator."

"And I'm an archaeologist," Kari added. As she said it, she wondered if it were still true. So little of what she had done in the last few days was true archaeology. Discovery, yes; archaeology, no.

"You two are our only link with the Shura mind. If you cannot convince it to help us, we are all doomed to remain here and face whatever fate the Shura decides for us."

The weight of responsibility felt like a 5-G acceleration pressing down on Kari. She had linked with the Shura, but both halves, sane and insane, had toyed with her mind. How could she be certain which half she asked for help? One wrong command could destroy the Aishaitia ship and everyone aboard it.

"Does this ship have weapons?" Sidthuri asked Clutep.

"The Aishaitia encountered no hostile races during their explorations. It is unlikely their ships were armed, but this is mere conjecture on my part. There is dissent on this matter among my people. Systems not designed as weapons can often function as such."

As they spoke, Fitzhugh approached Kirkurk. "Where is my friend Sung?"

"Sung didn't make it," Kirkurk replied. "He died half an hour ago not far from here."

"That's too bad. I shall miss the cantankerous old fool. He was excited about the prospects of discovering a living alien." He held out his arms to encompass the Amasha. "Here we are surrounded by them. Life can be cruel."

"We'll probably be joining him soon enough," Kirkurk replied.

Kari exploded. She faced him with her hands on her hips. "How dare you give up after all we've gone through? A Shutaish took me captive, but here I am. We're going to get out of this. You have to have a little faith."

"Faith?" Kirkurk snickered. "You mean that after all you've seen, the deaths you've witnessed, you still believe God is watching over us?"

"If you don't believe in God, believe in the Shura. Part of its function was to welcome and to test visitors. That means they intended to impart some portion of their wisdom to visitors that passed the test. The insane part of it, the protector, warped that directive. You must have faith that the sane part of the mind can help us."

"Ah, Kari. Your youth blinds you to the way of life. The Architects want supplicants, species to admire them. That's why they left signposts throughout our sector of the galaxy. They do not intend to give away their deepest secrets. Poor Sung was right about that. They intend to take it to their graves." He shook his head. "The Church was wrong. I've been a fool."

She realized that Kirkurk was an Interventionist. His attitude suddenly made sense to her. He had come expecting to see the face of God. Instead, he found that his God was dead and had left an insane angel to watch over his grave.

"You're wrong. They hoped other races would someday follow them into the void between universes. They could have given away their secrets, but they wanted us to earn them, to be certain we were ready for such knowledge. They might have thought themselves superior to other species, but they did not resent them." Having spoken her mind, she walked away before an argument ensued.

Amanda Collins knelt beside the body of one of the sailors killed by the Shutaish. Her shoulders jerked as she sobbed uncontrollably.

"Amanda, what's wrong?"

Collins did not reply. She had shut off her radio to cry in silence. Kari touched her shoulder and motioned to turn on her radio. "What's wrong?"

"Dale. He's dead."

"Oh, I'm so sorry." She didn't know what else to say. So many people had died that one more death didn't affect her. For Collins, it was different. Her world had ended. She was alone.

Collins sniffed. "It doesn't matter, does it? We'll all die soon."

"You can't think like that. The Amasha will help us. We'll reach the Aishaitia ship and go home."

When Collins looked at her, the distress in her face shocked Kari. "No, we won't. This place will never let us go. It's like some horror movie. We'll wander around, dying one-by-one until only one of us is left. We shouldn't have come."

Collins rose and walked away to join the others, her grief surrounding her like a cloud. Kari didn't know what to tell her. Her loss had devastated her. They couldn't even take McLaren's body with them. Kari had no one close to her to lose, except Hitochi. Would his death affect her so deeply? She had to believe they would make it back to Earth. Anything else was too horrible to contemplate.

While Sidthuri rounded everyone up to start them moving again after the reunion, Clutep dispatched eight Amasha to retrieve the carts and what remained of the Amasha's possessions. He directed them to rendezvous with the group at the Dome. Kari felt a cold chill as she surveyed the group, a pitiful collection of 18 humans remaining of the original 35. Almost half the company of the *Worthington* was dead. They had paid a heavy price for the scant knowledge they had wrested from the Band thus far. The Amasha had paid an even heavier price for helping them. She wondered how many genetic lines had been irretrievably lost to the Amasha hereditary history.

She noticed the look of anguish crossing Sidthuri's face, as he motioned for the group to start walking. He moved with a pronounced limp, but despite his pain, he set a robust pace. She could not guess at the severity of his injury, but he made no complaint. He moved among them, encouraging them forward, as a good leader should.

She fell into line beside Hitochi. He smiled and reached out his hand to her. She did not hesitate. She took his hand and interlaced her gloved fingers with his. The close contact, even through the heavy gloves, comforted her. She knew they were going to make it.

22

Kari had read about the Trail of Tears of the Cherokee Nation banished from their homes in Northern Georgia and Tennessee to the Indian territories in Oklahoma back in the 19th Century. She imagined the Amasha felt much as the displaced Cherokee had, driven from their home of 2,500 years to march the dark, endless corridors of the Band. The Cherokee had faced privation and starvation. Thousands had died along the way. The Amasha faced a gauntlet of hungry Shutaish and a legion of deadly repair drones. Many of them had already died. She feared many more would die before the end.

Her people had suffered as well and would do so again. Whatever fate awaited the Amasha would not spare her people. Without the Amasha, they could not survive. Even with their combined firepower, their chances were remote. Even now, the Shura had them under observation. If the dark side of the dual personalities of the Aishaitia artificial intelligence was in control, an attack would come soon. She hoped the saner mind was observing them. She wanted to go home.

Clutep informed them that they were less than two kilometers from the Dome. He deliberately chose a roundabout route down one of the smaller corridors hoping the Shura would expect them to make haste using the most direct route. So far, their luck had held.

"What are you going to do when we get home?" Hitochi asked her.

"Have a greasy cheeseburger," she replied.

He chuckled. "That sounds good. Mind if I join you?"

She stared at him through his face shield. His smile gave her hope for the future. "I would like that very much."

He squeezed her hand tighter. "Good."

Clutep raised his hand to stop the group. Kari peered ahead but saw nothing out of the ordinary. "What is it?" Hitochi asked.

"It is a voice on the frequency used by your suits. It is very faint. It is calling for help."

Kari gasped. "Josh! It must be. He's alive. We have to rescue him."

Hitochi was more cautious. "We left Luntz over 2,000 kilometers from here. How is possible he can contact us? Did your modifications enhance the receiving range of our radios?"

"It is doubtful," Clutep replied. "The signal is weak, but its source is nearby." He paused and pointed down a side corridor. "In that direction."

"That takes us away from the Dome," Chaca noted. "I smell a trap."

Kari couldn't believe what she was hearing. Was the sergeant suggesting they abandon Luntz? "We can't leave him," she insisted. "He might have gotten away and used the slidewalk just as we did."

"I am afraid the sergeant is correct," Clutep told her. "It is unlikely he escaped the Shutaish and located us so easily. The Shutaish have employed similar tactics before. To attempt to rescue him places more lives in danger."

"Please, Hitochi," she pleaded. She didn't think she could live with herself if they abandoned Luntz to his grisly fate. Could any of them? She looked at Captain Sidthuri. "Please, Captain." The ultimate responsibility lay on his shoulders. He had seen so many of his crew die. Would he sacrifice Luntz for fear of placing the others in danger? She held her breath as he made up his mind.

Finally, he nodded his head. "Sergeant Chaca, you and Lieutenant Rigolini lead everyone to the Dome. I'll take Hitochi and two volunteers and search for Mr. Luntz."

"No, sir," Chaca answered. "You're still in charge, and you don't hide your pain very well." He smiled at Sidthuri. "Your injury would hold us up. Ryder, Holmes," he glanced at Hitochi, who nodded, "and Hitochi will go with me after Luntz. Don't wait for us. If you manage to get the Architect ship operational, leave." He turned to Kari. "You, Mbala, and Collins seem to have a handle on this Architect technology. Get these people home."

She looked at Hitochi. "Ken, I ..."

He shook his head. "Don't fret. We'll take the two lasers Collins built. It's a simple in and out mission, right, First Sergeant Chaca?"

"One, two, three," Chaca answered.

"I and one other will accompany you," Clutep announced. "You will need our firepower."

"That's six," Hitochi said. "That should be enough to get the job done."

Kari was torn. She didn't want to see Hitochi risk his life; yet, it had been her plea that placed him in danger. "I'm coming too."

"No way!" Hitochi snapped. "You're needed to get the Architect ship operational." He held out his flechette rifle. "This may turn into a firefight. You're out of your element with one of these."

"But I –"

"Forget it. Now go." He pushed her away.

Her stubborn streak began to rise. She didn't like anyone telling her what to do, even Hitochi. Before she could argue, Captain Sidthuri placed his hand on her arm.

"Miss Stone, you have your duty before you. Will you abandon it and condemn these people to remain here and die."

"I …" Her anger fell away. She was being foolish. What could she add to the rescue expedition? The Shura mind had chosen her and Mbala. It might require both their talents to succeed. "You win, Captain. Ken Hitochi, you better stay safe."

He smiled at her. "Will do."

As she turned to walk away, the Shura mind contacted her, booming in her head so strongly she almost fell. "Go with them."

She stopped. "The Shura told me to go with you."

Hitochi stared at her, studying her face. "Is that true, or are you trying to worm your way into our party."

"It's the truth," she replied. She did not tell him she wasn't sure which part of the Shura mind had spoken to her.

"I hope it knows what it's doing," Chaca said. "I hope you know what you're doing."

"So do I." She turned to Mbala. "You can do this as well as I can."

"I will do my best," Mbala answered.

Kari took one last glance at her fellow *Worthington* passengers, wondering if she would ever see them again. In the five months they had been together, she had come to consider them family, even Kirkurk and Fitzhugh, whom she thought of as the crazy uncles who showed up for Christmas and quickly overstayed their welcome. She had not yet had time to sort out the deaths or properly grieve over them. That would come later. If she could help save Luntz's life, she had to try. She joined Hitochi.

"Do you think it's a trap?" she asked him.

He looked at her but did not reply. She could tell by the look in his eyes that he did. Did it matter that they might be walking blindly to their deaths? They had been running from death since they had first entered the Band. She didn't think one more trip would make that much difference.

"Holmes, you lucked out. Miss Stone is taking your place."

"No, really, I'll come along if you want," he said, but he looked relieved at his reprieve.

Ryder reached out and slapped the side of his helmet. "Go with the others, Holmes, but save me a seat up front by the driver. I get carsick at the back of the bus."

"Do it, Marine," Chaca said. "Captain Sidthuri needs a good marine by his side if the shit hits the fan."

Holmes looked at the ground and scuffed his foot. "We're not going to bring back Paisley's body, are we?"

"It doesn't look like it. I don't think he'd mind. Our priority is getting the living back home."

"Yeah, well, you and Ryder better not be late, 'cause we ain't holding the bus for nobody. Once we hotwire that sucker, we're out of here."

He turned and joined the group headed to the sphere. Kari, Hitochi, Ryder, and Chaca joined Clutep and one other Amasha and took another corridor, one that was narrow and wound upward toward the Band's surface. Half a kilometer along the way, Clutep directed them to a small circular alcove tucked alongside the corridor.

"This is an elevator into one of the buildings dotting the surface of the Han. I have entered one of the buildings only once. You will enjoy the view."

His cryptic message intrigued Kari. "Then they truly are buildings?"

"Many were residences for the Aishaitia when they arrived on the Han. They did not commit themselves to stasis immediately. Perhaps they took a moment to prepare themselves."

Finally, she would get to see an Architect residence. To see how they lived would give her a glimpse into their personalities. If she were lucky, they had left behind artifacts unaffected by the passage of millennia. The elevator operated similarly to the one with which they had entered the Band. The floor rose rapidly with no sense of motion. It stopped amid darkness. When she stepped off the platform, the walls began to glow. The space was large, but not cavernous. The walls were graceful curves supporting inset, curved benches. The room contained no other furniture or possessions. Disappointment made the visit to an Architect domicile bittersweet, but she had expected it. In 500,000,000 years, furnishings constructed of anything other than the ebony material or the durable gray metal would have rotted away.

Clutep walked to the far wall. One of his lasers rose from his suit and scanned the wall. The beam intensified, and the wall became transparent. She recognized the Dome and several other buildings nearby. They were inside one of the conical buildings at the edge of the City they had attempted to explore. Cyclops blazed overhead, muted by a filter within the wall. Its somber crimson light illuminated the Band. The

Band and the City silhouetted against the blazing edge of the Milky Way Galaxy presented a remarkable sight. She remembered to shoot a video with her helmet cam.

"It's beautiful," she said. The view was awe-inspiring. If not for the deaths, the view alone would have been worth the long voyage. If not for the need to save Luntz, she would have insisted on exploring.

Hitochi came to stand by her. "We've been trying to get inside one of these buildings for months. Now, we're here."

"We're not here to sightsee," Chaca reminded them. "We have a mission. Which way, Clutep?"

Clutep pointed toward a black wall. "Beyond that wall." His and his companion's remote lasers rose from their suits at the same time and scattered out in front of them. Kari braced herself for an attack and followed Hitochi, as he, Ryder, and Chaca moved toward the wall. Even so, she was not prepared for what she saw when the wall vanished, revealing another dimly lit room beyond. Luntz sat in the middle of the floor facing the outside wall staring out over the City. He noticed them and began backing away on his behind, whimpering. When he recognized who they were, he began sobbing.

"Josh!" Kari cried out.

She took a step toward Luntz, but Chaca laid his arm across her chest to stop her. "Are you alone?" he asked Luntz.

Luntz fought to control his runaway emotions. He took several deep breaths before replying. "They brought me here. I ... I thought they were going to eat me."

Kari shuddered. She knew how he felt.

Chaca made no move to approach Luntz. Kari wondered why. "How many were there?"

"I don't know ... six or seven. They ... they seemed frightened."

"Wraiths frightened of us?" Kari asked.

"Not of us," Luntz corrected her. "Of the ... whatever controls the Band."

"That makes no sense," Chaca said.

"I saw them." The tenor of Luntz's voice changed. Now, instead of fear, she heard awe in his voice.

"Saw who, Josh?" Kari asked him.

"The Architects. Millions of them!" His voice rose until it boomed; then, as if realizing what he was doing, he glanced around the room and whispered, "The shadow creatures were eating them. It was disgusting."

"My God," Kari burst out. "No wonder the Shutaish are frightened. The Shura will exterminate them for violating its charges."

"Shutaish? Shura? What are you talking about?" Luntz paused, as if noticing the Amasha for the first time. The fear crept back into his voice. "Who are they?"

"They're friends. I'll explain later. We have to leave now."

Still, he did not try to move or rise from the floor. "They spoke to me," he said. He began chuckling hysterically and clamped his hands over his the side of his helmet as if trying to cut off their voices. "Oh, my God."

"You understood them?" she asked.

"Not their language. It showed me things, bad things, images floating inside its body like a holo screen."

"What did they show you, Josh?" she asked, almost afraid to learn what had driven him over the edge of sanity.

He shook his head. "I shouldn't tell you. They won't like it."

She appealed to his vanity. She felt dirty for doing so, but she had to know what the Shutaish had revealed to him. "Maybe they want you to tell us. Maybe they wanted to use your skills as a photographer to describe them to us."

"You think so?"

She took a step toward Luntz. "I'm certain."

As she took a second step, Clutep called to her. "Look out."

Six Shutaish emerged from the wall and fanned out across the room. Josh saw them and crawled toward her, whimpering. She reached out her hand toward his, but before he could take it, one of the creatures lashed out at him with a pair of elongated tentacles, slashing open the back of his suit. The violent hiss of escaping air and his dying scream echoed in her ears, as he landed face first on the floor, his back sliced open to reveal his spine. He looked up at her and groaned one last time before dying.

Hands yanked her backward and held her – Hitochi. Three of the remote lasers focused on the Shutaish. It tried to escape, but the high-energy beams broke down the bonds giving it form, destroying it in a spray of black vapor. Ryder and Chaca opened up with their lasers. The Shutaish raced around the room, passing through walls and back into the room to spoil their aim. Hitochi released her and aimed his flechette rifle.

Clutep saw the useless rifle. "I am placing one of my laser drones under your control. I have linked it to your suit's computer."

The drone flew over and hovered beside Hitochi. "I didn't know you could do that."

"It has become ... necessary."

The laser drone bounced around the room like a lure on a fishing line as Hitochi learned to control it, but seconds later, he was firing at a Shutaish. Kari crouched beside him to stay out of the line of fire. Three of the creatures were dead. The intense laser barrage kept the remaining Shutaish off balance, but they did not flee. The sight of Luntz's blood freezing on his cooling body drove them mad with hunger, but they could not come close enough to attack without exposing themselves. She could sense their rage.

Hitochi and the others made the mistake of thinking in two dimensions. They forgot the Shutaish could come up through the floor as easily as passing through a wall. One of the creatures rose through the floor less than two meters from her and launched a tentacle in her direction. Stunned, she had no time to move to avoid it. Before it struck, she fell sideways as Hitochi shoved her out of the way. She glanced back to see the tentacle penetrate the front of his suit and emerge from the back, rupturing his oxygen tank. He stumbled and fell. A plume of escaping gas turned to frozen powder and fell atop his body. The laser drone he had been controlling lost power and dropped to the floor.

He was not dead. She could hear him panting and groaning over the radio. Chaca saw what had happened, shoved his laser against the creature's head, and fired. The Shutaish exploded. She was kneeling at Hitochi's side before the black mist of the dead Shutaish dissipated.

"Hitochi!" she cried out, holding his head in her hands. She examined the hole in his suit. It was small but judging by the angle, she knew it had ripped through his lung. His breathing was ragged as he gasped for what little air remained in his suit. She barely noticed the diminishing activity around her until Chaca knelt beside her and applied sealant patches to Hitochi's suit. He activated the small, undamaged reserve tank, and Hitochi's breathing eased as his suit inflated. They could do nothing to staunch the flow of blood or treat his damaged lungs until they could safely remove his suit. His reserve tank would last only 30 minutes.

"Lie still," she whispered, as Hitochi tried to rise. "We'll get you back."

"No," he gasped; then coughed blood onto the inside of his face shield. "I can't make it. Go. Now! Leave me."

"No." She would never leave him. She could not live with herself if she did. "No," she repeated.

She looked up and saw Clutep standing above her. Ryder and the second Amasha stood across the room facing the walls, ready for another attack.

"Can you do anything?" she asked him. She watched the laser drone Hitochi had been controlling rise from the floor and land on Clutep's suit. He held out a device scanning Hitochi.

"His lungs are filling with blood. Unless we can clear them, he will die soon."

"No, he can't."

"Then you must contact the Shura and ask it to create a habitable environment in this room. If not, he will perish."

Exposing her mind to the Shura was the last thing she wanted to do. In her state of mind, if she contacted the wrong one, it would rip her apart. She had no choice. She tried to control her rampant emotions by concentrating on slowing her breathing and heartbeat. Images of Hitochi lying on the floor flashed through her mind. She didn't know if they originated in her thoughts or came from the Shura. Gradually, her heart rate slowed. She took a breath, held it, and opened her mind to the Shura.

Its thoughts hit her like a tidal wave. A rampaging torrent of images and emotions flooded her mind, grinding her synapses like rocks dragged along by the current. A fish swimming upstream, she tried to grasp one and follow it back to its source. When she thought she had made contact, she sent her plea into the jumble, hoping the Shura would understand. Too late, she realized she had contacted both parts of the dual mind. The anger and outrage of the half-mad part lashed out at her, a lance of fire searing her brain. The other part of the Shura mind quickly shielded her, but not before she understood its anger.

An image of thousands of stasis coffins lining a part of the Band lodged in her mind, the Aishaitia awaiting their reemergence beyond the barrier of death. Hundreds of the coffins were open, the bodies of the Aishaitia exposed. All that remained were unidentifiable shriveled husks. In their hunger, the Shutaish had sucked every drop of moisture from their corpses. She wondered what could have driven them to desecrate the tombs and then devour the beings that had created them.

Images of the interior of the Band flashed through her mind, millions of repair drones at work separating sections of the Band. With the Shura's help, she understood the Band had become unstable. A small black hole had passed through the system eons earlier, dragging much of the Oort Cloud material with it in its gravity wake, material the Band needed for repairs. It had been cannibalizing sections of itself for millennia and had finally decided to reduce its size in a Herculean effort to re-stabilize its decaying orbit.

The drones had herded the Shutaish into the sections of the Band destined for jettisoning. Betrayed by their creators, they sought revenge in the manner they knew best, by feeding on them.

"You must leave," it told her, pressing a sense of haste into her mind, along with a stream of data too large for her to interpret.

She regained consciousness with Ryder holding her upright and her head pounding. She heaved and threw up; realizing only then that her helmet was off. Chaca had stripped Hitochi's damaged suit and was busy sealing the hole in his chest and back with synth-flesh epoxy. Hitochi's eyes were closed, and his face was ashen, but his chest rose and fell more evenly.

"You did it," Chaca said. "We have air."

"How long was I out?"

"Five minutes." He stood. "I think he'll make it, but he needs professional medical help."

"We have to leave. The Shura is jettisoning part of the Band to correct its orbit. It is driving the Shutaish into that area to eliminate them at the same time, killing two birds with one stone. The sunward side with the buildings, where we are, is one section destined for destruction. I don't know how much time we have. I think very little."

"Help me."

Together, she and Chaca maneuvered Hitochi back into his suit. She tried to be gentle, but she was certain they hurt him. When they had completed their task, Chaca bent over Hitochi to lift him. "I'll carry him."

"We can do that," Clutep said. The remote lasers detached from his and his companion's suits and hovered over Hitochi. Kari gasped, unsure what Clutep had in mind. The decagons lowered and attached to his suit. His body lifted from the floor suspended by the decagons. Kari could not hide her amazement. She glanced at Clutep. He explained, "The suspensor fields will not handle the strain for long, but we should reach the ship safely. It will allow us to proceed more quickly."

"What if the Shutaish attack again?" she asked.

"Then we must drop your friend to defend ourselves."

She figured Hitochi would accept a few bumps and bruises if necessary.

"We will have to push fast," Chaca told them.

Kari only hoped they got there in time.

23

Captain Sidthuri followed the Amasha into a dark corridor. As it slowly illuminated, he saw that it was a long, curving room. Unlike any other room they had passed through, this one held rows of electronic equipment of a design that, despite its exotic alien origins, he recognized as the bridge of a spaceship. He faced the curved black wall. Leanu Mbala came over, closed her eyes, and touched the wall with her right hand, gently rubbing the surface as if caressing it. Sidthuri almost cried out in wonder when the wall became transparent. He stared out into the void revealed, watching the dark sphere in its center rotate.

She opened her eyes and smiled at him. "Kari was right. This is so wonderful."

"Can you operate the ship?"

A brief pained expression swept over her features. "No, not yet. I sense some reluctance from the Shura. I'll try."

"Please," Sidthuri asked. "You're our only hope."

"When Kari gets here ..."

"Kari and the others might not return. It may all fall on you." He prayed they did return safely. He sensed something special about Kari Stone, perhaps because she had been the first person to link with the Shura entity. Their chances of escaping the Band improved with her present.

To his surprise, Mbala smiled. "She'll make it. They're on their way here now."

He took her at her word. "Good. We need to leave ASAP."

He looked at the group of survivors, both his crew and the Amasha. He didn't have the heart to tell them that all their efforts might be for naught. He didn't know about the mysterious Amasha's nutritional needs, but his people did not have enough food to make it back to Earth or any colonized world. Even if he dared try to reach the shuttles and the stored supplies, it still would not be enough for the months-long journey.

Mbala had been working as he mused about their fate. One part of the screen displayed a schematic of the sphere. It appeared as if the shell of the large sphere was the engine. A thin band encircling the five-kilometers-in-diameter ship contained the control room, or rather several control rooms, sleeping quarters, and empty spaces that could have been for storage. He doubted they would find clean sheets and soft mattresses after millions of years, but at least they would not have to huddle around the control panels.

"I need technicians, engineers, and weapons specialists to remain here." He looked at the Amasha. "That includes any of your people. The rest of you kindly follow the diagram to the crews' quarters and try to make yourself comfortable. As soon as we can learn the controls, we'll be leaving the Band."

A few cheers erupted from them, but most were half-hearted, born more of desperation than of hope. As they left, he saw that Kirkurk and Fitzhugh remained. *Damn. I don't want to deal with them right now.*

"Gentlemen, I don't believe your skills are needed at this time. If you will please follow the others –"

"Neville says you intend to destroy the Band," Fitzhugh burst out. His nostrils flared as he spoke. "Such a thing would be reprehensible. The U.N. Council –"

"Is months away," he reminded them. "You may file your protest. They might court-martial me, but I'll gladly pay the price. This place is too dangerous. They have real-time observations of Earth and our other colonies, so they know where we are. How do we know this is the only ship left, or that the Architects can't build more and fill them with weaponized drones or those damnable wraiths? No, gentlemen, I will do my duty to protect Earth."

Kirkurk joined in. He made no effort to hide his contempt for Sidthuri's decision. His thinly stretch lips curled slightly upward in disgust. "The Architects are dead, and the Shura hasn't attacked Earth in half a billion years. Why would it do so now?" He folded his arms over his chest, pleased with himself for his burst of logic.

"Over half of my crew is dead, murdered by these creatures or by the Shura. Miss Stone has said the Shura has a split personality, one of them half-insane, the other totally so. If the insane portion achieves dominance, I don't know to what lengths it might go to protect itself and its charges. That could include eliminating any species that has contacted it. You are the one, are you not, who connected the demise of the two races we have encountered, before we met the Amasha, to the Architects? You accused them of meddling in species evolution. Were you wrong then or now?"

Kirkurk's smug look vanished at having his own words thrown back at him. He uncrossed his arms and waved his hands in front of him in agitation. "I was simply conjecturing. We are talking about a species that spanned the length and breadth of the galaxy. The store of knowledge lost because –"

"We'll have this ship," he reminded them. "We'll have to be satisfied with what we can learn from it. Now, if you will join the others, I'll try to fly this thing."

"We can't allow you to destroy the Band," Fitzhugh whined. "The Architects are too far beyond us, superior in every way. We owe our existence to their benevolence."

He had suspected the structural engineer was an Interventionist. That increased his contempt for Fitzhugh. "Can't allow? If I discover a way to destroy this place, I intend to do so. I don't see how you can stop me."

Fitzhugh produced a pistol from his pocket. "I'll shoot you if I must to prevent such a desecration." He waved the pistol. "Please step away from the controls."

Kirkurk backed away from Fitzhugh with an astonished look on his face. "Bonner, what are you doing?"

"What I must."

Sidthuri wasn't sure if Fitzhugh had the guts to pull the trigger, but he did not want to test him. He saw Holmes edging forward and shook his head. Holmes might disarm Fitzhugh, but Sidthuri wasn't certain if stray bullet might damage delicate controls. He could not take that chance.

"This is stupid, Bonner. I'm a member of the Church, but I can't condone this act of barbarism to prevent another such act."

"Someone must protect the sanctity of the Architects."

Kirkurk shook his head. "Not this way."

He stepped toward Fitzhugh. Fitzhugh swung the pistol to point at Kirkurk. Holmes bounded across the room and tackled Fitzhugh, knocking the pistol from his hand. He rose from the floor holding a dazed Fitzhugh by the scruff of his neck.

"Should I chuck them out the airlock?"

Sidthuri smiled. "We have no brig, but confine them both somewhere out of the way."

"I tried to stop him," Kirkurk protested.

"I'll keep that in mind, but I don't have time to deal with either of you at this moment."

Grinning, Holmes said, "The captain wishes some alone time to think about saving our asses. We'll call you if and when we need you."

He nodded at a Navy ensign. "Put these two somewhere and watch them."

As the ensign escorted them away, Holmes said, "Those two are going to be trouble. I could accidentally leave them behind."

Sidthuri chuckled. "I think they understood the gist of your message."

"Just saying. No trouble at all. I don't like that Kirkurk asshole. He reminds me of a politician. Fitzhugh is just plain ape-shit crazy."

"I share your opinion, but he is an eminent scientist. Try not to hurt him."

"If you insist, sir."

One of the Amasha approached them. "Clutep and the others are near. He advises that we proceed quickly with our preparations to leave. Events are spiraling to a conclusion."

"What conclusion?"

"Destruction of parts of the Han, more pointedly, specifically the portion we now inhabit."

"Damn." Sidthuri turned to Mbala. "Do what you can. We must leave."

She nodded and closed her eyes. A few seconds later, many more lights on the control station panels lit up. She pointed to one station. "That is the flight control station."

He nodded. "Then I'll see if I can coax this ship into cooperating."

The Amasha's sense of impending doom hurried his actions. The controls were unfamiliar and the language indecipherable, but he studied the controls intently from a pilot's viewpoint. "I can do this," he whispered to himself.

* * * *

Kari, still weak from her mental encounter with the Shura, struggled to keep up with the others. Her legs felt wooden. She watched Hitochi as he floated along suspended by the Amasha remote lasers, searching for any sign of recovery. His severe wound worried her, but she feared any exotic alien microbes the Shutaish might harbor. If his wound became infected, his frail body would have no defense against them.

"My people inform me we must hurry," Clutep said. "Scouts report many Shutaish and repair drones moving toward the Aishaitia ship."

"Why doesn't it just let us leave?" Kari shouted to the walls. "Why kill us?"

The bipolar Shura's actions confused her. One side welcomed them, while the other considered them interlopers and a threat to the sleeping Aishaitia. It had to know they were leaving. What drove it to kill them?

"The ship is a storehouse of knowledge. The Shura is afraid of what we might do with it."

"We just want to go home." She didn't whimper, but she felt like it. Everything was beyond her control. She felt like a dust mote in a hurricane.

"The sane part of the Shura mind is aiding you, but the reconfiguring of the Han and the desecration of the Aishaitia by the Shutaish has given the insane portion greater control. I fear it may eventually sublimate the sane part of its identity and assume its powers for total control."

That dire thought hurried her steps. As they neared the Aishaitia ship, they encountered half a dozen Amasha scouts. After advising the humans to continue to the ship, Clutep stopped and spoke with his companions for several minutes. The conversation was private, but she sensed dark undertones.

Captain Sidthuri greeted them at the entrance to the ship. He spoke to Kari, "Miss Mbala says she needs your help. We must get this ship operational now."

She watched Chaca and Ryder lay Hitochi gently on the floor of the control room. Immediately, the Amasha lasers returned to their owners. She wanted to go to him, offer what comfort she could, but the safety of the entire crew compelled her to follow the captain to one of the control stations.

"Mbala says this station controls the engines. God alone knows what powers them; I can't even locate them on the schematics. Mbala says the sense of urgency she feels is increasing. I take that to mean we don't have much time."

As Kari touched the controls and allowed her troubled mind to meld with the Shura, the sense of urgency almost overwhelmed her. The internal struggle between the two parts of the Shura's mind became fierce, as the assertive portion stripped power away from its more docile counterpart. The mad mind was winning the battle.

Her fingers, almost unbidden by her conscious mind, danced over the controls, activating more of the ship. She felt rather than heard the engines engage. Their power source was so esoteric it was beyond her comprehension, but she sensed that Sung had been close to the truth with his theory about low-temperature vacuum eddies. Luckily, she did not have to understand them, only to control them.

Kari felt Mbala's presence in the mind meld, aiding her, accepting subroutines, while she concentrated on the task of readying the ship for takeoff. As she summoned the tremendous power of the Aishaitia engines into life, she allowed a small portion of her mind to wander through the ship's schematics in search of an infirmary or whatever medical lore the Aishaitia might have. She located a medical bay and directed Chaca to carry Hitochi there. Then, she submerged herself in the flux of the Shura.

She struggled to retain her consciousness in the maelstrom of thoughts. If the Shura tried, it could overpower her with little effort, but it was engaged in too many things to bother with her. Activating sensors around the ship, she detected a massive influx of repair drones and Shutaish in the nearby corridors. The drones were there to stop them from stealing the Aishaitia ship, and the wraiths had come to devour them.

A hand touched her shoulder. She glanced up to see Clutep standing beside her, his helmet off. His eyes held a deep sadness.

"The unmolding of ship and Band will take time. The energy must dissipate slowly. The drones and the Shutaish will arrive before you can move the ship. We cannot keep the Shutaish from entering the ship, and there are too many to stop them all. Several of my people have elected to remain outside to guard the ship until it can leave. I will remain with them."

"I can keep them off the ship," she replied and knew she could. She could reconfigure the energy fields of the walls of the ship to prevent the Shutaish from entering. Then she saw the weak point that the Shutaish would eventually find and use – the engines. When operating, the EM field became weaker to allow the engines to manipulate space-time. The half-energy Shutaish would sense the change. Clutep was right. Someone had to keep the Shutaish away.

"You cannot sacrifice yourself," she said. "Your people need you."

"I have guided them for many centuries. A new age requires new guidance. Others will assume that position. I can only continue doing what I have always done, protecting them to the best of my limited ability. I regret the brief time I have had among humans, but our two races have many common desires. I foresee a bright future for both our peoples."

She wanted to argue more, to make him see reason, but she knew her efforts would be in vain. He had made his decision, and as much as she hated it, it was the right one for all their sakes. The Shura mind was calling her back in. She could not abandon her post, as he could not abandon his.

"I'm sorry." It was an inadequate thank you for what Clutep had done by saving her, but she knew he would understand.

"A good life to you, Kari Stone," he said and walked away.

She saw First Sergeant Chaca, Gunnery Sergeant Ryder, and Private Holmes following him. Each man carried a laser rifle. They, too, saw their duty as remaining to ensure a safe escape for the others. So many had died, and now more were willing to sacrifice themselves for the safety of the group. She could find no words to convey her pride. She nodded to Chaca with a tear in her eye. So many who had come on the expedition would not be going home. She hoped the knowledge they brought back to Earth proved worth the sacrifices.

She activated the outside surveillance cameras, fascinated to see the walls themselves acted as receivers and transmitters for a wide variety of data, including audio and visual spectrums. Clutep and the others placed themselves in formation in front of the main entrance of the ship, hoping to draw all the Shutaish to them. Three humans and seven Amasha stood side by side between escape and death.

She could not watch the battle; or rather, she did not wish to watch the battle. She had witnessed enough death for the remaining years of her lifetime. Seeing people she cared for killed would not help her concentrate on the job at hand, saving the others. The battle between the two conflicting personas of the Shura raged on the fringes of her mind as real as the battle between man and creature outside the ship. She knew the insane persona would win. Chaos is stronger than order. It was simply a matter of time. Did they have time enough to get away?

"For you," the sane Shura voice said. A bolt of white-hot energy seared its way into her mind, ripping through neural connections like tissue paper. The data burst was more than her human mind could contain, threatening to explode her head. She felt portions of her past memories disappear as the new information sought a place to lodge. She knew it was important both for their survival and for the future of mankind, but her past was who she was. What would she now become? The pain subsided. She now found she could manipulate ship systems without the need for physical contact. She brought ship's systems on-line – power, environment, and engines. She realized Captain Sidthuri's fears of starvation were unfounded. The Aishaitia ship could reach Earth in hours, rather than the months it had taken them to reach the Band.

She sought the Amasha home world in the data banks, found it, and brought up an image of the blue-green watery world on the projector. She felt the indrawn breaths of the Amasha as they glimpsed their almost forgotten home. She knew it was a current image. The Aishaitia had discovered a way to use space itself to view distant worlds in real time. She resisted the impulse to find Earth. It had not changed much in eight months. She plotted a course that took them to the Amasha home world first. The Amasha had been in exile for many centuries. A few hours delay to deliver them safely home made no difference to her.

"Everyone prepare," she announced over ship's comm. "We're leaving."

The sphere, the Aishaitia ship, broke its bonds with the Band and hovered above the surface. She felt the dismay of the Shura mind. They had won their freedom, but at great cost. With one last look at the red dwarf Cyclops, she engaged the engines, and the Band disappeared. They were going home.

23

The Band shuddered as the ship broke away. *Thank the spirits someone will go home.* Chaca accepted his death stoically, as did every soldier. He was a Marine. His job was to kill for his country, his planet, and die when necessary. It had become necessary. He was in good company. The Shutaish had attacked in an ebony wave. Three of the Amasha were dead. Holmes sustained a serious wound, but even dying he continued to fire his weapon from a prone position. The Band's drones attacked the rear of the Shutaish, driving them forward in a killing frenzy. Chaca was not worried. Now, no matter what happened, the others, both human and Amasha, would make it back home and with a fancy new spaceship.

A Shutaish launched itself at him from the floor. He withheld his fire until it was almost upon him. As it solidified for the attack, he fired. The laser beam penetrated the creature's ebony shell, shaking it apart like a bulldog with a rag doll, but not before he felt a fire lance into his side. He glanced down to see blood spilling from his battle armor. The creature had managed to pierce his side. Oddly, he felt no more pain. He knew that wasn't good. He glanced around to see hundreds of black forms advancing like a thundercloud across a black plain. They had killed dozens, but it had barely dented the Shutaish horde.

Clutep was gone. So was Ryder. His weapon lay on the ground where he had stood. Holmes lay still. As he watched, the last Amasha went down beneath a clot of black bodies. The light in the room flared briefly, but he knew it was not the light itself but his vision. His wound was mortal.

He lifted his laser with one hand. In his other hand, he held the remote detonator for the half-dozen Claymore mines he had scattered around the room. "Come on, you dark beauties!" he yelled. "Come get a taste of this!" He pressed the trigger of the laser and held it down, sweeping it back and forth through the Shutaish. When the advancing line of dark bodies got within five meters, he pressed the detonator.

Explosions rippled the crowd, dispersing them. He laughed; then, the dark cloud enveloped him, sending him home.

24

Kari sat on the floor beside Hitochi, who lay nestled inside a transparent sarcophagus, as fluid dripped into his body through tubes inserted in his chest. She hoped the machine was saving his life. His color was better. She felt like a deflated balloon. All that she had been was gone. She remembered everything of the last few years, but her past, even her parents' faces, had been erased to make room for the store of knowledge bestowed upon her by the last bit of the good Shura as they departed. She hoped mankind used it wisely, but she had her doubts. Misuses of power and knowledge filled her species' history.

Hitochi stirred and opened his eyes.

"Hello," she said.

He glanced at the tubes entering his body and the enclosure embracing him. "Where am I?" he asked.

She smiled. "You're on your way home."

He returned her smile, closed his eyes, and lay back. "That's good. You owe me a meal."

She had so much to tell him. She had watched the Band break apart. The Shura's attempt to save it by dividing it had failed. The disassociation between the two parts of the Shura mind had doomed the procedure. First, the sunward side split away, becoming a second Band. Without a power source, much of the ebony material disappeared, leaving a metal core falling into Cyclops. Within months, it would reach the sun and melt away from the intense heat. The Shutaish would cease to be, ending their long hunger.

The remaining ring of the Band settled into a stable orbit around Cyclops, but by using the ship's computer, she calculated the stability would last only a few centuries; then, it too would take its death dive into its sun. The Aishaitia's dream of eternal life would end in dismal failure, as she imagined all such dreams ended. Life would continue, but only for the living.

They had dropped the Amasha on their home world. Surprisingly, Kirkurk elected to remain among them until Earth could establish permanent relations. He made a strange ambassador. She hoped the Amasha didn't declare war on Earth over some slight. In a few hours, they would reach Earth. It would be a homecoming she had never imagined in her wildest dreams. She did not know what would come next, but looking down at Hitochi, she knew what she hoped.

With their new ship, humans could go anywhere in the universe. She had made her last trip into space. The Aishaitia artifacts that had woven a spell over her no longer lured her. Too much death marred their beauty. Others could take her place. Earth still had her secrets, hidden tombs, lost cities. To others, it might seem mundane, but it would suffice.

The End

CHECK OUT OTHER GREAT SCIENCE FICTION BOOKS

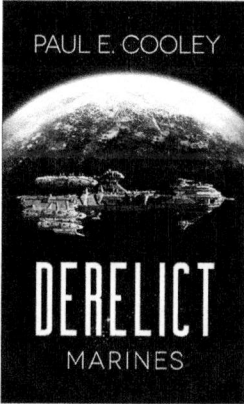

DERELICT: MARINES
by Paul E. Cooley

Fifty years ago, Mira, humanity's last hope to find new resources, exited the solar system bound for Proxima Centauri b. Seven years into her mission, all transmissions ceased without warning. Mira and her crew were presumed lost. Humanity, unified during her construction, splintered into insurgency and rebellion.

Now, an outpost orbiting Pluto has detected a distress call from an unpowered object entering Sol space: Mira has returned. When all attempts at communications fail, S&R Black, a Sol Federation Marine Corps search and rescue vessel, is dispatched from Trident Station to intercept, investigate, and tow the beleaguered Mira to Neptune.

As the marines prepare for the journey, uncertainty and conspiracy fomented by Trident Station's governing AIs, begin to take their toll. Upon reaching Mira, they discover they've been sent on a mission that will almost certainly end in catastrophe.

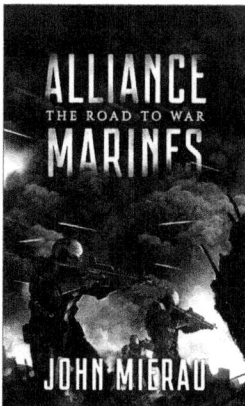

ALLIANCE MARINES
by John Mierau

One by one, all of Earth's colonies have gone dark and silent. Reach, the last colony, teeters on the verge of civil war against its Earth-loyal overlords...and Reach-born rebel Lee Zhang has sworn to push the planet over the edge.

As the colony descends into total war, a convoy from Earth races across the galaxy, carrying news of a threat unlike anything mankind has faced before. The colonies have all been destroyed by a vast alien horde, and now Earth has fallen, too. Time is running out for sworn enemies to learn to trust and unite, or the human race is extinct. The Takers are coming to destroy mankind. If we don't do the job for them first.

CHECK OUT OTHER GREAT SCIENCE FICTION BOOKS

SPACE MARINE AJAX
by Sean-Michael Argo

Ajax answers the call of duty and becomes an Einherjar space marine, charged with defending humanity against hideous alien monsters in furious combat across the galaxy.

The Garm, as they came to be called, emerged from the deepest parts of uncharted space, devouring all that lay before them, a great swarm that scoured entire star systems of all organic life. This space borne hive, this extinction fleet, made no attempts to communicate and offered no mercy.

Humanity has always been a deadly organism, and we would not so easily be made the prey. Unified against a common enemy, we fought back, meeting the swarm with soldiers upon every front.

PLANET LEVIATHAN
by D.J. Goodman

The cyborg commandos of the Galactic Marines are the greatest warriors in the galaxy, but sometimes one will go bad. Too unstable to be let back into the general population and too powerful for a normal prison to hold them, there is only one place they can be sent: Planet Leviathan.

CHECK OUT OTHER GREAT
SCIENCE FICTION BOOKS

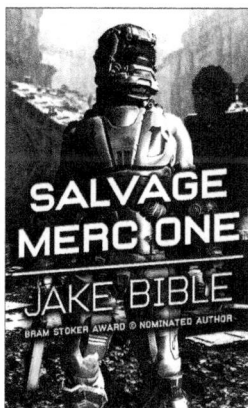

SALVAGE MERC ONE
by Jake Bible

Joseph Laribeau was born to be a Marine in the Galactic Fleet. He was born to fight the alien enemies known as the Skrang Alliance and travel the galaxy doing his duty as a Marine Sergeant. But when the War ended and Joe found himself medically discharged, the best job ever was over and he never thought he'd find his way again.

Then a beautiful alien walked into his life and offered him a chance at something even greater than the Fleet, a chance to serve with the Salvage Merc Corp.

Now known as Salvage Merc One Eighty-Four, Joe Laribeau is given the ultimate assignment by the SMC bosses. To his surprise it is neither a military nor a corporate salvage. Rather, Joe has to risk his life for one of his own. He has to find and bring back the legend that started the Corp.

SERENGETI
by J.B. Rockwell

It was supposed to be an easy job: find the Dark Star Revolution Starships, destroy them, and go home. But a booby-trapped vessel decimates the Meridian Alliance fleet, leaving Serengeti—a Valkyrie class warship with a sentient AI brain—on her own; wrecked and abandoned in an empty expanse of space. On the edge of total failure, Serengeti thinks only of her crew. She herds the survivors into a lifeboat, intending to sling them into space. But the escape pod sticks in her belly, locking the cryogenically frozen crew inside.

Then a scavenger ship arrives to pick Serengeti's bones clean. Her engines dead, her guns long silenced, Serengeti and her last two robots must find a way to fight the scavengers off and save the crew trapped inside her.

Printed in Dunstable, United Kingdom

66434672R00129